NO FINGERPRINTS

Sona Mahtani

Bijlee • **Mantra**

5 Alexandra Grove
London N12 8NU
Text copyright © Sona Mahtani

Printed in Great Britain by BPC Wheatons Ltd, Exeter

For Naina

ACKNOWLEDGMENTS

Writing can bring out the worst in you. Everyone has a touch of Ruddles fever lurking inside them. I would like to thank the following for limiting my worst excesses.

Ram, Dru and Ama Mahtani for inspiration and knowing how long a piece of string is.

Raj Shukla, Sunil Mahtani and the Sohanpal siblings for willingly submitting to torture with every draft.

Asian Action Group for putting the brakes on the Ruddles factor from Day One.

The Brown Buffaloes for kicking some in the process.

The whole team at Mantra for their support and encouragement, and Judy Gough for her precision editing.

I hope you all enjoy it!

CONTENTS

CHAPTER 1   Saturday Night
with the Crew   7

CHAPTER 2   Small decisions,
Big mistakes   19

CHAPTER 3   The Big Break   33

CHAPTER 4   The Enemy   64

CHAPTER 5   The Regime   87

CHAPTER 6   Till Death Do Us Part   108

CHAPTER 7   Down and Out!   129

CHAPTER 8   The Intruders   150

CHAPTER 9   Swallowing the Bait   168

CHAPTER 10   Outside Operators   186

CHAPTER 11   Trial on a Tightrope   207

1

SATURDAY NIGHT WITH THE CREW

The three of them avoided corniness like the plague. It was difficult to pinpoint what else superglued The Crew at the hips. Everyone around them speculated. The Shell Suit Brigade reckoned they had it sussed.

"Maybe they're into kinky stuff..." said the Pink One.

"Yeah well, there are three of them," agreed Red and Green Dots.

"But he's gorgeous and those girls are so ugly!" winced Shimmering Puce.

The Crew couldn't be bothered to think about it. Too much thought hurt. What was all the fuss about anyway? Shoulders shrugged and victory signs silhouetted from the back window of their modus transporter, the Busby Telecom van. They "just were" and if they weren't they'd probably still live, so it was no big deal. Mind you, if you were a misfit amongst a college full of purple puce, you'd look for somebody a little off-beat, wouldn't you? Maybe even somebody who was on-line...

It was Saturday night in North London and The Crew were on a roll. At that precise moment it was a very long roll, straight down Crouch Hill. Simeon was at the wheel and sweating manfully in his black leathers. "Jeez, the clutch's gone!" This wasn't quite how they'd planned it.

Amber had the night mapped out in the space between her ears. From the day that computer screens around England flashed up with the words, "HACKING RAVE IN THE COUNTRY!", she'd replayed her vision of the party over and over. She had everything covered, right from the way her hair would have one orange streak peaking out from under her Crew cap, to the way that other drivers would stare at this ramshackle Busby Telecom van. Naturally, they'd be thinking, "I wonder where they're going. God, I wish I wasn't going to Auntie Ethel's for tea. Man, I wish I was with these cool geezers." In reality, being 'cool' came close to being pretty smelly. Having the petrol tanked up and the burgers packed in one house-on-wheels, created a horrendous stench in the back room.

It wasn't your average rave. For starters, there was a lot of hush-hush around the location. A deserted house in Freezywater, could mean only two things. Three hours of driving around lost. Plenty of parking under street lamps, possibly getting done for kerb-crawling. The map was so into secrecy, it didn't actually give you the address. Amber didn't care. More time for foreplay. The three of them would cruise around like incredibly sussed, cocky, confident Somebodies.

This involved plenty of swanky dangling of one chubby arm out the window, shouting "I'm a really BAD girl!" at rich grannies from Muswell Hill who always looked mortified and dropped their bagels. Maybe some innocent revving at Robin Reliants at the lights, if they got lucky. Definitely not hurtling at this pace, scaring the exhausts off BMWs.

Meanwhile, Suki was having a fit in the back about her frequency. She never missed an opportunity for a hack even if it meant bumbling on the metal ribs in the boot of a van. All the swerving around parked cars had thrown her on her back and her legs tangled in amongst the wall of telephone wires and switches.

Suki's most distinctive feature was a shorter left leg, which was causing considerable problems now as she pirouetted like a mobile at the mercy of a cable. The fact that she also had a gob full of burger dripping at the same time didn't help.

"Mawhellzzon...inillygoatscop onzajam-n-zenwe..."

Amber, with a BA in Burger Talk, knew that roughly translated into, "Man, what the hell's going on? I nearly got some cops on the jam and then we're..."

"Vertical!" shrieked Amber, her eyes pinched.

The sound of a police siren broke through the screech of brakes. "Goddamn Muswell hillbillies!" muttered Simeon.

"Somethin' tells me we're gonna be late."

¥ ¥ ¥

At the police station, Simeon was short and gruff. The desk officer was getting on his nerves. The peaky-nosed trainee had silently looked at his driver's licence for five minutes, peered up and asked in a slow, irritating drawl, "Is your name Simon Powell?"

Simeon's suggestion went down as "uncooperative behaviour" in the book. This phrase is also known as "black yankee git looking for a bloody good hiding."

"If you were down the Stoke, you'd get lynched," growled the desk officer, who was very sensitive about his reading ability. He was itching to club this black dude around the head with his brand new Home Office truncheon...but there were too many witnesses, never mind it being his first day behind the desk.

The moment passed. Simeon was not pleased with half his wages going on a speeding fine but, more than anything, he could feel embarrassment creeping into his face. Suki was pacing up and down the corridor, tutting, totally oblivious to the drunken occupants of the police bench.

"We're late, man," she called. "It's the one night in the year...you're totally unreliable. I could be cruising into some serious frequency, and I'm here. With you!"

There was such venom in her voice. If Suki had suggested it, Simeon would have also considered taking full responsibility for World War III. Behind this leather machismo image lay a pulsating heart that beat in time to only one computer keyboard. And that was Suki's.

He had tried to rationalise it. She wasn't all that good looking, was she? He knew he could walk into a string of night-clubs and walk out, well, actually tear himself away, covered in lipstick and bites. He also knew he'd never meet Suki in The Hippodrome. That just wasn't her kinda dive. She'd be hanging loose inside some bar, swapping passwords on beermats, scaring the holies out of any barman who dared to ask if she was under age. They walked to the car-port Simeon's keys were in his hand, his thoughts wandering. There was something really sexy about the way those John Lennon's hung on her nose, those darting little eyes...the smile when she'd cracked a code. Christ, he had to get a grip on himself.

Suki gently interrupted his train of thought. "You shaken up?" Her hand was in his back-pocket. Woo! Could this be the same life?!

"Uh uh." He couldn't keep the glee from his voice.

"Stop flashing your money around then. You don't have to cop the lot," insisted Suki. "Amber, twenty from you too."

Predictably, Amber grumbled. It was a genetic trait she got from her father. With the memory of Suki's hand charring his behind, Simeon floated his way to a hacking party that he'd never forget.

¥ ¥ ¥

They arrived at a deserted road junction. The skyline was marked only by streetlights and a petrol station.

"This can't be it!" said Amber, looking at the corner house. "The lights are out for starters. And there's no music and no..."

"Well, it's the only place for miles and it's opposite a petrol station," explained Simeon. "And that fits with the directions."

Suki's eyes shone in the dark. "It's perfect. Just the best. What are you lot waiting for? An illuminated sign saying 'Come and Hack Here'?" She tutted. "I'll check it out and let you know."

She made a fast exit out of the back. Through the side mirror, Simeon quivered at the sight of Suki's slight frame limping towards the side door of the ominous looking house. For a moment, he had delusions of chasing after his loved one before she was in real danger, but as he knew, Suki was more in control than any of them. She waited for a couple of minutes at a dilapidated wooden side door. The letter-box suddenly creaked open. Her heart leapt. Two glaring eyes stared out sharply.

"Where you from, sister?" asked a gruff voice. "School?"

"I'm here for the stack, lumber-jack," Suki answered nervously. If a standard hacker code didn't work, they definitely had the wrong place.

"And who you got wid ya?" The eyes looked suspiciously past her towards the van.

"Aw, just The Crew," said Suki, smiling. She gave Simeon and Amber the thumbs-up. "We've got a reservation, so why don't you quit twenty questions? We look more suspect standing out here."

"Yeah, yeah, OK," replied the voice, eyes rolling. "You mighty cocky for your size, sister. Sign the book, and I'll show you around."

"It's OK. I know a few people. Is the Mean Machine here? What about the Oil-Burners?" rapped Suki excitedly, looking at the forty odd names in the book. Each name was virtually unreadable. Hackers had to protect their identity, after all.

"Hey baby, this is an England gig, you know," said Rolling Eyes, rolling them yonder into a dark, smoke-filled room. "Not international."

"Listen, dickhead, do not call me 'baby'!" Suki snapped. This bouncer scene always irritated her. "Do I look like I even possess a shell-suit?!"

Rolling Eyes looked pretty mystified, and went to

see who was causing the commotion at the door. Nobody had ever told him about the baby-shell-suit connection. He had to think about it. The sound of pulsing grooves thumping through the floorboards led Suki away. As an after-thought, she called after Rolling Eyes. "Hey, it's OK it's The Crew. They're with me." She paused. "Ask them to bring in the burgers."

"Damn hackers, always think they're somebody," muttered Rolling Eyes.

Simeon and Amber had entered the gateway into another world. It was their first hacker's party and they were amazed. The smell of incense and other strange aromatic substances shot through their nostrils. It was like they'd walked into a time warp. The furniture was out of a 1950s front room, pictures seemed to be hung at deliberately wayward angles and the odd Bauhaus poster was peeling off the wall. The paint just chipped. Mattresses lined the floor for when hackers ran out of energy. "It looks like a brothel," whispered Amber.

"You'll have a great time," grunted Simeon sarcastically. He would not, he could tell, and he was right.

A punk, with a singularly vertical green spike and a pair of Dr Martens, walked past in an intense argument with a girl who looked like she'd walked off Vampira's film set. They were talking about electronic conductors, as if life hinged on them. A hippy sat quietly in the corner, playing with his lap-top and under Simeon's gaze, whipped out a lump of hash where the batteries should have been. He looked up, suddenly aware that he was being watched.

"Want some?" he asked, with a thick German accent, putting forward his herbal offering.

Suki emerged from the basement stairs, armed with a few cables and a manual. "Come on down, guys."

"Not tonight, Josephine," Simeon motioned to him, self-consciously. The hippy shrugged his shoulders.

"What's your heritage?"

"Uh?" lurched Simeon, turning around. "You want my family tree? Well, my father's a blue-box man..."

"He means what's your speciality," explained Suki. "You know, what are you into. Is it programming, password-catching, code-breaking..."

"Yeah yeah, that's what I figured," lied Simeon. "I'm a telephone man. Any line, any time, anywhere. I can tap into the White House, the Kremlin, last week I got Tina Turner. And you?"

"I'm a philosopher," he said casually. "Call me Jung." Jung held out his hand and they shook. "Tell me more about your family tree..."

"Yeah well, my pa's a blue-box man, whistled across the States, tried to get a job with the telephone companies." Simeon was slightly embarrassed at this openness. "No-one would give him a chance, see, cos he knew the A & T system better than they did." He paused. "He's blind, right..." he continued, rather defensively, waiting for a reaction.

"Does he smoke?" asked Jung, pointing at the funny cigarette in his hand.

Simeon laughed. "My pa?"

"He should," advised the hippy in all seriousness. "It's very good for eye diseases. But only in huge quantities."

At this point, Simeon turned to look for Amber to save him from this guy who obviously devoted his life to marketing drugs as health products. "So you're a philosopher?"

"Yeah, computers man, they're only a tool," Jung said, taking a drag. "I read this book a long time ago about how the computers in the world are networked in a conspiracy. The system knows everything about us, and it's only right that we use them to wreck the system..."

Amber spotted Simeon's signal for 'get me out of here'. A tight fist held behind his back. She called him

13

over.

"See you later, man," said Simeon, relieved.

"That guy's off the planet," he whispered to Amber. "He reckons that computers are going to cause a revolt."

One of the other long-haired dudes must have heard his criticism. He staggered up from the floor, a beer can in his hand, all of which Simeon found pretty intimidating. It occurred to our telephone hero that here he was, trapped in a strange house in a deserted area with the strangest folk. A particularly formidable tall, long-haired animal was leering at him. Right now.

"It's true," said the young man, staring at him with eyeball to eyeball intensity. "We've got to be free! The system's eating us up and we've got to get inside it." He threw his hands about wildly in front of a rigid Simeon before collapsing in a pathetic pile of more beer cans.

"Gee, my father's a blind man and he can walk straighter than you," smirked Simeon, certain now that this weedy pile at his feet was no opposition.

"One look is all it takes," he whispered to Amber, as he led the way down the basement stairs.

The basement was obviously the Action Room, littered with all kinds of technical equipment, from computer screens, aerials and modems to synthesisers. People focussed around bulks of equipment, engaged in counter-culture conversations.

Amidst the sound of vibrating house music, they found Suki.

"See him over there, that's Heart-Attack Jack," she whispered. She pointed to a mean-looking white guy, immersed in a technical conversation about programming. "He got caught trying to do a bank and pretended to have a heart-attack. They stuck him in an ambulance and he ran off."

Suki felt more alive and awake than she had done for ages. Being surrounded by kindred spirits gave her a buzz. It was like a three-year-old being released into Hamleys. The night promised to be a long one and some big names were bound to turn up eventually. Even if they didn't she could compensate, she decided. As time passed, the basement became jammed and people wanted to see some action. Amber and Simeon looked well mixed in with everyone. Jung had followed Simeon downstairs to pursue the discussion about how computers should be used and probably to get the right telephone number for the Kremlin. They could look after themselves.

Suki's generous spirit quickly established her credibility with other hackers. Her big project for the night was setting up a program for everyone at the party. Using it as an electronic bulletin board, people sitting two feet away from her were able to contact hackers they'd only heard about and have a chat. This spiky-haired kid could really do the business!

"Who's next?" Suki shouted out hoarsely, at about four in the morning.

"I haven't had a go yet," said a stranger's voice.

Suki looked around. Everyone except this guy seemed to have dozed off. She didn't recognise him, whereas Amber, half-collapsing on a mattress in the corner pricked up her ears. She knew that voice. She had heard it at a party in much the same circumstances as this. Meanwhile Simeon's head had dropped between his legs. Undeterred by this apparent lack of interest, Jung was about to launch into the virtues of yet another herbal remedy.

It was late, and it was dark but, in any case, Suki didn't miss the fact that this guy looked like he'd walked out of a male model catalogue. It didn't really do anything for her. She logged the fact that a good looking guy was approaching her with a smile on his face but that's as far as it went. What really impressed Suki was his ease with the system. Amber, meanwhile, was already lifting herself up from the mattress unable to believe her eyes.

She nudged Simeon. "Look at that," she whispered. "That's Ivan. I went out with him about two years ago. Well, it was a long kiss, anyways. Isn't he gorgeous?"Amber felt like she'd just found a diamond shining out in the light, beckoning her. Ironically, this was exactly how she'd planned it in her epic, "Saturday Night with The Crew". The lights would be low, just like this. There'd be no one else around. Well, Suki in front of a computer and Simeon, doped up on the mere smell of hash equated virtual solitary confinement. Amber was pretty thick-skinned. It didn't matter that Ivan was about to peak on an intense keyboard flirt with Suki.

He cut a striking figure, even in the twilight. He was tall. A grunting, semi-awake Simeon disagreed. Maybe, dangly like a mosquito or a dragon-fly. Dark, although Simeon noted that he wasn't nearly dark enough. And handsome? Amber dodged the slap. "Get serious!" snapped Simeon.

The odd thing is that Suki didn't even wise up to the flirt. Ivan just seemed like an interesting guy, a nifty hacker who was quite good-looking. It was natural that they had lots to talk about because they were into the same scene, you know? Admittedly, Suki's link with her libido could only be measured through a computer cable. But, the time, the atmosphere and the mental intensity on the system had turned off her usual vetting of strangers.

"Did you hear about that guy that got caught?" Suki exclaimed. "They took him to court and everything!"

"Yeah, he was a friend of mine," said Ivan casually.

"Yeah? The school-kid, his mother didn't even know what he was up to? Parents are blind, man."

Simeon winced. That hurt. He could feel his muscles tightening. His machismo was slowly taking over his brain cells. If this guy even laid a finger on his girl he would...Simeon knew he was a complete wimp. Like the time when there were mice in the kitchen, it was his father who chased them out. Simeon was on the table, holding his leather trousers tightly round his ankles and screaming the place down. And here he was contemplating an attack on a member of the male species who was taller, more muscular and looked totally fearless. Why was life testing him this way? He had to follow through for once, just once...to see if he could do it. Maybe Suki would actually treat him with some respect then, and take his advances seriously.

"Hey, Simeon," whispered Jung, beckoning. "I've heard that the Government's got the education system..." He tightened his fist. "Like this. They're after us, you know."

"Not now, Josie," snapped Simeon. "I've got a headache."

Jung's head lolled like a puppet. "You wait, brother... You wait."

There was a lull and heads turned to catch the tail end of their conversation.

"Wait for what, man?" asked Ivan. All eyes suddenly turned to Jung.

Simeon kicked himself. Ivan just rotated everyone's attention like a telephone dial.

"Well, I just heard a rumour..." said Jung, arousing curiosity on purpose.

"Go on," urged Suki. She loved worming out secrets.

"They got all us on file," said Jung, leaning forward to this suddenly attentive audience. "The education system, they got us on a big network. The system's on the chase and it's looking for us. You and me."

"Well, it ain't going to touch me," said Suki, laughing at this hippy's hypothesis. "I'm a free bird."

"Me too," muttered Amber. She'd seen her chance. "Ivan! Hi! Remember me?"

"Uh?"

Ivan didn't look as if he remembered jack-shit, thought Simeon. His mind was elsewhere, obviously.

"Amber? Right, yeah, vaguely..." Ivan looked slightly embarrassed and gave Amber the Big Elbow signal. It set Simeon on fire. Casually, Ivan slipped his arm around Suki's shoulder. From the other side of the room, Simeon yelled, "Asshole!" and leapt forward. Something had just snapped inside him and he was a wimp no more. He was a caged lion bursting out of his cage. His manliness would be demonstrated to this unknown predator in a moment of shocked surprise. Suki would fall into his arms and praise him, yelling "Asshole!" over his shoulder at this creep. That was the film version and as Amber was fast appreciating, reality never quite got televised.

Momentarily, the Basement War came to a halt. From upstairs came the sound of doors being rammed open and hippies shouting, "Hey man! What's your problem?" It was a badly timed moment for fisticuffs, but Simeon didn't care. He was in his prime and nothing was going to restrain him. He bundled Ivan into the corner, facing the full force of Ivan's muscular frame. The sound of thumping feet coming closer won through.

"Get out of here!" screamed Suki.

The cops had arrived and were looking for easy pickings. Ivan lurched for the window. With a bloody nose, Simeon scarpered through the exit and rammed his van into gear. The back door was still flapping open and Amber, too bulky to run very fast, scrambled into the moving vehicle. It was a raid, it was insanity but they'd made it. Only when the sound of sirens had faded did Simeon realise that Ivan, the source of his anguish, was also sitting in the back of his van... Some party that turned out to be. Running into the cops twice in one day. Philosophers always have this knack of talking turd and being right, he thought to himself. The system's definitely on the chase, and they had better be careful. Never a wiser thought had crossed his mind in a long time.

2

SMALL DECISIONS, BIG MISTAKES

1993 was to be the year that The Crew would look back on and tell their grandchildren about. That is, if Suki ever decided to breed with something other than a computer chip. This was the Year of The Hack. Nothing to do with Chinese horoscopes. Luckily, we've all even been saved from a plot about the life and times of a lumberjack. Wicked twist of fortune that, it has to be said. This year brings something far more terrible, and yes, sinister... Incidentally, 1993 is also The Year of The Hacker. As we all know, the tea won't make itself. And it all began, when the government found itself in serious debt trouble...

¥ ¥ ¥

Of course, Rupert Mumford MP would have been quite philosophical about it all, if he'd known. Needless to say he didn't ever fully realise that he was a mere pawn in a much bigger game than his Wiltshire constituency. He was largely untouched by how intimately he was entwined in the saga. Mind you, Rupert had quite low expectations of life. If he managed to pull out a red pen when he needed one, it felt like a new day had dawned and the world was his oyster. Crisis? What crisis? Seen it, done that, and someone else wrote the manifesto anyway.

This fifty-year-old Cambridge swot was indeed flying high. He had only just been plucked from the backbenches to occupy one of the most prestigious posts in the Cabinet. Those who'd been panting at the Prime Minister's heels for decades rocked in hysteria at this seemingly insane appointment. Rupert himself privately revelled at this quantum leap and perpetually tripped on the concept without any aid from Jung's herbal remedies. On the hardened earth, a whole generation of young people was in danger of being scarred for life, hackers included. Why? Rupert was the Minister for Education. As irony would have it, his name popped up quite arbitrarily during a Prime Minister's meeting. It was apparent that Rupert's appeal lay more in his inabilities. The Permanent Secretary, the brains behind the Prime Minister's smile, had a devious plan tucked under his cuffs to get the government out of this particularly tight corner. Check mate.

¥ ¥ ¥

"The crisis is such that for the Education Plan, we'll need someone anonymous and discreet," remarked the Permanent Secretary candidly. "Someone quite decidedly brain dead."

"Permy! You've got that look in your eye! Who is it?" The PM was beginning to enjoy himself at last. He was more inclined towards EuroDisney and the friggin' House of Commons didn't even come close. "No, let me guess. Walter?"

"No, sir, not Walter. He's about as anonymous as Mary Poppins in hell," muttered the ageing Permanent Secretary.

No other PM had ever left him feeling quite so disconcerted. But Permy was not to be swayed by the whims of a wayward employer. He had weighed up the options. Once upon a time on the little isle of Great Britain, the buzz word was "recession". Now, it was "emigrate". The debt crisis was of such magnitude that there was no money for teachers' pay after next term. Permy had been frantically scouring industry for investors in the educational field with some success. An American multinational, Bucks Times Bucks, had been courting interest. Yes, in this climate of devious manoeuvring, an imbecile Minister was infinitely better than a half-wit. No questions would ever be asked, and in any case, Permy would ensure that the answers were scripted.

The PM guessed again, this time eliminating the long shot tactics with a photograph of all the government's MPs and a gigantic marker from Hamleys.

"Basil, I bet it's good old Bas!" he cried hopefully.

"Nope, he's in Defence, Prime Minister." Permy was fast losing his patience. "And his bazooka fetish means he's staying there. It's..."

"Oh don't spoil it, Permy! Just one more go!" squealed the PM.

The twilight hours arrived, way past the PM's bedtime. Permy was asleep, his head sprawled across the desk, gently snoring.

"I just don't get it, Permy," said the PM, sucking his pen. "I've gone through 119 names, haven't I? I'm well and truly stuck. OK, I give in."

Permy stirred from the deepest of murderous dreams. "Hmm, sir..."

"Oh God! I've just realised! There's only one name left and it just can't be Rupert Mumford. That's beyond a joke!" moaned the PM. "Come on, he's so bloody boring, he never has any affairs or anything. How can I have Boring Smelly Pants in the Party, let alone in the Cabinet! There'll be a revolt. Every time I go into the House, he leaves a trail of saliva behind me. He's such a slimy little shit..."

"Exactly, sir. He's perfect..." mumbled Permy.

The following day, an American gentleman tweeked Permy's ear. His name was Sky Moores, the Director of Operations at Bucks Times Bucks. "Any news, amigos?" asked Sky.

"Yes sir, the new Minister for Education is Rupert Mumford."

Sky, a tall striking figure, put the phone down looking bemused. He pressed his intercom. "Abraham, get a file on a British MP. The name is Rupert

Mumford. Who the hell is this asshole?"

Rupert had flaws that Permy had not even accounted for. Amnesia was one of them, but it never scarred his respectable image because nobody ever gave him anything important to do or remember. Penny, his wife, did all the shopping. She was also his secretary, his motivation, his meal machine and...there's no way round it...his smell-gauge. Yes, Rupert had a distinct personal hygiene problem. "Move up. Here comes Old Smelly Pants," his colleagues whispered on the backbenches.

The problem centred around the seizure of Rupert's memory cells at the end of the day. He frequently forgot to change his clothes when he got into bed at night and the following day, rushing to meet that appointment, changing out of that musty brown suit often slipped his mind. Penny was a bit scatty herself, but that was simply because she did everything herself, literally without a break. People at dinner parties often commented, "Those two are so well suited, don't you think?" Widespread 'nodding dog' impersonations revealed that it was impossible to imagine who else would have either of them.

Rupert heard the glorious news of his appointment from a hospital bed. He had accidentally double-booked himself by inviting to his office an entourage of militant New Age Travellers, and his friend, Lord Clapperton. He'd forgotten that the travellers were occupying the Lord's land at the time, which created a mild furore, directed mainly at Rupert himself. The end result was a friendship lost, a broken arm and a brutalised sense of self.

The word 'humiliation' did not often enter Rupert's vocabulary. Over the years, he'd rarely caught the whispers and wrinkled noses. He did not raise the issue of why Jehovah's Witnesses knocked on everyone else's door, except the Mumford cottage. Penny, a devout Catholic, was thankful. Foolishly,

Rupert did not even think to ask why he hadn't been chosen for the Cabinet earlier. Well, he just wasn't the paranoid type. So just imagine his joy when a 'get-well-soon' bouquet of flowers arrived from the PM, a man who had yet to give him the time of day. His life catapulted into another dimension when Penny bustled in, her eyes shining.

"Penny, I got a bunch..." he began, before she showered him with kisses. Rupert was startled. Penny had been far too busy for kissing...ooh, since they'd met.

"Rupert darling!" she yelped. "Wonderful news! At last! You're going to be a Minister! And you're my husband! All mine!"

¥ ¥ ¥

The Permanent Secretary had made a rare but fatal misjudgement of character. Certainly, Rupert was an incompetent in comparable proportion to the rest of the Cabinet. His Cambridge pedigree would help him settle in, among old friends no doubt. His directorship of Paperlace added minutely to his credibility, even if he did inherit that little number from his father. The difference with Rupert was that a position of serious power was stimulating parts that hadn't stirred in years. No erogenous zones, we're talking grey matter here. Some things are, after all, beyond repair. Rupert was making a decisive stab at being a sensible politician. His dismay was understandable when, thrust into a Cabinet meeting, he discovered that the agenda was set in the strangest way...

Clearly, the PM was in no mood for polite welcome speeches. He cracked open his briefcase and whipped out a plastic frisbee. "Gentlemen, this shouldn't take too long, please. 'Die Hard 5' is on in...ooh, exactly twenty two minutes. Ready?"

He threw the frisbee into the air. Grown men in suits

dived into the scrum around the huge oak table. All except our noble friend, Rupert, who had yet to acclimatise to the decision-making process. Miles Remmington, the Minister for the Environment, caught it.

"Bravo, bravo, Miles. Anything to report?" asked the PM.

"Just good news. Toxic waste levels have dropped since we changed the law."

"I would have agreed to it earlier, of course, but Permy was being such a pain about it," grinned the PM.

"Maybe we could fund some research into wind power or something? They say that oil isn't going to be around forever..." said Miles, basking in the glory of the catch.

"Let's not rush into things today. We don't want to spend, spend, spend, do we boys? We've only just got back in!" said the PM, knowing Permy would hit the roof.

"But really PM..." interrupted Miles, looking injured.

"OK, OK we'll let the Select Committee look into it, hmm?" conceded the PM, knowing that those boys spent more time playing cricket than protecting the environment.

"OK. You're the PM!" said Michael.

"That's right, I am, aren't I?" laughed the PM, holding up the frisbee for another throw.

This time Rupert was on the ball, or rather on the frisbee. He dived three feet and managed to scramble half way up the table to catch it. It was the athlete coming out in him and the sweat showed. Catch or no catch, the PM wasn't feeling charitable.

"Mumford, give it to Dick," he ordered sternly.

"But..." wheezed Rupert, about to argue that this really wasn't how cricket was played.

Dick snatched the frisbee, much like a spoilt child in a playground, and the Prime Minister proceeded with the meeting. Rupert crawled back to his seat in total humiliation whilst the comradarie continued, without his athleticism. A thought crossed his mind. Here he was a grown man, a Minister of Education, no less. And he was on duty.

"I have something to say," he trembled.

The Cabinet turned in shock. Who would dare interrupt the game? Ah, the new boy!

"Out with it, out with it!" thundered the PM.

"I'm meeting leaders of industry next week about the Education Plan. I hope to raise..." As ever, Rupert was overtaken by events.

"Time's up. Die Hard. Thank you Rupert, welcome to the club," grinned the PM, snapping shut his briefcase.

Rupert was left in the empty meeting room, tears rolling down his ruddy cheeks to the sound of sneers and laughter in the corridor.

As Penny snored like a Trojan later that night, Rupert lay awake with expressionless eyes, recalling his past with amazing clarity for a man with such a short memory. In a determined effort to use the filofax that Penny bought him for Christmas, he marked that day as a major turning point in his life. He no longer felt like the same man. He slithered out of bed and began careful preparation for his meeting with Sky Moores at Bucks. He knew instinctively that it was going to be the second most pivotal event in his mundane little life. Penny understood none of this. She was even mildly irritated by the new zeal in Rupert's approach.

"Why must you suddenly know where everything is, darling? It's not like I'm going anywhere," she crooned, the next morning.

Sky was similarly doing his homework. "What do you mean, there's nothing? Get in here, Abraham, and I'll show you something about data-analysis." He slammed the phone down.

"Goddamn college grads! Shit for brains."

Moments later, Sky was glancing at a computer print-out and a photograph of Rupert. "Aged fifty. Christ, he looks pickled. Married to Penelope Hooter-Mumford. No brats, hmm, at least we've been spared that tragedy. Bad sex life or he's sterile. Any affairs?"

"Nope. He's clean." Abraham, Sky's assistant, was smug and it showed.

Sky suddenly swivelled his chair around and looked coldly through a withering Abraham. "I get the feeling I'm casting pearls before swine. If you want to stay in this job, quit smirkin', sonny. It's dangerous. Do I make myself crystal clear or are you on the end of a very long dole queue?"

"Very clear. Sorry sir," said Abraham, nearly saluting.

"OK, we'll just have to dig a little deeper, is all," said Sky, rising to the challenge. "Local government councillor for ten years. Greatest achievement is what?! A Private Members' Bill giving greater powers to traffic wardens. Jeez, I bet he's a gas at parties! Any money interests?"

"Paperlace & Co. Honorary place on the board," said Abraham.

"Paperlace? The same Paperlace that supplies fancy paper and pencils to all the high street stores? This guy's on the board? Jeez Abraham, I think I've found just the carrot I need. Though it still beats me how this boring bum got there. Everything in place for the meeting?"

"Yes sir," said Abraham.

¥ ¥ ¥

Sky squinted at Rupert across the table with a mixture of amusement and disbelief. Rupert the Bear, he thought. Bucks Times Bucks had been planning for this meeting for decades, whereas most multinationals were like blind bees, sticking around only if there was any honey-money in the pot. No sweeteners on the bank balance sheet and they were off bumbling somewhere else. But Bucks was different. The corporation had a plan for the future, named Operation Acid Trip. It was dangerous, it was secret, it was international and it was the perfect challenge for Sky Moores. After all this, they've sent me Rupert the Goddamn Bear, he laughed to himself. In that instance, the Operation's chance of success seemed assured.

"Good. Very good. Are you all clear on the plan, Minister?" he asked politely.

"Well, I have read all the papers if that's what you mean," said Rupert sarcastically.

Permy almost choked. He had yet to find a Minister who dared to be so deliciously rude to a multimillion pound American giant. It was like swearing at God during mass. The other major plus was that a Cabinet member had actually read all the papers he'd given him. Permy excused himself from the room to recover from his coughing fit, and to give a quick progress report to the PM, who was busy playing carpet golf.

"If I've read it all correctly, Mr Moores..." Rupert started.

"Oh please, Minister, call me Sky," Sky interrupted.

He, too, was marvelling at a man whose political reputation was built on traffic wardens, yet did not seem frozen rigid in his presence.

"Uh, very well," Rupert continued, wondering what possessed parents to choose such obscure names for their children. But that's Americans for you, he thought. "As I understand it, the plan is that Bucks Times Bucks will invest ten billion pounds in an agency that runs the British education system."

"The agency is called RETROBASE," interjected Sky, reminding himself this was his plan not Rupert the Bear's. The Minister looked annoyed at being interrupted yet again.

"There will be offices in all major schools and colleges, am I right?" asked Rupert.

"Totally, sir," Sky decided to play the small man. "Keep it local. Avoid any aggro from people thinking some Big Brother's calling the shots, know what I mean? Every local office will have the latest technology that connects them to these Headquarters. Computers are amazing at..."

"And the job of the agency is to test every child from the age of six until eighteen?" interrupted Rupert, not really giving a toss about computers. After all, he had only just mastered a mobile phone. Rupert came from the generation that had the wireless not the Sony Walkman, the manual typewriter rather than the IBM. Unbeknown to Rupert, his name was on a little file in Sky's database. If he had paid a touch more attention to detail, 1993 may not have been The Year of the Hacker. But then, Rupert was Rupert. Change had swept through him in recent times, though ultimately, how much could a man with the foresight of a blind-bat change?

"Six is a bit young to test for things, isn't it?" he asked, remembering very vaguely what a meaningless little six-year-old he'd been himself.

"Not really, Minister. Well, kids are so advanced these days," Sky rambled. "You know, my six-year-old can speak Japanese? Hell, he's got a job made for him when he graduates, don't he?" he chuckled, with a false sense of pride.

Sky lied with remarkable ease. He wouldn't let a baby's nappy within a ten feet radius, but that wasn't going to stop him getting what he wanted. He had seen the Treasury's confidential report. He knew the government had insurmountable debt problems. With Rupert the Bear sitting right here, the government was playing right into his hands.

"Sure we've got to lay up the dosh right now," Sky had once said to his boss. "But when the honey-money rolls...it's rolling straight down to us."

Whilst everyone else was walking around moaning about having no honey-money, Bucks was in spend-spend-spend mode. He didn't want to screw it up now or get screwed by some cartoon Minister. As a matter of course, government people should be bullied in Sky's world.

"This whole goddamn plan is about getting the best out of all the nation's children, sir. Not just the ones that went to Cambridge, d'ya get my drift?" Sky said, hoping to niggle Rupert. "The time has come for industry to take its rightful responsibility, sir. We've been letting the government carry the can for too long. We're in a world recession now, and it's time we paid attention to the education of the "riff-raff". That's where the future lies, sir, not in eight fellas that can row a goddamn canoe!"

Sky waived his hands about casually, certain that anyone, even someone as thick as Rupert Mumford, would rise to the bait. But Rupert surprised him yet again.

"I quite agree. Well, Cambridge does breed some prize Dicks these days, doesn't it?" His thoughts wandered to some of his Cabinet colleagues. "Now, I see why you've got this compulsory Work Study option for 14-18-year-olds. Four weeks of the year getting on-the-job training with a company that the school or college finds. Excellent. And the student can go back to that employer when they graduate. Wonderful! One certificate will give all the details for the employer's convenience and..." Rupert rambled on.

Permy had recovered fully from his coughing fit, and found refuge in an empty office with a phone. He was communicating his new-found respect for smelly old Rupert. Permy was unperturbed by the rotations of a reel-to-reel machine recording the meeting. This was standard practice in the event of the need to make

Ministers toe the line. In fact, Permy found it extremely helpful. He could hear everything even though he wasn't present.

"Yes, Mumford is quite unbelievable, sir. Far surpassed my wildest dreams. I think I, I mean...er...you, sir, made an excellent choice. Listen to this..." Permy held the phone up to the tape-reels.

Rupert carried on, unaware that he had the undivided attention of anyone except Sky. "I really like the agency's plans to get truancy under control. So much of the country's talent is going to waste on the streets..."

"Our thoughts exactly," said Sky, relieved that, at last, he was going to get the chance to say something in his presentation. "We've already got some pilot projects up and runnin' around the country, just to show you what we can do. They're compiling records of the little runts, even as we speak. And that's all at BTB's expense, of course," smiled Sky.

Permy put the phone down and left the room. The conversation took a different twist.

"I was wondering," asked Rupert as nonchalantly as possible. "Who exactly is going to supply the educational materials, paper, pencils for this enterprise, Sky?"

"Well, we've got a number of companies on our books. Any suggestions?" Sky asked innocently. The carrot dangled like a hypnotic pendulum.

"Well, let me see..." Rupert pretended to think very hard and didn't fool a soul, let alone Sky. "I do have excellent connections at Paperlace. You must have heard of them? They do very good-quality HB pencils," he said seriously.

"Paperlace? Oh Lord, no. They're far too expensive for Bucks. This is a national project after all," Sky swung that carrot for all it was worth. And catch! He had Rupert exactly where he wanted him, if ever the need arose.

"Oh, discounts for national orders, Sky," smiled Rupert shyly.

"Well, in that case, Paperlace it is then. Good to be doing business with you, sir. Now, there's one small detail that needs changing, Minister."

"Oh really?" Rupert raised an eyebrow.

"Ten billion pounds is a lot of money. We're investing in the nation's future here. With all due respect to the British government, we want to make sure things get done properly."

Rupert understood instantly. It still amazed him how the country had not yet sunk in the North Sea with a PM that valued "Die Hard" over decision-making. Little did he know that in financial terms, Good Ol' Blighty had virtually settled on the sea-bed.

"Bureaucracy is an alien word to us in business, sir," insisted Sky. "We'd like to take the hassle out of doing this project for you and handle it ourselves. Obviously, we'll need access to the files in your department, sir."

"Well, I'm an understanding man, Sky. As long as the public think..."A knock on the door. Permy entered and retook his seat quietly.

"...the Education Department is how did you put it 'calling the shots' by involving RETROBASE? Hhmm... But that's seems such a big burden for a mere ten billion, don't you think?" Those Board meetings were paying off for Rupert. He had witnessed the Chairman haggle with W H Smith. And boy, was the Chairman going to be pleased with this wapping new contract! HB pencils for every school in the UK...wow! Sky smiled. He'd love to have the government fronting the Operation. Nobody outside the government need know who was funding the RETROBASE. Perfect. Rupert didn't know it but Bucks was going to pay whatever it took for the name and background of every child in the country. "I've spoken to a couple of other big guys, who've said they'd be interested in investing five billion each. So that's twenty billion," Sky said, agreeably.

Permy's eyes nearly bounced off the table.

"That's more like it. Twenty billion. Can I have regular progress reports, please Sky?" asked Rupert.

After profuse handshaking, Permy nearly ran out of the room.

Nobody knew how such a moron could do it, but Rupert was hailed to have pulled off a fantastic deal with Bucks Times Bucks. Nobody asked why a big drug manufacturer like Bucks was so hooked on helping the British government. Everyone was too busy getting excited. Rupert's ratings shot up in the Cabinet. Deciding that he could only carry on doing his duty if Penny was out of sight and out of mind, Rupert made that her last day in the office... And he even considered having an affair with his new secretary, who had just bought him some deodorant. The PM welcomed him to The Club with open arms, and gave him a specially engraved gold frisbee, that read, "Rupert the Great".

Outside this tight circle, Rupert had changed the lives of thousands without really thinking about it. He was just doing his duty after all... It was quite ironic that while Penny had been made unemployed, one of the world's unknown sources of energy, one of the masses of "riff-raff" was going to find a job at last. Her name was Monica Ruddles and she was going to make an explosive impact on everyone around her...

3

THE BIG BREAK

It was lunchtime on Crouch Hill. Suki lingered by the door of The Cave, a conventional burger bar with an unconventional menu, named after its owner, Mr Cavallares.

"Aye Suki! In! In!" A large man, Mr Cavallares, recognised his best customer. He motioned to her from behind the crowded take-away counter.

Wiping his hands on a white apron, he smiled and handed her a smaller plastic menu. "Menu for midgets. Take that pain outta your face. I ain't got time. Don't sit and think. Just eat."

"It's all too good," mused Suki. "I'm trapped. Stake-out Breaker or a Whopper-Cropper? What d'ya reckon?" Mr Cavallares had a short memory. Their conversations always started in this way and today was no different.

"What do I care? Your father's a cruel man. I could barbeque your ribs. Have both!"

Suki held out a fiver, but he waved it off. "OK OK, on the tab. Give me some news. Who's Amber with this week?"

"Who knows?" Suki garbled with a mouthful of Whopper. "No wonder Wimpy went bust. These taste better every time."

"See, she tells me nothing," he grumbled. "You watch out for my girl, OK? She's crazy. Now where you going?"

"College," smiled Suki.

"You! Pull the other one! You and Amber, you're both the same," winked Mr Cavallares. "Next! Come on, come on. Not a bus-stop. Don't think, just eat."

Suki sauntered to Crouch End Community College with its grey blocks of buildings, and cars shimmering like diamond ants in the sun. Sky Moores' research had shown the college at The World's End to have one of the highest truancy rates in the country. Suki was one of the ten-percenters.

College, like school, held few attractions for her. It was all too predictable. Take the first two weeks of term. Instinctively, she knew that the busiest place in the college would be the cafeteria. The public myth of keen students rushing around the library, poring over reading lists was still alive and kicking. In reality, people wore their best trainers and Giovanni jumpers, and recreated fantastic holiday romances that Mills & Boon would find banal.

For Suki, Preeti Seekh was an ideal case study. The girl was convinced that she's had the wildest summer of her life. "He bought me an ice-cream. We went back to the tent. He nearly kissed me then but I didn't really like raspberry ripple." Really rampant stuff. "All this was happenin' while Mum and Dad were in the next tent..." The urge to vomit was too great.

Suki hastened her steps towards the computer centre in the library. Computer Room 101A was a large open-plan room, the walls lined with PCs and printers. Surprisingly enough, it was relatively untainted by wittering humans. Suki was pleased. In no time at all, the atmosphere radiated with the aroma of barbecued beef. Suki was quite prepared to be caught, despite being a regular at the college computer centre. You must understand that "regularity" in Suki's book, was a highly elastic term. Daylight did not suit her and she had her own version of a "do not disturb sign". If anyone intended to approach her, they would think twice. Firstly, she sat in a wheelchair, which instantly sent a signal. Here sits a dedicated student, not an individual deranged through lack of sleep from all-night hacking parties. This diligence is a mark of a model pupil, not concerned with the cafeteria. And what's more, she's struggled up the disabled ramp that's more designed for The Abseiling Society.

Suki discovered that the wheelchair made an effective disguise. This hulk of metal on two wheels had a way of making other people maintain their distance. She was sure people worried that they wouldn't be able to understand a word she said through the spit and avoided finding out.

There was the swot factor, of course. Swots were the only people in the library at the beginning of term. The only time swots looked up from their work was to wonder about the person in a wheelchair. It would dawn on them that despite this modus transporter, here she was with a college place. They decided that Suki was probably one of those super-swot boffins who was cleverer than they could ever be, which eliminated the need to impress. Suki stared at the computer screen with a worshipping intensity. It all pointed to one distinct conclusion. Leave me alone. There was a good reason. The best burgers in the world were best consumed alone and progress was being made on the biggest intellectual brain-drain that could shake the world. Meet CONTACT 2000.

Suki suffered grossly from being misunderstood. People had this impression that computer programmers were weird and lacked style and panache. If popular folklore was to be believed, programmers existed as a bunch of skinny boffins in skin-tight drainpipes when flares were in and wore sweatshirts with a "University of Edinburgh" motif, even when they'd never been there. Of course, it would be quite unreasonable to expect them to have a conversation with anyone unless it revolved below the boredom threshold. This baseline gravitated around things like, ooh...programs and such like.

The myth got bitchier and bitchier. Programmers all listened to the Rolling Stones or other really weird music that stopped being in the Top 40 at around 1970. The worst of it was that real head-case programmers were so out of it that they hadn't even heard of Bobby

Brown! Really deprived lives, eh? People think "progs" prefer to meditate in front of computer screens than be in The Happenin' Nerve of the Planet ie the college cafeteria, lying out of their teeth. Curiouser and curiouser...

True to form, Suki had on an Edinburgh Uni sweatshirt and did not really care for the likes of Bobby Brown. Alas, this was because he'd never be a Rolling Stone. But Suki was a little different to the rest. Unlike ordinary fanatics, Suki was in love. Simeon, had he known, would have jumped to wildly inaccurate conclusions, starting optimistically with a lovelorn smile. Break that heart. Suki's wild passionate affair was solely with CONTACT 2000. Unlike Preeti Seekh's mob, CONTACT was a real living experience in her life that made her heart lurch. At that moment, Suki had love-trauma on her mind. She was soon to experience trauma of quite different proportions.

¥ ¥ ¥

The news spread like wildfire, right through the country. People sat in pubs, talking about it. Crowds gathered in the town library to confirm the word on the grapevine and fists flew at every newspaper stand. It was like the gold-rush! A vicious rumour went round a few years back about one being spotted in a shop-window in Gateshead. But no member of Geordie society went untouched by this latest flurry.

Outside the Metro Shopping Centre, Newcastle-upon-Tyne, two old biddies gossiped at a bus-stop. The bus arrived. "Na, you're having me on, love," said the one with piggy eyes, preparing for the civil war against school children ready to board.

"Audrey, I'm telling ya, I saw it in the paper with me own eyes!" said the other. She knew full well that any mention of eye-contact would convince her near-blind mate.

"Right then! Forget shopping," said Piggy Eyes, with a stomp, nearly amputating a twelve-year-old's foot. "I better phone and tell our Monica. Madge, that a phone there?" she asked, squinting at a parked car across the road.

A job in the North was like a shooting star, now you see it, now you don't. So, Sky Moores' full-page job advert in all the daily papers was causing an absolute furore. Nearly everyone north of the Watford gap dropped their pints, their spud peelers and their knickers and went for it. Unemployed lekky men, brickies, teachers, scientists, refuse collectors, film-makers, bus drivers, typists, security guards, just about everyone. No refuse collectors got interviews though.

"There's riff-raff and there's trash, ain't that so?" Sky had said to Abraham.

RETROBASE was leaving almost no stone unturned in its search for staff. Vacancies were advertised in local areas, regional centres, villages, inner cities, suburbs, in semi-suburban inner city areas where cockroaches only came in on Tuesday afternoons. Every conceivable place. And everything seemed so right about it. The pay was a lift from a dole cheque. Respectable work too. The advert said you'd be working for a government agency.

"And that'll give our Monica a better start than working in a chippy," said Audrey Ruddles to the fish-and-chip shop owner, where Monica worked the odd evening.

Thanks to Ma Ruddles and her wily ways, Monica got an application form despite the rush and struck lucky at the place to be, the Big Apple of Britain: London. It gave everyone who knew the Ruddles family a lot of heart: if that Monica could get a job, then surely their daughters could too. Mrs Ruddles boasted the happy news to everyone and threw a massive going-away party for her lass.

"Get on the blower, Maurice," she ordered her grumbling husband. "Tell 'em our Monica's going to work in Oxford Street."

Mr Ruddles was a bit slow on the uptake, so Audrey took total control. In a funny way, Penny Hooter-Mumford and Audrey Ruddles were cut from the same cloth.

Somehow, Audrey had the impression that the very heart of London throbbed in Oxford Street. Monica refrained from breaking her heart by telling her that she was as near to Oxford Street as Audrey was to 20-20 vision. No, Monica was going to make her big impact in Crouch End Community College as Student Officer. The Ruddles' phone-bill shot up. With Audrey's eyesight, a lot of them were wrong numbers and in the end, there were more gatecrashers than family.

Getting a proper job dramatically changed Monica's life. It gave her the chance to do all the things she wanted to do with her life: get away from her mum and dad, for starters. She hadn't really had the chance to use her psychology degree before, but then again she'd only filled in four thousand nine hundred and ninety-nine applications. Admittedly, this was a pretty pathetic figure amongst Northerners. Monica's nervous, scatty disposition did not aid her in stressful situations like interviews. Her handwriting on application forms made her Rs look like Ps so she usually spent the first five minutes explaining that her name wasn't Puddles.

If Monica's only medical problem had been nervous incontinence she could have coped. Her particular condition was far more damaging, embarrassing, and there was no known cure. At three hundred out of the volume of applications, she actually got interviews. The problem was that she often left a bomb-site behind her quite by accident. Damaged property, equipment, injured people. Usually they called to thank her for applying, sorry that she was unsuccessful on this occasion before landing her for a bill to pay for collapsed walls and bazookad photocopiers. Of course, they then wished her well for the future and wiped their brows. Ma Ruddles took out a second mortgage to cope. Monica's medical condition stemmed from the rapid build-up of gases in her intestines. It led to her having a seriously deprived or even depraved childhood. Maybe that's why, when Monica met The Hacker, they could relate. Monica was a lonely timid girl but bullies shook in their shoes and stammered in class when our plump little friend sat near them. Her playground nickname had been Hurricane Ruddles, thanks to her reputation for mass destruction. The medical name for Monica's problem was RBW, otherwise known as Really Bad Wind.

Given her track record, Monica lacked optimism about her chances with RETROBASE. A fatalist at heart, she suspected that once something good happened, then something bad was undoubtedly around the next corner. The good thing was that her mother had got hold of an application form, against all odds. The bad thing would be that she wouldn't get an interview. And if she did, then she was bound to accidentally wreck the interview room with nerves.

One feature of the application form really worried Monica. It said that the applicant had to be able to drive. This was pretty bad news as Monica had failed her test three times and been banned from all the driving schools in the North East. On each occasion she'd wrecked the life of a driving instructor with her accident-prone tendencies. The first one had a nervous breakdown after the first lesson, which distressed the whole Ruddles family because he was a good friend of her father's. The second instructor committed suicide but luckily no-one missed him. A bit of a pervert, he often mistook Monica's knee for the gearstick. The third time was the last. She drove straight into the chip shop, after badly timing a wave to her boss whilst parking the car. Newcastle's Fast-Forward Driving School complained that they were going backwards with Monica on their books. She wrecked their Ford Fiestas and scared off their staff.

Ma Ruddles failed to see any difficulty. "So? Of course you can drive lovey, if you had one instructor who had the guts to teach ya. You just tick the 'yes' box and learn in London. Driving round Oxford Street's not something you can learn on the Tyne."

Encouraged by her mother's convictions, Monica kept her cool, telling herself she'd probably get caught for lying on the form but that's the worst thing that could happen. It was a case of five thousandth time lucky. Like Rupert Mumford, Monica Ruddles got the job by accident. She didn't know anything about the crisis in RETROBASE's Personnel office. Their problem was that no one wanted to work in Crouch End. They would have gladly given interviews to refuse collectors, had it not been for HQ's elitism.

The Personnel Office had neglected to conduct medical reports in their rather rushed recruitment programme. If they'd bothered, they would have discovered that Monica was a sitting time-bomb.

¥ ¥ ¥

Suki had a paranoid streak, particularly focussed around things she cared about, namely burgers and CONTACT. CONTACT was definitely not the run-of-the-mill, slow-dance-at-the-youth-club kind of affair so she had to be extra careful. CONTACT captured Suki's imagination to the point of obsession. She was a gifted individual and it would have been her chosen subject on Mastermind, if Magnus would let her. CONTACT was actually christened as CONTACT BURGER MONSTER 2000 (filename: CBM 2000). The strange friendship Suki had struck up with CONTACT made it incredibly difficult to get quality time alone. Had anyone found out about the intensity of their relationship, they would inevitably be forced to split. The justification would be "We didn't want you to get hurt in the long run," or some other such foolish excuse. Half the problem of keeping the whole thing a secret was that Suki was a Crew member with the two most inquisitive investigators on the planet, Simeon and Amber.

Simeon's telephone skills gave him an ear for a secret conversation. "It's in my genes," he would always say, modestly.

Telephones didn't really interest Amber unless the line was plugged into Dateline. Her full-time occupation was falling in and out of love. "You make a spring rabbit look frigid," Suki had once said.

Amber and Simeon wouldn't mind something fishy in the least. In fact, A Very Fishy Project made the world bearable. The three of them lived a life that revolved around other people's secrets. Holding back some of your own would have been classified as breaking The Crew's oath: Thou shalt tell all. Taking a bite from her Whopper-Cropper, Suki could foresee problems. If she told Amber and Simeon, they would plead for CONTACT to be introduced to all and sundry as soon as possible. ASAP was way too soon for a perfectionist programmer. Suki had to make sure every introduction had finesse and a purpose.

Let's be clear. Suki wasn't the kind of girl to indulge in casual flings. She had cultivated this love affair for over four years. A recognition of the nature of true love came upon her when she read about Robert Tappan Morris (RTM), an American college student at Cornell University.

Far from being interested in this lad in trousers, Suki took exception to the virus 'worm' program that he let loose in Internet, the college computer network. Robert was into computer security and the best way to stop hackers breaking in was to find the loop-holes in the system. Like Suki and CONTACT, he fell in love...with a virus.

Internet connected researchers, universities and labs around the globe so that scientists could "talk" to each other about their work. Computers ran many programs at the same time, and they needed the space and the computer power that got taken up by RTM's virus. Viruses are short chunks of "randy" programming code without any condoms. They make copies of themselves wherever they go, hiding inside hard disks that store info and get transferred to floppy disks.

"Randy" computers, like the ones in colleges, have a lot of floppy disks fleeting through and can easily get infected. After RTM's virus took a grip, computers around the world, from University College London to New Mexico, got clogged up and came to a halt. Suki defended Robert to the hilt. He didn't mean to spoil anyone's day. His virus was a game, a challenge, to get a buzz out of how many computers could be reached by a tiny little program. It was supposed to be harmless. It just went badly wrong.

CONTACT 2000 was also a harmless virus program that was even more ambitious than the famous case of RTM. Suki had begun to design a CONTACT program that had several layers to it and could adapt itself and reach 2000 computer terminals. If CONTACT ever did get released on to a network, a person jabbering away at their terminal would see the words, "Burger, burger, give me a burger." The whole screen would fill up with the words until it appeared that files were destroyed by a burger-hunting virus.

After a while, the virus would give in and say, "I hate McDung burgers anyway. Gimme a real burger any day," before disappearing to another terminal. You could save yourself from the Monster by typing the word, "Burger", in which case, the program would very politely say "Thank you" and disappear, leaving you with your original data on the screen.

So the aim of CONTACT was never really to destroy other people's info but to have some fun. To stop people taking their work so seriously and realise that there was more to life. And along the way, to stretch out across the network links, skip-jump-hopping from one to the other...right around the world.

Like RTM, Suki was using the UNIX operating system. An operating system is like one of those old-fashioned traffic policeman standing solemnly on an island waving his arms around letting some cars, or programs, run whilst others are put on a temporary hold. UNIX is popular amongst colleges and universities, industry and some government networks, because it can think "uniformity" where others veer towards "hey, I'm from a different planet to you". It was designed to adapt itself to different computers in a network so that they could hang loose and have a chat.

Other operating systems were more elitist and said, "Hey Sinclair! Forget it, you pleb, we're not having you!" RTM's dad was a bit of a computer boffin too and worked on UNIX's maths programs, so RTM got into it as a kid and after a while began to find flaws in the system. It eventually dawned on him that, instead of being a real square and sowing up the loop-holes all the time, he could be a little naughty and exploit them by running a "fun" virus program. Suki sometimes envied Robert's relationship with his dad. Her father was definitely not into anything marked 'latest technology' and would have had a heart-attack at having a microwave in the house, let alone embracing a computer program with open arms.

RTM had been so anxious to see whether his idea would work that he became sloppy towards the end of his program and made mistakes. One of his major errors was not to do a test-run. Suki wasn't about to make that mistake. She set up three of the computers in the room so that they could talk to each other on the floppy disk. If anything went wrong, nothing got infected except a cheap floppy...

Just as she was about to type >TEST RUN, she heard familiar voices. Simeon and Amber had finally tracked her down. Mildly irritated, she exited from the program, whisked her disks out and chewed the last of The Whopper, with a marked look of innocence.

"There she is! Caught you!" Amber shouted, excited. "What the hell are you doing in here? Listen, Sucksy, you've got to..."

"Jesus! Turn down the opera, will ya?" hissed Suki. "Library, man. Silence signs, you know, like no noise? Can't you read, eh?"

"Yeah, and you can?" jibed Amber, looking at the hamburger wrappers from her father's burger bar.

"Hey, what the hell are you doin' with a wheelchair? Are you hurt bad?" asked Simeon. Had something terrible happened to the love of his life? "Have you got a cell lose in there?" snapped Amber, who wasn't making much headway with Ivan at the moment. Watching Simeon batting his eyelids at Suki just made it all the more frustrating. "Ivan called. Apparently, a new timetable's really screwing up. There's a tube crash around four and he can't stop it..."

"What?" asked Suki in shock.

The Library Monitor, a man with baggy eyes, made his entrance.

"What's going on 'ere?" He glanced shrewdly at the burger wrappers. "Which one of you has been eating in here? Give me your names now," he ordered, getting out a note-pad.

"Actually my name's Santarinosova Jenamilia Anastassia Beluchi and I'm a daughter of the Russian Tsar," boomed Amber in a Russian take-off. "Are you always so rude to your guests, huh? What makes you think I would CHOO-OO-SE to come to a place like this?"

"You're not even at the college?" He was horrified. "I'm calling security."

Only a miracle could save them now. Luckily, one was on its way.

"Ow...ow...ow," cried Suki, clutching her legs.

The Library Monitor was alarmed. Simeon half-hoped that Suki was having an orgasmic sensation just being near him, and half knew it was a game.

"It's happening, it's...coming back. It's really coming back, guys! Hasn't anyone got the brains to help me up?" snapped Suki.

Amber clicked and went into overdrive. She had the gift of being virtually anyone on command, including the caring nurse type with a touch of Jesus. "Is it really, baby? Are you sure? It's a miracle. The Lord listens every time. Take it slow now."

"Shall I call an ambulance?" asked the Library Monitor desperately. The library was rarely the venue for a spiritual experience.

"No, you're doing fine," encouraged Suki.

She edged her way out of the wheelchair and stumbled around the room. "Bit stiff, like. You're in the wrong job, d'ya know that?" she said seriously, turning to him. "You'd put Billy Graham to shame, man."

The Library Monitor watched them from a window whilst he stocked shelves, as they ventured slowly down the ramp. The back of Suki's black leather jacket read, "I'm a Rolling Stone." He mistakenly inserted a "bird-spotting" book under "trainspotting". "Maybe she's right, I am in the wrong job," he muttered half to himself.

Outside the college gates, Suki lost her rag.

"What tube crash? Another bloody King's Cross! Why the hell doesn't somebody do something?"

"Exactly!" rejoiced Amber and Simeon.

"They think it's a hoax," explained Amber, taking

Suki's arm. "There's only one person that can fix it and that's you."

"A hack?" laughed Suki nervously. "Come on! Haven't you learnt anything? If you're going to hack into a live system you can't learn on the way, you need to get it right first time. System manager passwords, operating system, the lot. And all for your love life? Forget it!"

"Ivan knows the passwords, the operating system. Don't worry about that. I've got some morals, guys. This for the people stuck on the train. Not me," pleaded Amber, clutching that aching hole in her chest.

"Well, why can't he do it himself?" asked Suki, suddenly suspicious.

"He doesn't want to get caught. Look, he's got a problem with jobs. This is the first one he's managed to hold down for a while. He needs someone else."

"Suki, there's people at stake, here. You can do it," said Simeon in a whining voice.

"Who am I, Mother Theresa? Stop being such a drip about it," snapped Suki.

"Think about the headlines: 'HACKER STOPS TUBE CRASH. LONDON TRANSPORT FAILED TO HEED WARNING,'" rebutted Simeon a little hurt.

"That's more like it. OK, OK. Let's give it a shot," sighed Suki.

¥ ¥ ¥

Monica's day at work was also being disrupted by things happening out of the blue. Her job hadn't turned out to be as brilliant as she had hoped. Anything built up to be paradise just wasn't as good as the advert. After only two months, Monica hated it. She had spent most of the summer typing into a VDU. The green screen was giving her a lobotomy.

Her 'work with young people' involved spying and

hounding them down around London at all hours of the day. Hence the stipulation for someone who could drive. Nobody guessed she did her rounds via the London Underground, although her office colleagues spent the whole day spying on each other to see who broke the unofficial office rules which were six-fold:

1. Dress smartly. Clients won't respect someone who looks like them. (Monica's own pertinent thoughts on this one questioned a seventeen-year-old's ability to respect someone in a flowery blouse.)

2. You must wash your mug before you finish at the end of the day.

3. Empty your bin in the black bin-bag at the end of the corridor.

4. Don't speak to senior staff unless they speak to you. (In any case, Monica found it astounding that anyone wanted to speak to her boss, Paper Tiger.)

5. No talking in office hours unless it's an emergency. Idle mouths aren't high-achievers. (This was a blatant attempt to stop people having a good time.)

6. Don't be late. Ever. (Christ, this is worse than bleedin' school! thought Monica.)

¥ ¥ ¥

It was a packed tube train, stuck in a tunnel between stations. People were tutting. Monica was fidgeting like a gerbil on heat. Her brain was stuck between two problems. Both were making her head hurt and her body sweat so hard that her seat was damp.

Today, the Midday Pervert Society had sent an elderly City gentleman as their representative. He gripped 'The Times', but was too busy peeking over at Monica's sweat-stick red blouse to read a word. She was too engrossed with Problems #1 and #2 to really notice him or anyone else.

She dived for relief into her red handbag and came up trumps. Grasping a chewy Nurofen, she paused only to pull out a few strands of hair from it before she panicked again...

Problem #1: She had broken Rule 6. She was already thirteen minutes, eight seconds late returning from lunch. They would make her the topic of conversation in the office...

Flicking momentarily to Monica's office, the whole place had an exam room atmosphere. People sat burying their heads in computer print-outs of student records. Petra, a colleague from a neighbouring office, was frantically searching for Monica. Nobody knew her whereabouts, and no-one was going to hide it. Heads pointed at the clock, as if to say, "That Monica! She deserves to get murdered for this."

Petra sighed loudly outside Paper Tiger's open door, using up more oxygen than was rightfully hers. "Ohhhhh! That Monica! I to-o-old her to file that ten tonne truck of pa-a-aper this morning. Where could she beeee?" she breathed. "Ssue-ue-e..."

Petra annoyed the Tiger. No-one escaped her wrath for any length of time as it would jeopardise her reputation. Admittedly, Panting Petra's hot breathy sighs in the right ear-hole was enough to fire up a saint.

Monica twitched in her seat. Aggravated by Petra's spit clinging to her right lobe, Tiger would probably unleash her attack on those brainless morons in Personnel. In Tiger's book, all her staff problems could be laid at the door of RETROBASE's Personnel Department. It was not her fault that they employed brainless morons like themselves "...to do jobs that a dead cat could do better", was her usual condemnation.

Paper Tiger had five cats and were deemed by their owner as the sole source of planet intelligence. Even dead ones, obviously...

Monica secretly suspected that a Very Brainless Moron gave Paper Tiger her job. Indeed, maybe a dead cat in a glass box was more suited to the job. And it would be far more pleasant to say a cheery "Good morning!" to a stuffed tabby, than those bubbling varicose veins on Paper Tiger's ominous face. Being new, Monica didn't dare joke about these things in the canteen. Cats had ears and nine lives...and looking at Paper Tiger, she was obviously only into her third or fourth.

¥ ¥ ¥

Tottenham Court Road Station. Three impatient people.

"He's late," grumbled Suki.

"Only a couple of minutes," said Ivan, tapping her shoulder.

A tall, tanned and well-worth-the-wait Ivan had appeared from nowhere in an incredibly sexy navy-blue London Underground uniform. "Are you going to be my buddy on this?" he asked Suki.

She nodded dumbly. His strutting features had been his entry ticket into practically every job he had. Many a bod sweating outside the interview room felt their chances had been killed by the appearance of Ivan the Stud, even though intellectually they knew more about cleaning cars or sweeping roads. The only thing that let Ivan down was his inability to stay away from company computers. However, his charm had repeatedly saved him from being pushed out with a bad reference.

"I was just checking to see if the terminal was free. Hi Amber," he smiled. "Follow me."

They walked in twos through the maze of "Private" areas, with Amber and Simeon doing their level best to keep up with Suki's shuttling pace.

"Heard of any new boards?" she asked.

"Oh, just the usual," he replied. "Data Thieves is the best though. It's about the only one where no dork is going to ask for free numbers to 10 Downing Street and stuff like that." Ivan smiled. "I'll give you the connect code later if you like."

Entering a door marked "Technicians Only", Ivan took the driver's seat on the terminal. "Just give me two secs."

He logged in. Suki's photographic memory made a note of the code.

"The Boss's just gone for a sandwich. Moron thinks he's smart," he said casually. "Caught me sniffing around for his password. Says, 'Forget it, Ivan. You'll never get your hands on the control. I use my National Insurance number to enter. You'll never find it'. I just hacked into the Inland Revenue."

Suki was impressed. The Inland Revenue was a difficult manoeuvre.

"Now, do you want the good news or the bad news first?" he asked, relaxing a little.

"Good," said Amber.

"Bad," said Suki simultaneously.

The ever-watchful Simeon said nothing.

"OK, bad news is that we don't know how long we've got. Good news is that Jim's gone for lunch."

"What's he like?" asked Amber out of curiosity.

"Shut up!" said Suki and Simeon together.

If a nuclear war was going to break out, Amber would have no problems deciding how to spend her last minutes on Earth. Suki and Simeon turned their minds to more important things.

"You mean it could crash any minute?" asked Simeon, gulping.

"Where's it going to crash?" asked Suki, feeling the

prickle of excitement.

Ivan pressed a button, shooting up a map of the Central Line. He pointed at the Tottenham Court Road junction. "Right there. Under our feet."

"OK, let's get cracking," said Suki. "The system runs on Coral, right? What's it like as a program? Can they trace the hack?" She had lost her nerves. "What's the bloke in the Control Room like?" she asked as an after thought.

"That's what I just said!" grizzled Amber.

¥ ¥ ¥

On the tube, Problem #2 was beginning to dominate Monica's existence. She cursed her luck. If she had avoided trying to do a Linford Christie in her lunch-hour, the situation would have been more manageable. But Mam had rung and insisted it was an emergency...

Personal calls weren't allowed unless someone had died. "It's OK, I won't tell anyone," Petra half shouted.

The Eyes popped up from behind VDUs and filing cabinets, staring at Monica.

"Aw, Mam...Auntie June? Really? That's terrible!" Monica improvised loudly.

All The Eyes disappeared back under paper. Boring, boring, boring, somebody died and that was allowed.

Audrey had yet to appreciate Monica's difficulties. "June? There's nought wrong with our June. Listen now, Monica. There's a sale on in Underwoods and I saw a pair of lovely beige trousers for your dad...course by the time I found the fitting rooms they'd bleedin' locked us in! Lexy wants some more of those lovely tights from Richard Shops and..." She reeled off a shopping list.

"You can manage that in your lunch hour, can't ya pet? It's only up the road."

"Right, yep the funeral's tomorrow then. Yep, got that," continued Monica, wishing she could tell Mam the truth.

"Don't leave it till tomorrow now, pet," Ma Ruddles warned. "That beige pair went shooting out of Underwoods."

"I'll see what I can do, Mam." She shoved the list into her handbag and faked upset. None of this would have happened if she'd told her mother that she didn't work anywhere near bloomin' Oxford Street.

In a civil war in Underwoods, men's flared beige trousers were at the height of fashion. Leaving no time for a proper lunch, Monica bought a greasy hamburger that still twitched in the wrapper. She knew that she might regret it later, but otherwise the thought of no food all afternoon might rupture her interior.

She fought her way to Oxford Street tube station, racing against the clock, and heard the train entering the platform. Monica favoured Scrabble over the decathlon, but this time she surpassed herself. Belting down the escalator, the doors were about to close but she stuck her handbag in the way and they opened again. Another battle to find a seat, amidst threatening looks from other passengers. Monica figured that the state she was in, she needed it more than any of them.

As the minutes ticked by, the train gave no indication of moving any closer to its destination. By this time, Monica was in agony. The burger had hit her stomach. RBW was taking over her intestines and in danger of breaking out any second.

Over the years, Monica had tried to get treatment for RBW. All the shrinks she'd ever tried in Newcastle called it 'free release'. 'Free' gave the impression of being cheap, easy and painless. The vicious fart that was working its way through her colon threatened to blow away at least a month's wages, after a lot of effort from her to keep the worst of it in and God, was it painful! Her therapist suggested that she look forward to the moment of release. "Let yourself go,

Monica. Repression is self-destructive." Simple enough, isn't it? OK, if a girl's gotta fart, she's gotta fart. This was a gross over-simplification. Monica's eruptions were violent and lacked that silent quality that would have at least remained anonymous. Worst of all worlds.

For years, Monica felt there was something uniquely wrong with her. She was right although she only realised that everyone else also broke The Eleventh Commandment (Thou shalt not release freely in public) quite late in life. As a chubby twelve-year-old, Monica detested PE and crouched behind a bush, only to find herself next to a fellow truant, Mona The Groaner. The sound of leaves rustling violently and Monica yelling for a gas-mask got them a detention. Speaking later to Mona, Monica asked a choice question, "Cauliflower cheese, weren't it?" They collapsed in a sick pile of childish giggles and earned a punishing cross-country run.

Simeon got up to open the window. He felt like he was waiting for a bomb to go off under his feet. Teetering on the edge of this nightmare, he instinctively realised his final wish. Erotic thoughts filled his brain as he glanced at Suki.

"The signal's jammed. That's the third time we've tried it," Ivan said, irritated.

"Let's just send a message through to the platform. At least some people..." said Suki.

"Not just a pretty face, are ya?" Ivan nodded and typed quickly. Suki smiled at being appreciated. Amber looked horrified. Simeon gritted his teeth, moving behind Ivan's seat for the kill. Who the hell did this guy think he was? Just cos he knew how to operate a VDU, he thought he'd got the right to make jibes at Suki, the fantasy that he had been nurturing for years.

The screen read "URGENT NOTICE. PLEASE LEAVE THE STATION QUIETLY AND QUICKLY. URGENT NOTICE."

Seconds later, the message boards on all the platforms echoed this message in orange and black. Waiting commuters swore at the guard but left the station.

"Maybe if we gave them another call..." suggested Simeon, deciding that perhaps he should show he's not just the second best-looking guy in the room but the only one with brains too.

"Saying what?" asked Amber, knowing that she'd probably be the one doing it.

They were interrupted. The door opened, Jim walked in. The words slipped out of Simeon's mouth. "Terrorist attack."

Ivan sighed. Another job gone.

A headline flashed through Suki's head, "Hackers caught crashing the London Underground". But the worst was still to come.

¥ ¥ ¥

By now, everyone trapped into playing the waiting game, had lost their irritation and were looking at the experience as a story to tell. This was the first time Monica had ever seen people on the tube talk to each other. Plots to assassinate the Chief Executive of London Transport were being hatched and wasn't it awful when it was such a nice day and the last place you wanted to be was a hot, sweaty tube train, that kind of thing. A petition to complain circulated.

After a clean fifty-eight minutes of waiting, the train started to boil up. Monica relaxed her muscles with relief. Fatal. Suddenly, her body twisted and froze. The snowball was gaining momentum. She felt that she was at that familiar point of no return. Her mind whizzed through some questions: "What can I say? I'm the world's most dangerous wind-breaker, hold on to your briefcases?" It didn't seem adequate. She couldn't bring herself to open her mouth.

Monica's body contorted and she accidentally kicked

the neighbouring passenger off her seat. Amid the outcry, it suddenly just blew! The sound of a cracking whip tore the heart out of Monica's flesh. She could do little but scream and moan alternately. Toupees slapped the back of glass windows, newspapers danced through the air into the next carriage and noses shrunk into wrinkles upon wrinkles.

It was a case of wrong time, wrong place, wrong life. Like God hated Monica, Problem #3 emerged. The train was the sitting duck in a collision. A Really Big Bang shook the carriage. A loud rumble could be heard on the surface as the carriage belched forward and caved inward. The screams got louder as it keeled over. "It's that bitch!" screamed the elderly City lawyer, devilishly looking at Monica from a roof-top tube map. He wished he'd kept his mouth shut. His teeth fell out.

Poor Monica, hated by everyone now, blanked out to the sound of sirens. She had always dreaded this moment. Her last mutter was to Mam, apologising for eating that hamburger. Half-dead, half-cooked, half-eaten definitely, but still so full of wind. Right then, Chernobyl felt like a fart in a fuse-box.

"Terrorist attack! Relief for tear-gas. Now!" Sergeant Jenkins, first on the scene, barked into his walkie-talkie. A kindly old man had given him an eye-witness account. Jenkins smiled. He saw this as his first step in a meteoric rise to CID.

"She fits the description. The woman in red. We got her. Terrorist apprehended," said Jenkins into his radio.

"Sorry Mam, sorry Mam..." muttered Monica, as she was hauled out of the wreckage.

¥ ¥ ¥

Meanwhile, the gang of crazy keyboarders sat in McDung's in Tottenham Court Road clouded by depression. Not only had they failed to stop the crash, but they were witnesses to the mayhem. Why didn't anyone listen to the people in the know? In fact, Ivan had just got an on-the-spot sacking for meddling with a live terminal. Suki felt slightly sick at the fact that people around her were willingly consuming slabs of mad cow and did not even seem to mind paying for it. She was certain that her burger, sitting untouched in its wrapper, had just moved.

Simeon felt a little demoralised. Ivan gave him a pretty low-down scowl when "terrorist" slipped out of his mouth. Not only was this strange, six-foot tall git in a crass London Underground uniform nosing around in other people's computers wherever he went, he also had his evil eye on Suki. Simeon hoped that despite the smiling, Suki was trying desperately to put the jerk off the idea. He held on vainly to the thought that she was totally embarrassed that he was making a total prat of himself in front of her true love, Simeon. But this Ivanovavitch just didn't seem to catch the drift. As Simeon tried to nurse himself back to normality, Amber tried to interject on the computer conversation.

"This is the fifth job in a row, man," said Ivan, shaking his head.

Simeon wasn't exactly stretching his wires to be sympathetic. Hell, he don't deserve that job. London Underground don't even know it, but he, The Telephone Man had just saved them millions from this crook, he thought.

"What did you do before?" asked Suki.

"Bank clerk. One of the dorks that sits behind the counter and says, 'Ooh no, well I'm sorry you haven't got any money but that cheque's going to take at least three weeks to clear. And if you haven't got your card in the post you'll have to apply again.'" He laughed at his own jokes, noted Simeon in disgust.

"Really boring," continued Ivan. "Money was good

though. Me and a programmer set up a Salami Trap Door from this loaded account." A slight gleam came into his eyes. "Two pounds fifty used to come to my mate's account every night, just before the computer backed-up it's files. He got busted for five months."

"What about you?" asked Suki, horrified that anyone out there would want to use something as sacred as a computer for something as petty as money. "Didn't you get caught?"

"No, it was only my idea. I sure wasn't letting the cash into my name. I just got him the passwords," laughed Ivan. "I know how to come out of trouble."

"Smart, smart," said Amber.

"Sounds like daylight robbery to me," ventured Simeon.

Suki wasn't so sure on this damning verdict. If Ivan was a thief, then why would he want to try and stop the tube-crash? She gave him the benefit of the doubt. On their way home, Simeon pulled Amber to one side. "What the hell's a Salami Trap Door anyway? A burger or something?"

Amber shrugged her shoulders. "Hacker-talk. If you ever make it with Suki, your pillow talk is going to be weird!"

¥ ¥ ¥

Monica was summoned to The Paper Tiger's office, her arm bandaged and her face covered in cuts and bruises. Tiger was in a strange mood. She offered several times to break Monica's other arm after outbreaks of laughter. The Eyes were rotating shifts to peer through the key-hole of Tiger's door.

"Are you telling me you're late cos...I can't even say it. Ha ha ha!" she cackled.

"They tried to arrest me, saying I was a terrorist. It's not my bleedin' fault! It turned out to be signal failure. London's a mad place," sighed Monica.

"Don't you take that tone with me, girl. You're darn lucky to get this job. Those dim-wits in Personnel would employ refuse collectors if they got the chance," said Tiger grimly. "Terrorist or not. Tube failure or not. That's your problem. You can drive, can't you? You know the rules, one hour for lunch. Now come on, back to work."

Monica's face betrayed the wish to stick a fork in one of Tiger's green varicose bubbles. But she'd lose her job, be back in Newcastle, back in the chippy with nothing else to do. And her Mam had put so much into this London trip. She bit her tongue, determined to wait for her revenge.

"There you are, Monica," smiled Petra. "When you've done that filing...here's a pile of urgent visits. My, you look rough."

"Th-th-th-a-a-n-k y-you-you-u, Petra," breathed Monica sarcastically, giving Petra a taste of her own bad breath. All The Eyes nearly fell out and rolled under paper mountains. They now had really good material to bitch about! Monica parked herself in front of the VDU, squinting like Mam. Petra had left piles of requests to visit students in her END MAIL file. Monica preferred to stay local, exhausted after her experience on the tube. She often marvelled at how much computer data could reveal about a person. She picked a name that caught her eye by virtue of being unpronounceable. Sukhvinder Samra. The file showed that this student was of high calibre, but attendance was poor. She was recommended for urgent counselling. At the touch of a button, Monica knew Suki's life history.

¥ ¥ ¥

Suki's parents owned a market gardening business and they were slowly starting to make money, although they insisted it wasn't their prime motivation. Shanti and Janak were doing something that they believed in and were practising what they preached. Suki on the other hand was a lot more practical. Computers, software, printers, modems cost money.

Shanti and Janak didn't realise they had regular adverts over the computer bulletin-boards all around the London network. The more successful the business, the more Janak got paranoid about house security. Despite many rows with Shanti, he tried his hand at interior design. He stuck a few tasteful bars across the window, added five Yale locks to the front door that looked really nice in the dark. And although he'd be the last person to buy anything with 'latest technology' on the box, he got a security alarm, just in case a burglar realised the true value of his garden roses.

Number 39 Lime Road could have been a hostel for battered women posing as an average semi-detached brick box in suburbia. Visitors were rare, because they had to speak into an intercom at the door rather than to a person. If there was someone in, it meant waiting around for five minutes for them to open all the Yale locks. Shanti resented the negative affect on her social life. Very few of her Green World friends bothered coming round any more. The nosy neighbourhood on Lime Road thought of Number 39 as the house where screams and shouts came from...

"That weird man that never says hello..." commented Number 50.

"Probably beating up his wife and torturing his daughter," deduced Number 45 grimly.

"Look at her, she's already got one funny leg as it is," - Number 42, who always stated the obvious.

"Probably trying to get her to have an arranged marriage, you know what these foreigners are like..." - Number 45 could make any episode of "Neighbours" sound like a murder mystery.

Janak had heard this kind of talk and found it quite amusing. It saved having to socialise with them, sending Christmas cards when you don't even celebrate it. Let them think what they like...

¥ ¥ ¥

Monica pressed the buzzer, catching the sound of a bell tinkling throughout the house. She dawdled on the step, as hassling students was an act she despised even if it did take her out of the office. She noticed some of the neighbours peeking around their nets. She blamed the tube-crash for giving her that battered wife look.

Suki froze. Mum and Dad never forgot their keys. She had persuaded them to connect the door-bell to an ansaphone, for her own security against the neighbours. They were always checking up on her family, for some reason, probably boredom. It would only take one of them to call round on the pretext of buying a pound of tomatoes and ask her why she's not in school. Janak and Shanti grudgingly accepted the ansaphone was useful for the business. Monica listened closely to the message.

"No thank you to free newspapers, Jehovah's Witnesses and don't worry, we've paid our council tax. If you've come for the carrots, aubergines, tomatoes, spuds, forget it. You're out of season. I've got some cucumbers left, but you'll have to be quick. State your business and leave your number after the bleep." Ble-ee-eep!"Er, I hope I've got the right house," began Monica. "I'm the Student Officer from RETROBASE, from the college. Er, me name's Monica...Monica Ruddles with an R not a P. I've come to see er...oooh God, I hope I'm saying this right, like. I'm not sure how to pronounce this, right...is it Suckvender Sammy Ra...?"

Some of the neighbours were actually outside their

front doors, openly staring at Monica. "Oooh she's a brave girl, ain't she?" remarked Number 40.

Monica felt a twinge of nervousness, but nothing dangerous. She'd got used to being stared at over the years, she just hated ansaphones.

"Our computers tell me that Suckvender hasn't enrolled on her A-level course. Don't get me wrong like, I'm not saying she hasn't enrolled, it's the computers, right."

Suki stopped the ansaphone, erased the message and flicked on the computer with her left toe. Thank God she made sure she got the password for the Inland Revenue.

Monica rambled on, unperturbed. "It's the second week of term, like, and she really should be on the books. It's OK, not to worry though, I'm not going to pretend that it's really important or anything. I'll call back tomorrow, if that's OK with you?" She laughed sheepishly. "Course you're just a machine, so you can't really tell me, can ya..."

Suddenly, the sound of five quick clicks and a suspicious-looking Suki peaked through a crack in the door.

"You think you gotta a file on me?" said Suki casually. "Well, I gotta file on you too. Monica Audrey-Jane Ruddles, aged 24. Birthday, 5 May. National Insurance number NY 33 10 59 C. Five points on your driving licence and that's only as a learner. Now, what's all this stuff about college?" She took a closer look at Monica. "God you look a mess. Let me guess, another driving lesson or...not Tottenham Court Road. You don't believe all this crap about terrorists, do ya? Christ, you better come in. Fancy a cuppa... Sorry, Mum and Dad only drink camomile."

Understandably, Monica was stunned. Her students usually gave chase rather than cups of tea. She sat in Suki's bedroom, admiring the Indian mobiles with the same goggle-eyed expression. Her eyes cursored to the computer, which was on-line to a bulletin board. Suki paced up and down the room, deep in thought.

She stopped. "You mean my file says I'm a truant? A letter home to my Mum and Dad? But what about my grades, man. I mean I got ten As without going in. I mean what kind of right have they got to have a file on me!" Suki was getting loud and excited.

"They've got a file on everyone in every college in the whole bloomin' country," said Monica meekly. "Even me."

"You mean you used to bunk?" Suki raised an eyebrow, as she scribbled down a number of another bulletin board from the screen.

"Oooh yeah," said Monica, recalling how teachers had been too scared to approach her in case she got nervous and blew them away. "All the bleedin' time. I hated school, me."

"How come you ended up getting a job at the RETROBASE, then? I mean, it's like criminals joining the police force!"

"Well, it's all good experience innit? If you bunked yourself, you're more likely to be able to help, aren't ya? But I don't know why I got this job, man, worst mistake of my life. I mean, I can't even drive, like. I've nearly killed three driving instructors single-handed and I haven't even passed me bleedin' test, man! Me brother calls me psycho-killer! Ha-ha," Monica laughed. Suki joined in, a bit nervously.

"But me Mam would go spare if I jacked it in. She's runnin' round the North East saying, 'Our Monica's got a job in London, ya know.' I hate it so much, like. That bloody Petra woman heats up your neck when she's standin' over ya. And Paper Tiger, now she really is a dragon..." Monica was only just warming up.

Suki was the first person that actually seemed interested in anything she had to say. An hour later, Suki was still getting Monica's life history.

"The thing that changed it all for me was Mr

Goodman, me A level psychology lecturer. I never bunked a single lecture when he turned up. He was old enough to be me Dad, like, but he was lovely...whenever he'd speak, me heart would just fly oop to me mouth and I couldn't say a thing!"

"Hard to believe," said Suki grimly. "My brother's doing a psychology degree..."

"Yeah, I know. Edinburgh University, weren't it?"

"S'pose you got a file on him too. Yeah, he wanted to go as far away as he could from Mum and Dad..."

Sound of the front door banging, locks clicking. Suki stiffened. "They're back." Sounding desperate, Suki thought of a solution. "Look, if I promise that I'll enrol at college, will you tell them that you've just come round to make sure I'm settling in OK on my course or something? Don't say anything about the hamburger you had, OK? They hate hamburgers."

Monica smiled, thinking that she really had found a soul-mate. "I know, me Mam's the same."

Monica was eager to do just about anything to please her first friend in Crouch End. Suki didn't have to worry about having a clash with her parents. Monica was more than willing to slip out quietly into the darkness, and strolled back to her bedsit with a skip in her step. Suki slipped her brother's leather Rolling Stone jacket back in her wardrobe and sat down thoughtfully in front of the computer screen. So that hippy was right. For once, she couldn't concentrate on being with CONTACT. Monica had given her something far more urgent to think about.

4

THE ENEMY

Suki lounged in the front room at 39 Lime Road, half-watching the television screen, not really savouring the Whopper in her mouth. She flicked the channels absent-mindedly, delaying the inevitable. After Monica's informative little visit, Suki resolved to make an appearance at college that day. Being pushed into a corner generated resentment. She gritted her teeth. There was no rush, she insisted, it was only lunchtime.

A morning routine had evolved over the years. It was a pattern of deception that Suki undertook for her parents' sake rather than her own. It demanded energy, alertness and a flexibility that Suki had perfected robotically just when she was feeling quite the opposite. Shanti and Janak valued schools, colleges, education, homework, classes, exams, reports, wringing hands at parents' evenings - the works. "Probably cos you've never been forced to go there yourself!" Suki had screamed at them. "It's so boring!"

Janak attributed Suki's attitude problem to his wife's relaxed approach to motherhood. "At least I have an approach," Shanti had growled. She had accused him of loving his plants more than his children, marking the degeneration into a colossal row. Hardly a day passed when divorce was not on the cards. Suki nurtured her technical interests in this atmosphere, having immeasurable amounts of time to herself. She usually chose to fiddle with equipment languishing in the basement - an old television or the grandfather clock - previously lost to dust.

Shanti's pleading for an easy life gave way to a promise of the unthinkable. Suki agreed to make an effort in making regular appearances at school. She noted that she had made no such contract for her college attendance. Now, much to Suki's consternation, Monica had appeared like some kind of mind-reader to put nails in the educational coffin.

Suki groaned. She really did not need this kind of hassle. She lacked the zest for the usual twilight game of runaround. It invariably meant rushing at a frantic pace, cursing faulty alarm clocks and revelling in the mysteries of the missing biology textbook. Her stomach had rumbled for a Brekkie Whopper. Awaiting her presence on the breakfast table was a bowl of home-made muesli. It was an ideal solution to skid prevention on icy winter roads. Her gut had practically prayed for a bacon sandwich. Anything, just not milky gravel. It was a relatively difficult task to survive as a burger-loving, chicken-eating, ham-curing vegetarian with parents like Janak and Shanti. They were amongst the first bean-freaks and dhal-and-rice fascists in Britain.

On one occasion, Suki had smuggled several Cave burgers into her attic sanctuary. Being too gorged to move, she let the smell of fried onions linger on and the wrappers charred the bin. Their discovery led to Shanti's mild epileptic fit, and Janak's pathological hatred for Amber intensified. It's exact source was never clarified but Suki suspected that her father viewed Amber as the daughter of a meat-selling Greek tycoon. The Burger Find simply added to Janak's notion that Suki was being corrupted by That Man and His Family. Suki termed it The Traffic Light Reflex. Janak the Green, resented Amber because she just made him see Red. It was unfortunate but for Suki, hiding the extent of her friendship with Amber was just one more addition to a long list of hidden pleasures.

The art of living a double life as a vegetarian who ate meat was a perpetual source of difficulty. It would have broken her mother's heart to find that her daughter was a carnivore, seedily venturing out and salivating anonymously in burger joints. Suki thought about her options and went for the arrow marked "liar" if only to stop the hunger pains that no lettuce could cure.

Suki's skill at bunking from school was ironically never displayed in her results. The reports were so good you'd never guess. Suki's lifestyle was quite dismembered from her parents and they shared little, least of all her fascination with technology. Janak found it particularly distasteful. He could just about operate the video after he made Shanti stare at the manual for a couple of hours. He had, at one stage, had dreams of converting the house to wind and solar power but the thought of the windmill ruining his lawn quelled the ambition. The pendulum swung in Suki's favour when she offered to write a program for Janak to input the market garden's accounts. Shanti nodded happily and signed the cheque for a computer installation in Suki's room. Janak baulked at adding up two rows of carrots by himself and a computer would solve the whole problem. Shanti hoped they'd even argue a little less often...but alas there was no software on the market called "Marital Guidance".

If only to be seen and heard, Suki had grown to love a good scream. A scream to Suki was a fart to Monica. Pure therapy. If something was bothering Suki, her lung capacity could usually reflect it, making her a feared commodity. So, sitting irritably for "El Dildo" to start was an unusual experience. Suki was uncharacteristically uncomfortable with the prospect of going to college. It was a feeling that she suspected she might have to learn to live with.

The news bulletin...more boredom...but wait.

"...Government's plan for Education. Minister for Education, Rupert Mumford..." said the reporter.

Suki fumbled for the remote control. This was, after all, the enemy who had brought about this dithering streak in her.

Rupert Mumford was at the Government's Conference on Education, shining in the limelight, in a new suit and smelling of Lynx. A packed hall of journalists, snapping at his heels. Headmasters and school inspectors awaited details from this unknown quantity of a Minister. Permy lurked in the background, wiping his hands. He no longer suffered from nightmares, he was permanently awake. His doctor called it insomnia, Permy himself termed it an occupational hazard.

Rupert cleared his throat. Silence filled the auditorium. "This country's future lies in its children. It's time we stopped cheating our future, cheating our children. Let's give them the chance of a decent education. That, in a nutshell, is what the Government's Education Plan is all about."

As Permy's speech rolled off Rupert's lips, Permy pondered on why this charismatic genius had slipped Cabinet selections. The Prime Minister's capabilities had lowered Permy's expectations of any politician. Rupert continued with his plan, unaware that The Hacker had put a hold on the burger, and was tuning into his every word.

"The Plan is like a surgical operation. An operation to cure a disease. We have to cure old habits and replace them with better ones. Better ones like 'hardwork', 'discipline', 'punishment' and 'reward'. The discipline will begin when a five-year-old steps into a school right through until he walks out as a sixteen-year-old into the world of work."

Sky Moores smiled at his TV monitor. All the staff at RETROBASE HQ had been given an extended lunch hour especially to see the Minister in action.

"If we sow the seeds now," boomed Rupert, "Britain will become a garden of talent, an adventure playground for new ideas." He paused to stare into the camera, with illusions of speaking directly to the nation. "There's a hidden element of young people who have rejected education, ladies and gentlemen. Yes, it's uncomfortable but it's true. This element wanders the street, getting into crime, drugs, vulnerable to all kinds of evil, instead of sitting in classrooms and learning. It is wrong and we have to bring this element back into the fold."

Suki returned Rupert's stare. This maniac was calmly referring to her as an 'element'! Some kind of nasty chemical compound.

"We have to go back to basics, back to English and Maths and History. Measure our talent, test it, prune it. The Education Plan will create a Government agency to test and prune educational standards. That agency is called RETROBASE, Returning to Basic Education."

"REPROBATES?!" screamed Suki wildly.

"Britain is going to resume its rightful place as one of the world leaders with this plan. This takes money, ladies and gentlemen. And the Government is going to invest the sum of twenty-two billion pounds..."

A gasp filled the room. Headmasters smiled, the Minister had made a mistake, of course, he had meant to say "millions" which was a modest increase in itself. School inspectors looked simultaneously shocked and elated. Journalists knew this was incredible news, unmentioned in their briefing papers. Government plans tended to be rhetorical and short on cash. This was wild, this was new, this was amazing. This was the new Minister for Education.

"A price well worth paying to give our children a decent future..." Rupert finished, beaming. He could feel that a lot of very important people were pleased with him.

Suki was not one of them. She could feel her lungs itching for a yell. She replayed Rupert's performance, pausing on a photographic still of him with his mouth slightly open.

"Aaaarrrrggggggggghhhhhh!" Suki let rip. She knew

she was fighting a losing battle. The Government had twenty-two billion pounds at stake, she had enough in her pocket for another Whopper. The odds were stacked against her. If they thought they were going to drag her into the prison compound without a struggle, they were in for a surprise. That hippy was right. The system was on the chase. But they'd have to search with more than a fine toothcomb. If the Minister had a plan, so did Suki. The Hacker was a marvel of disguises and she was about to perform a disappearing trick.

Knowing the complex nature of this task, Suki realised she needed help. She plugged in her two-way radio to call Amber and Simeon. The Crew used a secret frequency and refrained from the urge to share it with anyone else. Today, it was failing her. Amber was engaged and Simeon was not responding.

Untouched by Suki's desperation, Simeon was engrossed in wire-tapping machinations opposite The Palace. The sound of the radio bleeper could not drag him away. He suspected it was Amber, they had intended to meet today. "Sshhh...I've got some Duke getting kinda' intimate." Amber was in a spot of similar urgency, trying to escape her father's clutches. She twiddled with her two-way radio, trying to put her coat on at the same time.

"Hey Ambereen! Five minutes! That's all!" shouted Mr Cavallares from behind the counter.

"Take it off my lunch hour!" shouted Amber.

"That is your lunch hour, girl!" he retorted, cursing to Mrs C.

"Christ, I thought slavery was abolished in 1800 something!" moaned Amber.

Simeon finally responded.

"Hey Sims, anywhere near your lunch-hour?" asked Amber.

"Damn Amber! I was on the verge, there," complained Simeon.

"Hey what do I have to do, huh? Wear Gandhi glasses and walk with a limp just so you'll talk to me? Are you into this or what?"

"Meet you outside the library in twenty minutes," muttered Simeon, embarrassed that his absolute adoration was so visible.

Simeon and Amber had made a pact. They were going to do something about their jealousy. Amber had reasoned that Suki and Ivan connected on a basic instinct, an intellectual interest in the electronic. There was only one way to challenge it and that was to improve their own levels of expertise in hacking. Suki's attempts to coerce them into the more tedious side of doing the groundwork had fallen on deaf ears in the past. It was only with the potential to thwart Cupid from plugging into this undesirable territory ie having one's best friend dating the love of one's life, that led to a visit to the library.

Amber charged her way through the queue to a terminal. "I'm a librarian," she lied to the perturbed twelve-year-old user on the keyboard, pointing to a forged name badge on her lapel. "The system's broken down. Do your homework at home."

"You're horrible," grimaced Simeon, as he typed in their choice of subject matter. "Computer hacking" appeared in green on the screen.

Amber pressed the <Return> button. A title, 'Hackers Handbook' was available. "By any means necessary," she grinned.

Suki was raging through the front-room, throwing her gear into a bag, wound up by the marked absence of The Crew in her time of need. She continued cursing her solitary predicament after banging the front door behind her. Five minutes later, a postman whistled past with the afternoon mail. A letter for Mr and Mrs Samra fell on the door-mat.

Suki speedily trotted down to the college. She had some hacking homework on her mind.

¥ ¥ ¥

A computer hacker with more than two braincells rarely wakes up to the thought of, "I fancy a nice juicy hack" unless she knows the ins and outs of a computer system. To gain entry at all, the hacker's computer has to "speak the same language" as the one being hacked. This involves having the same communications software. Otherwise, any information on the screen looks like Russian to an English-speaker. Hacking's not an easy business. The hacker also needs the name of someone who should be using that system and their password. Any moron that goes into it blind isn't going to be able to break in at all or find out much or worse still, get caught pretty quickly. These days, there's always someone watching...

The multi-million pound security industry is getting wise to hackers, and writing security devices into programs to lock people out when they start doing weird things. Most systems have a little program that says, "OK buddy, forget it. You've had three attempts at the password. I ain't got the time to be sitting around, waiting for you. I'm a busy computer, man, don't hassle me. You're either a hacker or some lazy bum who just don't have a memory like mine. Toodle-oo!" The computer lines disconnect.

When that happens it's a bit like that feeling of having your cashpoint card chewed up by the only TSB machine in Outer Cumbria, which you've walked ten miles to find. You're supposed to be on holiday, you haven't eaten for three days, you're broke and can't remember your number. If you're a hacker, then tough. You haven't done your homework.

Over the years, Suki drummed a few things into Amber and Simeon about hacking. No system is totally secure, loopholes can be found either in the programs or operating systems themselves or the way that people use them. But to find loopholes, you had to have access to a terminal. The only reason Suki and Ivan were able to hack into London Underground's central timetabling system, for example, was because Ivan had access to a terminal and the boss's password. Having a terminal like that, already linked up to the system, by-passed any of the system's defences to outside hackers.

People aren't as logical as computers. They make mistakes. They don't listen to computer security experts who tell them to use passwords that aren't real words. They don't keep them a secret. Remember that night in Outer Cumbria in a snow storm, when you were too cold and hungry and lazy to go and find the TSB machine yourself? You gave your trusty mate, Dingbat, your card and your number...OK Dingbat's not the kind of bloke to do the dirty on you, but the point is that you're no longer the only one who knows your number.

¥ ¥ ¥

Everyone had deserted the cafeteria. Understandable in some ways. The burgers tasted like slabs of baked dog-droppings. But most people who frequented the cafeteria had no taste buds anyway. Something was going on. Crowds of people were heading to the main hall. Suki eavesdropped en route. She rarely aroused suspicion as people saw her, they tended to assume that her limp indicated that she was probably deaf and dumb too.

"...I'm really worried. I haven't revised at all," said Preeti Seekh. "I didn't get the chance. Rob called me from Bognor Regis last night, and we were talking for at least three hours..."

Yeah yeah, sure. Suki veered away from the crowd and turned in the direction of the Administration Block, halted by a harsh voice. "Excuse me, where are you going? The exam hall is over here," boomed a lecturer, pointing back to the crowd.

Suki twisted around and the crowd of students stared. She made her way up to the lecturer. His frowning face revealed his hatred for under thirty-fives. He was better suited to the army but lack of fitness led to his teaching career. His name tag read, 'Brian Poulton. Chemistry Department'.

"What d'ya think I am, deaf or what?" seethed Suki, avoiding drawing yet more attention to herself by screaming. Trust her to get landed with a nasty compound like him for A-level Chemistry.

"You are heading straight for an Insolence Order, do you hear me? Get in line and see me immediately after the exam," he glared.

Insolence Order? Was that like a detention? Is that what that Rupert guy was on about when he referred to "discipline" and "punishment"? Old Poulton Pants was obviously a cast-off from the Nazi era. He probably taught the Third Reich a few things, like what gases to use in the camps, considered Suki, not knowing that the RAF wouldn't touch him with a barge pole because of his very dodgy affection for Hitler. Christ, school was a doddle. College was like the army. And what was that about an exam? Suki stood in line. The student brigade marched off to the exam hall. Hundreds of students entered the testing ground, some trying to look cool, others still revising, noses buried in their pencil cases.

"Testing, pruning, testing, pruning..." Suki muttered Rupert's buzz words.

Mr Poulton invigilated. "Silence! We're already running behind time. Paper One of the Start Exam lasts forty-five minutes and is a general knowledge paper. It is very important. Quiet at the back!" he barked. "It will decide which level you will be taught at, so I hope you've all revised thoroughly. If you haven't...well...tough." He almost managed a smile.

Preeti Seekh, sitting in front of Suki, started sniffling in her pencil case, annoying the jitters out of everyone. Suki managed to contain a scream, content to whisper, "Who left the tap on? Drip, drip, drip."

The lecturer handing out papers wandered towards Preeti. The strategy had worked yet again. Sympathy poured out. Preeti begged to be sent back into the exam but somehow, the nurse in the sick bay wouldn't hear of it. Everyone else had to suffer the nightmare of Paper One.

Suki's nightmares revolved more around being in the college grounds rather than sitting exams. She had grown accustomed to spending the least amount of time possible in school and still sustained the best grades in its history. No hacking was necessary. At thirteen, Suki had been interested in conning video arcades by remote control to avoid paying for a game. Preeti Seekh was sitting in a classroom at the time, giggling in a biology lesson cos the teacher had just said the word "vagina". It was a different level of thought and interest. At fourteen, Suki was sorting out why her Dad's 1969 Phillips TV didn't work. That was the day that Russian TV came to Crouch End.

If we flick back a few years to 1987, Amber's fat arm was dangling a heavy rope from the sky-light to a huge, collapsed TV aerial. The familiar sound of Janak in a state of hysteria pervaded the view from the basement. A younger Suki, screw in mouth, commented, "Still in quite good condition."

Janak was not impressed. "I'm going to have a heart-attack," he screamed. "I'm going to die. Christ almighty! My oldest TV! What are you trying to do to me!"

Shanti appeared at the top of the stairs, thumping feet and looking angry. "For God's sake, Suki, what's going on?"

"Dad's having a fit about an old TV set. Doesn't work though, does it?" she said, calmly. "Now watch this," she giggled, opening a window shaft. "Now Amber! Pull it now!"

Upstairs, Amber pulled the rope over her shoulder and like a dutiful mule, she plodded to the other side of the room.

Fuzzy pictures of a Russian newsreader appeared.

"How the hell..." Janak looked at his daughter with suspicion in those steely eyes.

"Now, what's the matter with you?" Shanti barked. "You! She fixes it and you still moan..." They argued.

Suki and Amber, hands cupped around chins, parked in front of the renovated television. Amidst the din, Suki eventually emerged victorious in the decibel war. "Shut up! Christ, can't even learn Russian in peace!"

After that, a Physics GCSE paper was like a family picnic in the park. Painful, what with only cheese and tomato sandwiches, but relatively unexacting.

¥ ¥ ¥

Suki was bored after half-an-hour and irritated. Other students around her were clearly developing brain tumours over silly questions like, "What is the difference between an amoeba and a mammal?" Suki's ideal response was "If your name's Mr Poulton, not a lot," but decided it would only make things worse. Her irritation stemmed from this exam hall diversion to her plan. Unable to tolerate the torture any more, she walked out, avoiding eye contact with Mr Poulton. Eyes lifted from pencil cases. At least someone else has found the exam so difficult that they've thrown the towel in, they reassured themselves.

"You! Where are you going?" shouted Mr Poulton.

Suki rolled her eyes. What, another Nuremburg? "I've finished."

"Yes, and I'm Napolean."

Suki didn't like to say it but with that 2 cm square

moustache, Hitler was a more obvious choice.

"Impossible. It's a 45 minute paper," he said suspiciously. "That's it. Go to the Administration Block. Ask Mrs Turner for an Insolence Order and wait outside my office!"

"Yes sir." Suki saluted and her eyes shone. It was her preferred destination in any case, and now she knew the name of a college secretary.

Inside the grey corridors of the college Administration Block, Suki ventured towards the 'Student Records' section. She was privy to an argument between a finance clerk and a student.

"If you don't live in the Borough, you shouldn't be doing a course here," snapped the bod.

"Yes, I know all that but that's cos the records aren't all there," replied the student huskily.

Suki instantly recognised his voice. Ivan! She noticed that she suddenly felt a lot happier, but tried to put that at the back of her mind.

"If you check your computer records, you'll see the fees are paid in full for the whole year," insisted Ivan.

"Have you got a receipt?" asked the clerk, reluctant to admit that he couldn't use a VDU.

"Oh come on!" says Ivan. "D'ya want my passport, my birth certificate, my NI number..."

"Hi," greeted Suki. Their eyes met. "Problem with my cousin?" she asked the exasperated clerk. "He's living with us, you know. Here's my student card."

The bod made a note of the address. "Why didn't you say so?" he asked Ivan. The clerk returned to his office and slammed the door.

"Thanks Suki," sighed Ivan. "There's some things computers can't do and that's give you an identity overnight."

"I was hoping to get rid of mine today," laughed Suki.

"Oh yeah? If I had an identity like yours I wouldn't throw it away," said Ivan eagerly. "What's the problem?"

"God knows why you want to come to college. I'm trying to escape. I feel like MI5's after me."

"No problem, I can fix MI5," said Ivan modestly.

¥ ¥ ¥

Suki knocked on the door labelled "Student Records".

"Mrs Turner?" she called, opening the door to see a wizened old face poring over a computer screen.

"Come in," called the secretary.

"Mr Poulton's having a few problems in the exam hall. He sent me to get you, Miss," said Suki, with a sense of urgency. "A few students were cheating and he wants Insolence Orders...It's a real mess in there."

"Oh no!" The secretary was horrified, snatched a key from a row of hooks and began locking the door.

Ivan bounced around the corner, clutching a few sheets of paper. "Hello, Mrs Turner," he enthused, as if he'd seen an old friend.

"Hello, yes...I'm in a rush," she said.

"Mr Poulton said I should put this in his pigeon hole. He lost my last essay so I've got to do it personally," smiled Ivan.

"Hurry up, hurry up," said Mrs Turner, unlocking the door again.

Ivan moved in and out in twenty seconds. Mrs Turner swept past them, muttering incoherently.

They moved quickly. Ivan had had just enough time to snatch a spare office key from the hook. While Ivan locked the door from the inside and opened the window, Suki called up the computer menu on Mrs Turner's terminal which had been left on in the rush. She searched for the right directory, conveniently called "RETROBASE". She began formatting her disk to copy the whole range of files.

Ivan was on another terminal.

"What's that?" asked Suki.

"Today was Paper One, right? Tomorrow's going to be Paper Two, right? Nobody's revised right?" he grinned.

"Ivan the Terrible," murmured Suki in shock.

"Ivan the Broke," he replied.

Fifteen minutes later, Mrs Turner was back in the empty office from her wild goose chase. "Oooh there's a chill in here? Did I leave the window open?" she said to herself.

On their way home, Ivan popped into the key-cutters. "I want an exact copy of this," he said handing over a rectangular piece of blue putty, embedded with the shape of a key.

"Never know when it might come in handy," he winked at Suki.

"Ivan, has anyone told you you're a crook?" she asked.

"Yeah, it's not an original line," he admitted. "It's OK. I don't take it personally. Is it my fault if they can't take a joke?"

"Well, I don't dig crooks. Especially when I get crossed by one," warned Suki. "If you cross me even once..."

"Suki, I don't cross people that have nothing, OK?" he said earnestly. "In the space of two days, we saved a whole lot of people from getting killed. I lost my job for it, right? You just got me a place at the college, right? We make a great team, right? Am I really going to say thanks by stabbing you in the back? No," said Ivan, his hands in his pockets. He pulled out some change. "Fancy a burger?"

"A burger? Do I like oxygen?" Suki laughed.

"Let's forget The Cave," he said. "Amber might get the right idea. How about McDung's or..."

"Forget it, anything else tastes like dog-shit," said Suki firmly.

They began having one of those killer computer

conversations that you need a degree in Advanced WINDOWS to understand.

"Got in the gateway," said Ivan, animating with his hands. "Great, no problems. Just needed to catch the password. One of those invisible password bastards. Couldn't go anywhere after that."

A little later, Suki and Ivan were still giving each other some hacking tips on how to get the best from a hack when Simeon and Amber appeared. "All right," Suki motioned to them, before returning to this tantalising technical problem. "Easy. Open the 'Suggest' account. Program it to give you a freeze and a screen clear. Bomb it at least 150 CPS."

"What the hell is this?" yelped Amber, fresh from a deluge of reading much of the same jargon. "Do we really need to talk in code?"

"Sshh..." said Simeon, trying to look as equally engrossed as Ivan.

"Overload it with garbage," continued Suki. "Open a log-in account, stick the garbage in there. Freeze, unfreeze. Catches the password in the buffer!"

"Brilliant!" breathed Ivan and Simeon together.

"Brilliant," grunted Amber. "Let me know when the English translation comes around."

"Too difficult if you're not a programmer," confessed Suki.

"There's other ways of getting information," smiled Ivan. He told them about their college adventure, earlier that day.

"That's illegal," confirmed Simeon and Amber together.

"So's listening in to other people's phone conversations," jibed Ivan, unimpressed by Simeon's lack of daring.

"And pretending to be something you're not," said Suki defensively.

"Everyone does it," said Simeon.

"Not me," said Ivan, about as righteously as a bankrobber can.

"If you had my job...hell, if you had any job..." remarked Simeon, spitefully.

"You are just a..." Ivan stopped as his eyes caught Suki deep in thought. "You OK?" he looked concerned.

"I'm going to kill myself," said Suki calmly.

Their attention shifted to shock horror. "Why, I mean your Pa's not all that bad..." cried Simeon.

"Bad? He's worse. When's the last time you ate gravel for breakfast and drank nettle wine at Diwali? Relax, no wrist slashing. I'm going to die on computer, that's all," laughed Suki. "I want to terminate. Act like I don't exist. Get this Monica woman off my case. She's cool but hey, they're all the enemy, right? I saw them on TV. You know what they called me? The hidden element! Like I'm ET or something!"

"Not far wrong," muttered Amber with hate in her eyes.

"Forget it. You can't do that," insisted Simeon, thinking back to what he'd read in the library. "You'll be chasing your files all round the mountains, man. Births and marriages, passport office, national insurance, banks, school. And your ma and pa's files. Too much hassle. Forget it."

"Yeah, but..." began Suki.

"Yeah, college isn't that bad. You could just enrol," admitted Ivan.

"Yeah, but..." said Suki.

"Yeah and Monica's already met you, right? Forget it," said Amber.

"Yeah but I hate classrooms!" shouted Suki. "I'm going to kill myself!"

"Hey Suki, don't shout! People will think the meat is mad cow!" yelled Mr Cavallares. "Not good for business."

"Yeah, kill the parrot first, will you?" said Amber, seeing her father roll his eyes. She turned to Suki.

"What did your Mum and Dad say?"

"They know nothing. Ignorance is bliss," sighed Suki.

¥ ¥ ¥

"What is it with you?" shouted Janak, waving the letter in Suki's face. "We give you everything you want and this is what we get? You're a truant! What is it with you?" His voice was hoarse.

"Janak, why do you always have to shout?" shouted Shanti. "In twenty years, we've never had a conversation. Not me, not your children. Shout shout SHOUT SHOUT SHOUT! What's the matter with YOU?"

Another row. Suki disappeared into her room, to psyche herself up for the result. Her father was about to do his usual "spoilt brat" routine of insisting on his right to "shout at my own kids or forget it. I'm not speaking to anyone in this house". And more importantly, The Big Problem remained. It seemed as if there was no option. The impossibility overwhelmed her. There was nothing for it, she had to enrol.

She switched on her computer and scoured the college communications disk for any enlightening information. She had mistakenly copied more than one directory, as often happened in a rather rushed download. The second one was marked "Confidential" but in any case, she lacked the user identification to enter it. She faced the future and dialled her modem into the local RETROBASE office...

¥ ¥ ¥

Monica had been working late in the office for over a week, her desk taking the shape of an over-sized in-tray. Petra had been deluging her with filing from a rainforest.

"Trees? I don't care about trees, I care about it being nearly three weeks into term and half our truants not being enrolled," said Paper Tiger briskly. "You care about trees? Go back to Newcastle, go back on the dole. There's plenty that'll take your place!"

Monica hummed to herself. Irrespective of her status as a victim of the Tottenham Court Road tube crash, despite her near arrest for terrorism, and that she nearly died yesterday, Monica looked on the bright side. She was alive, she had made a friend in Suki, she was definitely not a terrorist and what's more, she was in love...

Monica had found someone "nice" in the office, someone she would have liked to sit with in the canteen, someone who she suspected would appreciate her sense of humour, someone with the maturity and caring persona to understand her medical problem. Monica was either psychic or really perceptive. So far her contact with Gunster had been when he had opened the door for her as she was coming back from Petra's office with a skip full of paper for filing. Monica got a thrill from just thinking about him, with a touch of self-censorship. It's oooh, lovely! But ssshhh...don't tell anyone, it might be seen as breaking Office Rule # 4, "Don't speak to senior staff unless they speak to you."

Gunster rarely had reason to enter RETROBASE's Crouch End branch as he was responsible for the financial affairs of all the branches in the region. As the Regional Accountant, Monica saw him only when there was a query or when there was occasion to oversee Paper Tiger's boss's expenditure plans. Gunster travelled around the country with his job, with all the perks of an executive. The Eyes noted that the only time Paper Tiger displayed any signs of becoming human, ie started wittering on about her cats and her caravan in Kent, was when Gunster came in. And he was such a respectable man that he actually pretended to listen to her. Maybe cats were interesting when you got to that age...

Gunster was old enough to be Monica's father, but that did'nt bother her...

Mr Goodman was older if anything. Thinking about the lovely feeling that Gunster left in her heart, Monica got a real fright when the computer on her desk made a sound.

"Ooooh! Who's in here?" she whispered loudly, eyes twitching form side to side.

Nothing happened, nobody answered, except more sounds from the computer. Monica was a bit jittery but curiosity made her remove the paper piles. She watched the screen, which seemed to have a life of its own. It reminded her of piano in "The Dog and Duck", a pub in Newcastle. The screen read:

Please enter User Identification:
"Monica Ruddles" appeared like magic on the screen.

"Who knows me name?" Monica was amazed. This was incredible.

Please enter password:
The Hacker almost knew by instinct that this wasn't going to be difficult.

The word **"Monica"** appeared on the screen.

"Aw, come on. Gimme some credit, man. Try again," jeered Monica, playing the game now. She could almost imagine someone racking their brains about it on the other end.

The word **"Psycho-killer"** appeared. "That's it, man! Excellent! That's it! Aye, it's not our Danny, is it?" Monica wondered.

The menu appeared. Suki opted for "enrolment" and an enrolment card filled the page. Suki entered her details, feeling the urge for a Stake-out Breaker coming on. This was mega painful. This had echoes of going into a police station and saying "Yep, OK. Beat me up."

"Aye, it's Suki!" said Monica, seeing Suki's name appearing on the file. "That's brilliant! My first enrolment! What a mate! What a mate!" She reached for the phone.

"Suki! It's for you!" called Shanti. "Someone called Monica?" she said, her hand over the mouthpiece.

Suki gritted her teeth. "I'll take it upstairs... Monica? I feel like killing you. Thanks a lot for throwing me in it. Great mate you turned out to be. I've just enrolled. You're there...now? And you don't mind?" Suki was relieved. "Yeah yeah, I know computers are great. Listen, this bloody letter...how? I thought you said..."

"Oh that's terrible! I'm so sorry, like," gushed Monica. "Petra didn't say anything about the letters going out. I'm so sorry, like Suki, I'd never throw you in the crap like that."

"Petra, the heavy breather, so you didn't know anything. Well, my dad wants to kill me by force-feeding me with carrots but you're forgiven."

"Listen, is there anything I can do? You've enrolled now so maybe, if I ask Petra to send another letter explaining that the first one was a mistake cos she's the one that does that after she's asked Paper Tiger to clear it. Or what if I came round and told your Mum and Dad and had a chat..." Monica felt a pang of guilt.

"Tell you what, Mo, what bothers my parents the most is their daughter having a black mark against her name. That really bugs them, right? They're ashamed to go out in the street cos they think everyone knows their daughter's a crook, a criminal, a hidden element, vulnerable to every evil in society, right? That really wrecks their day, gives them bad vibes, who knows maybe their carrots won't grow the right way up now." Suki had an idea.

"Oh no, that'll kill their business," sympathised Monica.

"Yeah, and you know how hard they work," said

84

Suki, almost rubbing her hands with glee. "So, how about if we share a secret, just you and me."

"Oooh yeah," said Monica, her eyes gleaming. She loved secrets mainly because she could never keep any from her Mam. Except the one about Oxford Street and that hadn't turned out very well. Now, Suki, was offering her a tap-your-nose. In Monica's dreary life of pining for what you couldn't have, ie Gunster, any bit of excitement got a "Yes" vote.

"If I take the black mark off my name on the boss's computer...what's her name...Paper Tiger? Yeah, if I just rub it out like it didn't exist. Delete, terminate, kill. And then I stick in another letter, saying that the first one was a mistake..."

"Yeah, that's OK like, but I don't know how to work Tiger's computer..." confessed Monica.

"Don't you worry about that," said Suki, gleefully. "Don't worry about a thing, Mo, OK? You won't get into trouble with Paper Tiger cos I'll delete the second letter after it's been sent out, OK?"

"Oh that's grand," said Monica relieved. "I just don't know how their computers work, that's all it is, like."

"OK, listen very carefully," said Suki, reeling off a list of instructions about how to download a disk.

After an hour, Suki had everything she needed to get into RETROBASE HQ's files. "Mo, has Paper Tiger got anything written on her computer? On sticky tape or anything?"

"Well she's got a photograph of her cat. Is that what you mean?" inquired Monica.

"She likes cats, does she?" asked Suki.

"Loves 'em, man, more than any human," laughed Monica.

"What's her cat called?"

"Well, she's got five, like, but her favourite, the one in the photograph, is Pepsi. She's got one called Cola, one called Tango, one called 7-UP..."

"I get the picture, thanks Mo," smiled Suki. "This

will keep Mum and Dad really happy. The minute the next print run of letters goes through you just give me a call, OK? Leave a message on the answering machine, something like 'Terminate', OK so they don't guess? D'you fancy going for a burger, sometime? Sorry, I forgot...we'll go for a coffee."

Later Suki stood by her window, flashing her torch towards Simeon's bedroom. "Come on Simeon, you lazy bum. I'm giving you computer training like you're never gonna get and what the hell are you doing?" she muttered.

She tried to rouse Amber. "Hey Mr C? Yeah, I know it's late. I'm hungry, is Amber there? She's reading? What like, books? Come on, Mr C, you're having me on. Send her over, she needs the exercise."

Minutes later, Suki was on-line to RETROBASE HQ. This would at least disconnect her nightmares. Without realising it, Suki was about to begin another one that was more deadly than she could ever have imagined.

5

THE REGIME

Suki heard the door-bell. At last, Simeon and Amber arrived, looking bleary-eyed. Glancing over her shoulder, Suki snatched the burger package and stuffed it under her jumper. "Life-saver. Mum's got a vicious quiche brewing. What you been doing?"

"Reading," revealed Simeon. "Ow! I mean...er..." Amber kicked his shins.

"Nothing," smiled Amber through gritted teeth.

"Reading nothing, eh?" Suki smiled, getting the picture. "Listen guys, there's nothing like learning on the job."

Three faces reflected in the light of the green screen.

"Just watch this space," garbled Suki. A Super-Whopper Cropper hung limply from her mouth and her body raced with adrenalin.

"This'll give me cancer, man," muttered Amber, wiping the green-glow sweat off her face. "Ow! I mean it's great." She rubbed her ankle and glared at Simeon. "Just great."

Suki ignored them, engrossed. "I've got a funny feeling that the Paper Tiger's password is Pepsi," she whispered. "But I'm not sure. Let's have a go."

The system requested for the network user's ID.

"Shit!" screamed Suki in horror.

"What? What?" asked Simeon, looking around alarmed. Working in Suki's house, with parents like hers, made him paranoid.

"I don't know her name. Paper Tiger's name!"

"Who's Paper Tiger anyway?" asked Amber in a lazy tone.

"Supervisor. Monica's supervisor," said Suki, depressed. "Most of the time, people just use their names as NUIs."

"Office supervisor," said Simeon, fishing through a mass of photocopies. "Got it. Try 'supervis' or something."

"Let's see that. Hacker's Handbook, eh? You guys have really been working hard, haven't you?" smiled Suki, trying to whip up some encouragement. "I tried buzzing you today, where were you?"

"Library," replied Simeon, making sure Amber's size 10s couldn't touch him.

Suki typed in 'supervis'. The screen read "Re-enter NUI." Simeon was disappointed.

"Hang on, I've got an idea," exclaimed Suki. Another route became suddenly apparent. Find a cat called Pepsi and teach it English? Nope. Suki accessed Monica's files again. Employment contract, date of starting, her qualifications. A letter offering her the job. Perfect. It was signed by the notorious Paper Tiger, "Susan Wallis, Office Supervisor"

Simeon stood over the printer. "Hey, you were right! How did you know her password was Pepsi, babe?" He turned in wonderment.

"My name's not 'babe' and you can't learn everything in one lesson, OK?" snapped Suki. Was there something about her that brought out paternal instincts? Simeon looked like he'd been kicked somewhere very painful.

¥ ¥ ¥

Monica was not alone in working late that night. On the other side of London, Abraham, Sky Moores' personal assistant, was doing some overtime at RETROBASE'S Head Office. People thought it was strange for a young man of his calibre to be a workaholic. The lone-figure of Abraham pored over documents, plastered 'confidential'.

Stan, the night-watchman, sighed in disbelief. "Not you again, sir!" he said. "Shouldn't you be at a nightclub or something? You don't want to throw your life away looking at a computer screen."

"Just another hour, Stan," smiled Abraham. It was an inane grin from a martyr in seemingly painful but quiet suffering. In real agony at around twenty-five grand a year.

It irritated Stan, who had more mundane concerns than martyrdom, like the urge to lock up and go home to Edna. This office was practically the boy's home. Stan acknowledged that if he had a penthouse in Richmond, the last place he would be was work. But Abraham enjoyed working in the silence of the evening, when there was no scraping of finger-nails being filed and no eyes staring at him...

"Doesn't say much about himself, does he?" commented Donna, new on the typing section. "I mean, I don't think I've heard him say anything."

"No, he's so boring. What can he say? He doesn't do anything except work, work and bloody work!" remarked Jackie, whose eyes were suffering from winking conjunctivitis. Abraham was a lost cause for her. "I bet you he doesn't even know who Bobby Brown is!"

"Don't be hard on him. He's just an old head on young shoulders," said Sarah generously. She was equally uncertain about the significance of Bobby Brown.

"Yeah, old. Abraham Lincoln kind of old. He's just a college yuppie going nowhere but up Mr Moores' bum," said Jackie grimly.

Abraham was constantly aware of his position and his age. The two just did not match. He suspected in a cowardly way that, with a powerful man like Sky, he was in rather too deep. Material pleasures and raw ambition made him reluctant to face these facts. He had met Sky at Bucks during his industrial year at University, when he was a mere lab technician doing a few behavioural experiments. He had worked like a dog then too. And to his mind, it had paid off.

None of his University friends had a surprise phonecall from a multinational company offering them a job in the recession. None of them enjoyed the seduction of working on secret projects and none had the ear of one of the richest men in the world. So, for Abraham, sacrificing lunch hours, wine bars, evenings and night-clubs were just part of being a good old-fashioned, dedicated brown-nose.

Forgetting the presence of Stan, he walked into Sky's office and examined the view. Lights twinkled on the river, reflecting ugly architecture. Canary Dwarf. He too had delusions of joining the league of the richest men in the world...

A terminal outside bleeped. Romantically, Abraham imagined some other mortal was out there, competing against him, working just as hard, hungry for success. He thought nothing more of it. Abraham, with all his dedication to The Job had lost his curiosity. His mind was brimming with his running total of overtime hours, experiment results, the registration number of his new car and his bank balance. There was little room for being on the ball. Jackie had been particularly insightful, he was a boring little schmuck. He would live to regret it. The Hacker was about to dramatise his life too.

¥ ¥ ¥

The initial hurdle over, The Crew were into the system. Lists of files lined the screen. "Let's go for 'Testing Programme'," said Suki, recalling Mr Poulton's face. Details of testing programmes for six-year-olds and upwards reeled on the screen.

"What does a six-year-old know?" scorned Amber.

"Depends on the six-year-old," said Simeon sarcastically.

"Hey man, look at this!" breathed Suki. "IQ tests,

conformity tests. Conformity tests? Can you believe it! Someone, somewhere, actually sat down and thought, 'How do I make a classroom full of screaming brats shut up!'"

"Obviously didn't work with you," commented Amber tritely, pretty sore from the fact that Ivan had yet to phone her.

"Where do these guys get the money from, man, to do all this?" asked Simeon in frustration.

"Government. Twenty-two billion pounds," said Suki wryly, pressing the remote controls for the TV and video with one hand.

"Phew! That's a hell of a lot of dough," marvelled Simeon.

A stilled picture of Rupert Mumford appeared.

"Look at the brute, man, ruining my life," said Suki.

"Is he married?" Amber piped up. The other two groaned.

"What's that file, there?" she asked, pointing to "Finance".

The word "confidential" flashed on the screen, informing them that they lacked the user access to the file. "Enter the correct NUI:"

"Try sysman!" encouraged Simeon, hedging his bets again. Whoever installed the system might not have wiped off the NUI left by the program-writers.

No luck. It was a loophole that hackers looked for immediately and security experts had blocked. "Damn!" said Simeon, irritated that none of his reading was reaping rewards.

"Relax, relax. There's other ways of finding things out," soothed Suki, pressing the <Enter> key for a file called "Meetings".

"Bingo!" she said.

A list of four names who attended a meeting in March 1993 appeared on the screen, Sky Moores from a company called Bucks Times Bucks amongst them. Judging by the notes, he dominated the meeting.

Focussing on one line, their eyes simultaneously got larger. "90% - 100% investment of RETROBASE, pending progress on The Operation. Agreed that S Moores to act as Security Monitor for The Operation in his role as Chief Controller of RETROBASE."

"Ain't this a Government thing?" asked Simeon, confused.

"Where's Rupert the Bear on the list?" insisted Amber. "He's a Government bod, isn't he?"

"Weird, very weird. Bucks Times Bucks, I've heard that name somewhere. What's this Operation?" puzzled Suki. She jerked into reality. "God, how long have we been on? I don't need Big Brother watching me. I've got enough on my plate."

They looked at her plate, bad news. No Whopper left.

The sound of five clicking Yale locks indicated that Shanti had returned from her Green World meeting.

"Suki, aren't you hungry?" Shanti called. "It's curried quiche."

"You guys don't want to stay, do ya?" Suki pleaded, hiding the burger wrappers.

Amber and Simeon looked scared and made their excuses.

¥ ¥ ¥

Shanti and Suki sat at the table in silence. Suki tried to eat her quiche under Shanti's watchful eye.

"Dad?" asked Suki.

"Bed," replied Shanti, now immersed in a newspaper article. "College?"

"Great army camp atmosphere," said Suki.

"Good," answered Shanti, peering closer at the small print, eyebrows merging.

"What's up?" asked Suki, expecting another of her mother's Green World horror-stories about dead seals and barbecued Amazon snakes.

"Education plan?" muttered Shanti. "Another one?"

"Tell me about it," grunted Suki. "Oh yeah, Mum, do you know anything about Bucks Times Bucks?"

"Chemistry homework, is it?" smiled Shanti, relieved that she still knew something. "I think it was a drugs company in the 1970s. It sent bad vaccines to Africa and Asia and places like Liverpool. I remember going on a march when I was pregnant with your brother. Of course, your father wanted to put his feet up and do nothing... Is that the right one?"

"I don't know," said Suki, slowly. "Pregnant?"

"Yes, he was very heavy and I could just about walk. They forgot to get insured properly. Lots of deformed kids, lots of claims, especially from Liverpool. The insurance company collapsed," explained Shanti.

Insurance companies going bust? Bad vaccines? Africa? Asia? Liverpool? Drugs? Great reputation. Had Rupert Mumford sat down and thought, 'Wow! Great these guys are perfect. Let's get them to throw a twenty billion pound cheque into the education system!' What do they do, pump six-year-olds with drugs and then hit them with a conformity test?! wondered Suki.

"1976. Divorce," said Shanti.

"What?" asked Suki, puzzled.

"1976 was the year. Seriously thought about divorce."

"Mum you say that every year. Face it, it's not going to happen," grunted Suki. "Anyway, how would you have coped on your own?"

"Easily. Your father's only good with carrots, not children. Nappies? No way. Carrots? Horse manure? Any day," laughed Shanti, returning to her paper.

¥ ¥ ¥

"Good morning, everyone," smiled Gunster, strolling past.

"Good morning, Mr Robbins," murmured the whole office, minus Monica.

Monica's heart thumped. She smiled shyly as he swept past into Paper Tiger's office. Had she just imagined that nod he gave her? Gunster's presence brightened up everyone's day.

"Isn't he the n-n-i-c-est man?" said Petra.

The Eyes intervened to spoil the romantic atmosphere and the accompanying mouths started gossiping.

"Third time in two weeks," said one.

"Maybe he fancies Paper Tiger," giggled another.

"Maybe he's just doing his job," said Monica coldly.

"Ma-a-ybee he's not," snarled Petra, as she dumped yet more paper in her in-tray. "Do this by midday, sweetie, I wouldn't want to deprive you of a lunch break."

Breathers and Farters just aren't on the same wavelength. Maybe God decided that they just shouldn't hit it off, but stuck them together in the same office as some kind of test of religious devotion. Either way, Petra had been distinctly more vindictive towards Monica recently, if that was humanly possible.

Behind the closed door, in Paper Tiger's office, Gunster leaned over her shoulder. He was helping her with some number work.

"Well, Gunster, thank God you're here," gushed Paper Tiger. "I really wouldn't be able to work these figures out myself."

"Susan, take an evening course," advised Gunster. "Adult Education. They'll understand."

"And Pepsi? And at my age, going to a class. No, I'd be too embarrassed..."

"Well, everything else seems to be in order," smiled Gunster, anxious to get out of the room. It had a distinct musty feline atmosphere in there. "The first lot of test results have been inputted now, I suppose?"

"Oh yes, definitely," smiled Paper Tiger confidently,

crossing her fingers and her toes. "Despite the staff problems, I cope somehow."

"Problems?" enquired Gunster.

"Well, there's just no discipline here at all, Gunster. Take that Monica for instance..." moaned Paper Tiger.

"She seems like a nice enough girl to me," said Gunster casually, as thoughts overtook his brain.

Was Susan trying to tell him something? Had she guessed that the only reason he came over to help her with her arithmetic was to catch a fleeting glimpse of young Monica? Was it so obvious how he felt? He thought he had concealed his feelings relatively well. God, he had to escape from this woman...

A knock at the door saved him.

"You won't tell anyone, will you?" begged Paper Tiger.

Never see that beautiful girl again, her shy smile, her hair glistening in the sunshine? He couldn't bear the thought. Gunster shook his head.

"Who is it?" snapped Paper Tiger.

Outside the door, everyone's sensory organs focussed hard. Would she, wouldn't she? "Pe-t-r-a," said the Heavy Breather, holding a glass next to the door.

"I'm in a meeting, Petra," called Paper Tiger irritably.

"It's very, very import-t-ant. Se-c-u-u-rity alert," insisted Petra.

"This better move mountains," muttered Paper Tiger.

Petra, Paper Tiger and the unwitting Gunster pored over a computer print-out from the yesterday's computer back-up records. Clearly, someone had been using Paper Tiger's terminal out of hours, downloading important files.

"Well, I wasn't here last night. I was with Pepsi," snapped Paper Tiger.

"Well, someone's been using your terminal then," said Petra. "And Monica's."

"Monica's?" repeated Gunster innocently.

"Who?" barked Paper Tiger. "Who was doing overtime last night? Look on the list. Well?"

"Mo-o-n-n-ica," cried Petra happily. She couldn't have planned it better herself.

Gunster tried to control his shaking hands in vain. Monica didn't bother trying to control her own nerves. Not only was she being humiliated again, this time it was in front of him.

"Well?" Paper Tiger peered at a sniffling Monica. "You're late. You wear the same clothes every day, you hardly ever wash your cup, you never throw your rubbish out. You might even have terrorist connections for all I know. And now this! I don't think you're really cut out for this job, do you?"

Gunster cleared his throat. "Private word, Susan?" Monica shuttled out.

"Be reasonable, Susan. Does she look like a terrorist to you? Girl doesn't know anything about computers either. Nothing serious. Another chance? Maybe we could finish these figures today..."

"Well, OK Gunster," sighed Paper Tiger, feeling weary with the strain of having to do long division by herself.

Monica was let off the hook, but only just. And all thanks to good old Gunster.

Gunster made a call to RETROBASE'S Head Office. "Mr Moores, not in?" said Gunster surprised. "Strange...I've got a meeting with him. He's left you in charge. Report on the latest budget figures. Yes, I'll come in," he confirmed.

Abraham was sitting in Sky Moores' chair, looking pompous. Sky had left for an important meeting at Bucks Times Bucks and he was the boss for the day.

"I make it one-and-half hours," said one prying Eye, staring at Paper Tiger's door.

"What are they working out? Pythagoras?" wondered another. "Using the Karmasutra?"

"Must be love," insisted yet another.

Monica looked seriously depressed. She had lost him to a totally inhumane brute of a woman. All those dreams of taking him up to meet Mam evaporated... Who could she talk to? Suki! Oh no, her first enrolment would be at college now, studying her little heart out. Ironically, Monica wished that her friend wasn't.

¥ ¥ ¥

Suki had a similar longing. Mr Poulton had won Oscars for his part as Boring Lecturer. Suki was in a lab coat, standing in front of a mass of glass tubes. She could feel her levels of irritation brimming and her frustration reaching expressive proportions, and yet she couldn't scream. It seemed pointless to her to be doing experiments that had been done countless times before, particularly when she knew the result. She longed to have a therapeutic rap with CONTACT 2000. Her face revealed that she was merely going through the motions. Her mind was elsewhere, on an incident that had happened earlier that day.

Suki had edged past the cafeteria, on the way to the library with Bucks on her mind. She glanced up briefly to make herself feel doubly better about not being in the cafeteria circle.

She caught sight of Ivan's handsome frame. What was he doing in the cafeteria of all places? How bizarre. Surely he had more sense than Simeon gave him credit for. Worse still, he was engrossed in a conversation with...Preeti Seekh! Ugh! Yep, that's a sure sign of someone who's new to the area and doesn't know the scene. Either that or the wily one had cornered him ("I'm sure you're in one of my classes. Is your name Tom, Dick or Harry?") and he was trapped.

Although Suki would have claimed that she was

only going over to rescue him from Preeti's clutches, she was conscious that she hadn't seen Ivan since the day they gave Mrs Turner the run-around. She missed his company.

"How many's that?" muttered Ivan, leafing through his pile of cheat sheets.

"Jenny, Penny, Denny, Rene, Lenny. That's five," squeaked Preeti. "Oh Ivan! Don't forget me." She spotted Suki over his shoulder. Her expression changed to one akin to seeing flies mating in her soup. "Oh my gosh, what's that?"

Suki came closer. "Hi Ivan," she smiled.

"Hi," acknowledged Ivan, pleased to see her but slightly embarrassed at being caught in the middle of a lucrative deal.

"Didn't you try to bunk Paper One?" pouted Preeti.

"Didn't you sound like a dripping tap just before the papers came out?" asked Suki sweetly. "Waterworks City!"

"I was ill! I really was!" exclaimed Preeti, glancing at Suki's left leg. "Luckily no permanent damage."

Suki had been in situations when people said stupid things like, "Only pulling your leg!" and then fell over themselves apologising. Preeti did not even come in that category.

She was a member of The Really Sad Group which worried incessantly not only about their own love lives but also everyone else's, in case there was a connection. The only serious love connection in Suki's life was the hot-wire that plugged into the back of her PC. But Preeti wasn't to know that and in any case her favourite phrase was, "And I thought, who's going to fancy her?" She stared patronisingly at Suki, thinking her favourite thought. Preeti would have been mortified if she realised that Suki, despite being a programmer, scored a higher popularity rating than she herself could muster if she gave away all her Bobby Brown tapes for free. And Ivan wasn't the freebie sort.

"So Preeti, Paper Two times five..." calculated Ivan, working his way round to the money part of the deal. "That's twenty-five quid, plus a two pound fifty discount for you. Twenty-seven fifty."

"Ivan? I did get you five new customers," whinged Preeti.

"What's up, Sick Bay's kicked you out for squatting?" snarled Suki. "Daddy's money gonna pay for a cheat sheet now, huh?"

Silence. Preeti and Ivan looked like they had been hit with a baseball bat.

"Forget it Ivan, you can buy me an ice cream some other time," Preeti said, staring coldly at Suki. She bombed off to find consolation amongst like-minded friends.

"Hey! Hey, Preeti..." Ivan called after her in anguish. "That's twenty-seven smackers just gone!" he said angrily.

"Sales down? What about everyone who hasn't got dough?" snapped Suki. "If you're stooping down to the scum level, we're history."

"You'll never break any system without me..." he said between his teeth.

"Don't flatter yourself, Ivan." Suki could feel a scream coming on. "You're no hacker, you're a crook." She stormed off quickly.

Ivan looked depressed. In seconds, he'd lost a friend, maybe even something more, and was still broke at the end of it. Classification? A really bad day. Ivan wasn't the only one with that opinion.

¥ ¥ ¥

Paper Tiger's door opened. "Goodbye everyone," smiled Gunster.

Had he just winked in Monica's direction? She must have imagined it. After all, you only see what you want to, don't you? She remembered that from the psychology experiments that she had done at college. But how could Gunster go for such a cow? Mr Goodman didn't cover that under 'Interpersonal Attraction'. It was almost like 'nice' people just weren't attracted to cows, so there was no need to have it on the syllabus.

"Monica. In here," snorted Paper Cow. "Now."

"Oooh!" The Eyes were all ears. There might be something worth waiting for before dashing to the pub.

Gunster stood outside the florists looking into the window. The big bunch of red roses was screaming out to be bought. When his wife Jean was alive, she always accused him of being totally unromantic. He could never bring himself to kiss her in public or run out in his lunch-hour to buy a box of chocolates.

In the past week, he had been to the Crouch End branch three times. He had only walked past her desk, held the door open, perhaps smiled from across the canteen floor. That was it! And on the basis of such limited contact, Gunster suddenly had the urge to buy a florist and leave Thornton's without any stock. It was totally irrational.

But true love never followed the laws of numbers and balance sheets. Over the years, Gunster had discovered that breaking rules didn't make you the most popular person but even Office Rule # 4 which said, "Don't speak to senior staff unless they speak to you" held no weight. He looked at the roses. Should he, shouldn't he? Did she have a boyfriend, someone her own age? Was he making a fool of himself? Was there a chance that she felt the same way? Later, Gunster walked to the underground station. His finger traced the route on a tube map. Highgate Station down the northern line. Monica followed the same route on that fateful day she had gone shopping for her Mam. Gunster had more in common with her than he realised.

He could have driven, he had a company car. But Gunster had a medical condition that made him dangerous on the road for other people as well as himself. Epilepsy. His Harley Street doctor suggested that he avoid stress and if he was going to work in the City, then avoid driving like the plague. He hadn't had a fit since he had worked for the Treasury four years ago. Gunster's lips tightened. It was still a bad memory.

An empty corridor. A wall plaque read "Treasury Accountant". Inside, two men sat in an office. One of them looked confused and he was Gunster.

"I can't understand it. Nothing's balancing," Gunster said to his boss, perplexed. "The same amount's missing every quarter. £5437. Something's wrong."

"Leave it," said his boss. "It's nothing."

Later, the office was deserted, apart from a guilty-looking Gunster looked through his boss's drawer. A photograph of a woman standing in front of a Spanish villa with a receipt from an expense account. Close up of the figure. £5437. Flash-back to his computer print-out. £5437. £5437. A shadow fell.

"Robbins, you really should know better." His boss at the door.

A dishevelled Gunster at a typewriter, rattling out a letter. Close up of the words on the page. "Sadly, health problems have forced me to resign." Angrily, he quickly banged out the same word over and over again. "RESIGN. RESIGN. RESIGN. RESIGN. RES..." Suddenly, Gunster clutched his chest, fell off his swivel chair and writhed in pain on the floor.

¥ ¥ ¥

A less grey-haired Permy had Gunster's boss standing in front of him. He was looking at Gunster's letter of resignation and he looked concerned. "I see, I see.

Robbins is a good man. Most unfortunate. A sad loss. A transfer perhaps?"

Abraham sat in Sky's chair. Pip, RETROBASE's computer systems expert, was with him. Gunster knocked on the door and entered.

"Strange for someone to be working at that time of night," said the computer expert, looking at the print-out.

"Anything changed, amended? No," snapped Abraham. "Nothing to worry about then is it?" He was feeling the strain of wielding power for twenty-four hours.

"Well, it's best to be careful. There seems to be a spate of these break-ins," commented Gunster, thinking of his morning visit to Crouch End. He was forever a cautious man after the Treasury experience. In his book, prevention was always better than cure. "I've been down to one local office this morning..."

"There you go!" said the computer expert triumphantly. She was glad that at least someone in authority was taking her seriously.

"We'll discuss it later, thank you, Pip," said Abraham, asserting himself. The door closed.

"Have you told Mr Moores?" asked Gunster.

"He's at Bucks and he doesn't want to be disturbed with minor issues," said Abraham, annoyed that other people were interfering. Didn't they think he was capable of handling the situation? He would show them.

"Bucks Times Bucks? What's he doing..." Gunster said.

"Business. Just business," said Abraham, biting his tongue. Sky had told him not to say anything.

"Well, security is very important, you know," advised Gunster. "You've got some pretty personal student records. People should hug their passwords close to their chest, I change mine practically every week..."

"OK OK," snapped Abraham. Who did this guy think he was? He was only the friggin' accountant. "Let's have a look at the budgets."

Gunster tightened his lips. He couldn't stand smart little up-starts, especially when they were half his age. How Abraham contrasted with Monica, and they were practically the same age! She was so charming, so unassuming, so fresh, so alive. Gunster pushed her out of his mind and concentrated on work. The question of where Bucks Times Bucks fitted into the RETROBASE spun through his mind.

Like Shanti, Gunster was old enough to remember the 'bad vaccine' scandal that came out in the 1970s. 1976 was the year when his wife died of cancer. Unlike Abraham, Gunster was a man of honour and a man of soul. When he saw the news reports of people from Africa to Liverpool showing the first signs of cancer because of bad vaccines, he was appalled. He was shocked and angry when it turned out that the company was uninsured.

Sky was sitting with a secretary on a private jet, reading some papers. Over his shoulder, the words "Operation Acid Trip flashed up, privileged Access Only" in red print. The pilot's voice over the intercom crackled out. "We'll be landing in Palermo any minute, Mr Moores."

The telephone buzzed. Sky narrowed his eyes. "Bucks Times Bucks. Mr Moores office. Can I help you?" said the secretary.

"Mr Moores is busy right now, can I pass on a message?"

"Abraham? Christ, he couldn't get a dog to piss on a tree! Gimme that! Abraham? I said no calls, goddammit! Star Wars breaking out cos I've left the office for five minutes? What's up?"

Abraham rolled his eyes. He knew he should not have rung.

"Which terminal? Which files? Nothing wrecked,

right? Well use your brains, that's what I pay you for. Send a memo to all local offices about tightening up security. And do it on paper, forget the computers. Is that it? Christ! Only call me if the neutron bomb's landed on my desk while you're sitting at it. Got that?"

Sky slammed the phone down. "Goddamn college grads! I'm surrounded by complete morons!"

The secretary looked up.

"Except you, sweetie," smiled Sky. "You've got more brains in your little butt than the goddamn Premier."

The Hacker got let off the hook, but only just. All thanks to Abraham's lack of curiosity. He would live to regret it, but others might not get the chance...

And Sky was wrong. Not everyone was a moron. RETROBASE's Regional Accountant, for example, had a brain. Gunster made a fascinating visit to the library, whizzing through old newspapers on the microfiche. He chose a box of negatives marked, "The Financial Telegraph: 1976." With the whoosh! of the microfiche, the screen filled up with rolling black-and-white newspaper images. Gunster stopped the machine on one article. Close up. "Vaccine Multinational Cover Up: Mystery Virus Link to Africa". Like Suki, Gunster was doing his homework.

¥ ¥ ¥

Suki was at home alone in front of her computer, making up for lost time with CONTACT 2000. The phone rang. Without taking her eyes off the screen, Suki pulled a lever under her table. A pulley angled a table-on-wheels to her desk. On the small table was the phone. Laziness down to an artform.

"Yep? Hi Mo! The Cave? Seven-thirty? Great."

The phone rang again.

"Yep? Hey Amber! You? Jealous? With a capital J? I didn't even notice. Forget it. College. Yeah yeah, very funny. Preeti Seekh. Cheat sheets for money. He's a scummy crook. Forget him. Yeah, with Monica."

The phone rang yet again.

"Yep? Hey Sims! Yeah, college. Ha ha ha, very funny. You? Princess who? You're crazy. More like pervert found hanging around the Palace. Thrown in the slammer for a long time. Keep an ear on Rupert the Bear, will ya? Thanks."

¥ ¥ ¥

The Cave was deluged with customers and Mr Cavallares was frantically handling the orders. Amber had reserved the corner table for her ten-minute dinner break with Suki, who was making clear that she had no empathy for Ivan.

"Grants are bad, what can you do?" Amber said, throwing her hands up in sympathy.

"Rob a bank. Deal drugs. Bash a few grannies, why not?" Suki said sarcastically. "He's a first-class crook. We fell for it, now we know."

"Good looking, though," moped Amber.

"Skin deep," said Suki grimly. "Simeon tell you about the Palace?"

"Yeah, even the Duke's got more of a love life than I have," said Amber.

"So? Big deal. Stop being such a drip." Suki spotted Monica making her approach and called her over. "Hey Mo! Over here." She glanced at a sombre Amber. "It's a dry period," she consoled.

"Like a desert," sighed Amber. "Male famine. But Preeti Seekh? Jeez, he must really be broke."

Suki mimicked Preeti. "Forget it Ivan, you can buy me an ice cream some other time. PUKEDOM! Ah, Monica this is my buddy Amber, you'd better like the food, she's inheriting it. That's why we're like this." Suki knotted her fingers, screwing up her eyes.

"What can I get ya, Monica?" said Amber. "A

Whopper Cropper, a Weekend sandwich?"

"Coffee please," said Monica shyly.

Much later, the bar was dark and empty. Mr and Mrs Cavallares had gone to bed. "Only time of night you don't loose me any business." Famous last words. The three of them were the last customers. Suki was gorging a Salami Slammer, under Monica's envious gaze.

"That looks like heaven, man," she said.

"I've been bred on them," said Amber hoarsely. "From birth. Best in The Universe."

Minutes later, Amber fried Mo a Slammer whilst Suki slouched in the corner. "Tell me about yourself, Mo. Any men in your life that you don't want?"

"Well, the only one I want goes for a woman that makes me look like a skimpy horse-radish, like," Monica slurred.

"Well you've got to fight, Mo," smiled Amber. "That's what I'm doing. I'm going for a low-down dirty crook who'd knock off a lorry and say, 'See what I got you babe?'" She laughed.

"Oooh, he sounds like a handful," gasped Monica. "Oh aye, Gunster's well worth fighting for. But he's in love with the boss."

"Paper Tiger?" sneered Amber. "Come on. She doesn't stand a chance. And Ivan? He doesn't know what's going to hit him!"

Monica stared in wonder. These people were nothing like the Londoners in her office. Amber and Suki were human. If Amber could get her man, why couldn't she?

"Mo, the second letter been printed yet?" asked Suki, waking up from the state of burger-bloated happiness.

Monica's hand flew to her mouth. With Gunster on her mind, she'd forgotten to tell Suki to wipe it off.

"Nearly got the sack today, man. They traced it on the back-up file this morning," she said. "Gunster saved me, I reckon."

106

"Oh jeez, I'll do it tonight then," promised Suki. "Is RETROBASE a government thing or what? You ever heard of a company called Bucks Times Bucks? Or a bloke called Sky Moores?"

"Mr Moores. He's the Big Boss at Head Office but Bucks Times Bucks, ooh no, never heard of them, like," said Monica.

"On that disk it says that Bucks is funding the Commission with 90-100% of it's money, d'ya know that?" said Amber.

"I'll ask Gunster. It's his field isn't it, money?" promised Monica.

When she stumbled home to her crummy bed-sit, there was a bouquet of red roses awaiting her return, signed "Love G. R.". As Suki blearily erased any trace of the letter to her parents denying that she was a truant, Monica danced the night away with a pillow.

6

TILL DEATH DO US PART

Abraham was tired and it came solely from behaving like a brainless twat. Sky had given him the relatively simple job of sending out a memo to all the local RETROBASE offices, saying "watch out for security". He was still smarting about the fact that he'd got a dressing down from the boss on the security issue. Abraham had developed an affliction to ever being caught out. So, twattily, he became determined to produce a supremely brilliant memo that would demonstrate his worth. Yes, for money and recognition as the Assistant with a tongue that had the longest reach, Abraham ruined another of Stan's evenings, by being holed up in the office.

¥ ¥ ¥

Paper Tiger felt she now knew from personal experience what it must be like to have a brain haemorrhage. Her state of consternation derived solely from a laborious memo from Head Office that landed with a thump on her desk. In a paranoid mind set, Paper Tiger was convinced she was being persecuted by a higher authority for the irritating errors of others. Constant reference to "carelessness in computer security" made her shudder as her mind rambled through a maze of dead-end alleys, puzzling frantically over various questions. How did Head Office ever find out about the security breach? In the course of making the memo a literary masterpiece, Abraham had wasted nearly a tree-and-a-half, revising it to include just one more big word. The intensity of literary creation had blurred the reader's understanding of one crucial fact: it was Head Office's

108

computers that had experienced security problems. Missing this fact, Paper Tiger was flabbergasted that news of recent events in her office had reached the top and the consequences were tumbling down.

The memo was written in that academic bureaucratic style that made Paper Tiger feel small, inferior and just plain thick. To her it was obviously articulated by someone who had been to university. The kind of English they taught you at university might as well be another language and Paper Tiger just wasn't into foreign languages or foreigners for that matter. Monica was about as foreign as she could tolerate. Susan Wallis had a complex about intelligence and people who thought they had it. She made the classic mistake of believing the myth that people who went to university had brains and the people who did not had none. Underneath that powerful image, lay a depleted personality, ever fearful that her mathematical equivalent of dyslexia would be discovered. In her limited experience, university students never had that kind of problem and being surrounded by students in this job, there was one thing she was not going to let them get away with, and that was feel superior to her.

Yes, Paper Tiger was a twat in full throttle and her own insecurity turned viciously to find a scapegoat. The image of Monica was first in the firing line for doing all those strange things on her terminal, making her more trouble than she was worth. Ruddles was clearly another of Personnel's classic mistakes, a department full of graduates, and yet none of them could interview a decent candidate even if they shortlisted one. She, Susan Elizabeth Wallis Newton, had been to the University of Life. When Monica had heard this claim, she concluded that Paper Tiger must have been a perpetual truant.

Paper Tiger pressed her intercom. "Petra, in here. Now," she growled.

"Well act-u-ually, Sue, I wanted to see-ee you my-s-self," said Petra, rushing into Susan's office with the latest incriminating computer print-out.

Minutes later, she was poring over the security memo with an alarmed look on her face.

"How did Head Office find out about the stuff on my terminal the other night?" Paper Tiger asked, with steely paranoia.

"I don't know, S-s-sue-ue-e," gushed Petra. "I didn't te-e-ell them."

"Who did then?" barked Paper Tiger. "Where's Monica?"

"She's late," cried Petra triumphantly, pulling out her print-out. "And there's another strange piece of late-night activity. A letter's been er-r-as-sed on her terminal."

"That girl's treading on dangerous ground," grizzled Paper Tiger.

After a passionate night with a feather pillow, Monica was late getting into work again, but this time she didn't care. Gunster's love made her feel strong. Paper Tiger was guaranteed to do her nut and pop a varicose but Monica felt as if there was suddenly much more to life than getting stressed up about these minor trivialities. She had better things to do and taking life at a slower pace was one of them. Monica sat in her dressing gown and sipped her tea, smiling at her bunch of roses. She was planning what she'd do when she next saw Gunster. Would he come into the office today? He most certainly would. Gunster was half-scared of seeing Monica and yet burning to find out how she reacted to the roses. Had she thrown them away in disgust? Did she think he was a member of the Midday Pervert Society? Gunster came from that "chivalrous gentleman" category who found page three pin-ups quite depraved. Or, hoping against hope, would she give him a chance to prove that he really loved her? There was only one way to find out and that was to give Susan Wallis another elementary maths lesson.

Walking past pigeons and drunks and couples arguing in the street, Gunster wondered how Susan ever got her job. Her viciousness with Monica demonstrated her lack of skills in staff management. However, being a logical numbers man, Gunster would have been horrified to find out how staff appointments are sometimes quite arbitrary. In fact, Gunster might never have met Monica if it hadn't been for one of these little accidents in life.

"Good morning everyone," said Monica defiantly.

The Eyes looked up, shocked. "What's up with her?" they whispered. Late and happy? Impossible! Moments later, they were surprised to see Gunster again, so soon after his visit the day before.

"Good morning everyone," smiled Gunster nervously, his eyes tracing the path to Monica's desk.

"Good morning, Mr Robbins," came back the murmur.

Was it safe to approach her now? Could he disguise it as a work matter? agonised Gunster. He began walking, almost involuntarily, towards her desk.

Monica's thoughts were synchronised. How can I make it look natural? The Eyes were attentive as always. Amber's trusty words, "Fight for your man," blazed in neon in her mind.

She spotted a convenient corner by the coffee percolator, near the window and away from any desks. Monica was not really renowned for her chat-up lines but it seemed to fit.

"Good morning, Gunster...I mean Mr Robbins," she stammered. "Would you like a cup of coffee?"

The Eyes bulged in front of their VDUs. Monica was infamous for the black rings at the bottom of her mug, in blatant disregard of Office Rule #2. And now she was going to present the greatest authority this side of Paper Tiger with it. Hung, drawn and quartering material! Gunster looked elated. "Thank you,

111

Monica," he smiled back. He would have drunk out of a bidet if he thought Monica had just sat on it. Love blurred the line between obscenity and devotion. They stood twitching like lemmings on heat by the bubbling percolator, making inane small talk.

"Well, did that little problem with the computer get sorted out?" asked Gunster, in an effort to prolong the flow.

"Oh yes, thank you," gushed Monica, racking her brains for something intelligent to say. "I don't really know much about computers. I suppose I must have pressed the wrong button by mistake."

She cursed herself for seeming like a technological moron. Gunster didn't think so.

"Well, with good training they're not too bad," empathised Gunster.

He found Monica quite endearing. In the high-powered world of government departments, no-one ever revealed their vulnerabilities. Much was lost by empty posturing and proving that one was always absolutely correct. Take that Abraham for instance! So obsessed with doing things perfectly, he probably screwed up all the time. In any case, if Monica had said, "I'm a ding-bat with a killer wind problem", Gunster would have justified it somehow. A brainwave struck Monica. "I wanted to ask you something, actually, Gun...I mean, Mr Robbins."

"Oh please, call me Gunster," insisted Gunster.

The Eyes were straining to hear, unable to comprehend what in the world the squat-faced girl from Newcastle could have to talk about to Mr Robbins for so long. Paper Tiger would not be amused, if she ever found out. And of course, in an office like this, how could she fail?

"Gunster." Monica savoured his name on her lips, while trying to concentrate on her question. "Well, I don't know how I did it, like. But I found a file on the computer that said RETROBASE was 90 per cent funded by Bucks Times Bucks. I don't know anything about finances but I thought you must be the right person to ask. I thought it was a government company..." Monica batted her eyelids furiously.

Gunster was stunned. Not only did she have the beauty of a goddess, the personality of a saint, she also had brains. It was a rare combination. Why, it was only yesterday at Head Office that that nasty assistant had mentioned Sky's meeting at BTB... Gunster's mind catapulted into ecstasy! She had the same intellectual preoccupations. A match made in heaven! "That's very interesting," he mused. "I've been investigating that very question myself. We really must compare notes, Monica. Lunchtime, perhaps?"

Monica blushed. A date! "Yes, that would be lovely," she said shyly.

The Eyes stood out on stalks, craning forward. Did they or did they not hear a date being fixed up between the Regional Accountant and a lowly Student Officer? The click of the coffee percolator broke the mesmerising gaze that Gunster had fixed on Monica's rosy cheeks.

Paper Tiger's door opened in the distance and Petra weaselled out after a stressful half-hour trying to understand the meaning of all this strange computer activity. Seeing Susan sitting at her desk, Gunster remembered his official reason for being at Crouch End.

"In the foyer, 1 o'clock?" he asked urgently.

Monica nodded.

Gunster headed off to Paper Tiger's office with love in his heart. He had not felt so fit and agile for years. All that money wasted in Harley Street! The permanent cure had been found and it should be bottled on the NHS. Even the prospect of spending a dull morning with Susan Wallis did not dampen his spirits.

Susan, meanwhile, was ready to pop a facial varicose

vein in paranoia and frustration. Gunster had just the shoulder she needed to cry on.

"Look at this memo," she said tearfully."'Security breaches will be dealt with severely.' They think it's me. Mr Moores thinks I'm a security risk, Gunster. What am I going to do?"

"Paranoia, Susan, pure paranoia," consoled Gunster. "It's a standard memo sent by Head Office to all the local offices. I was there yesterday and it's a regular problem that they're getting with the computer system."

"It's that bloody Monica!" seethed Susan. "She's about as regular as crazy paving. She's trying to ruin me. Last week it was a disk from my file, then last night a letter went missing from her files. I'll have the parents storming up here and I don't know what to do..."

"Come now, Susan. Let's get these figures done," said Gunster, hiding his impatience. Time was short.

The Eyes were shocked by the flirtations around the percolator.

"Flaunting it," said one, wiping her hands in the ladies.

"I know, I know," said the other, hanging her jaw as she put on another layer of ruby red. "The minute she asked him if he wanted a cup of coffee, I thought, aye, aye, what's this."

"What was she asking him? Bucks Times Bucks or something," asked the other.

"Yeah, something about it not being a government thing," replied her gossip partner. "Doesn't really have anything to do with her job."

"Well, if Paper Tiger finds out, Monica's had it." She motioned a slit throat.

"Yeah, then we'll be stuck for laughs," giggled the other. "She's a weird one, that Monica. Can't think what Mr Robbins sees in her. He's such a nice man."

They left to the sound of a flushing toilet. Petra

emerged, her eyes gleaming.

¥ ¥ ¥

Monica chose the expensive French restaurant in the entrance to the arcade, risking severe rupture of her intestines, to celebrate their new-found love. Gunster, on doctor's orders, had avoided rich food in the past and shied away from ordering.

Monica took charge; perhaps a little of Audrey had rubbed off on her. Her only holiday had been in France with a schoolfriend and she had accidentally ended up at Le Pen's country mansion. Unexpected events were the story of Monica's life. She explained to Gunster that her Geordie-French improved considerably when she tried to ward off the bodily advances of the fascist's bodyguard. "He just wouldn't take no for an answer," snorted Monica. "I just blew him away."

Rather than take this statement literally, Gunster assumed that modern women were quite immodest about their seductiveness. Of course, in Monica's case, he was unsurprised. Gunster thanked his lucky stars that he was so well-blessed by the gods. He was impressed, like a schoolboy, by her knowledge of foreign food. He had half an eye on the burgers in The Cave across the road. Somehow they were the only burgers that never seemed to bring on his breathing problems. But perhaps Monica was right, it just wasn't romantic enough. His wife Jean would have said exactly the same thing.

Monica's French holiday had had a major impact, particularly when she found out that there was a touch more to French cuisine than frogs' legs. As Monica and Gunster got to know each other, they were oblivious to being beadily monitored from a window-seat in The Cave. Petra had followed them from the college gates and was savouring the sight as she breathed heavily into her Whopper. Things might have been very different if Monica had not been so intent on impressing Gunster that she was not just uncultured riff-raff.

Tucking into their poulet, Gunster probed a little into what Monica knew about Bucks Times Bucks.

"I don't really know what it was," she answered evasively, treading carefully in this minefield. She was conscious that she had not actually even seen the file. If Gunster discovered that the file was on Paper Tiger's disk, which she had let Suki download, it might cause complications for their relationship. Monica, caught in the very thrust of passion, knew that would be a tragedy of cosmic proportions.

"It just said that Mr Moores was from Bucks Times Bucks and that the company funds 90 per cent...oooh it might have been more, like. Maybe even a 100 per cent, I really can't remember," lied Monica with a confused expression. "I just thought it was weird because I thought RETROBASE was a government company not a private one. I don't suppose it's really that important, do you?"

Gunster recalled the newspaper article that he photocopied in the library about Bucks and once more recognised the feeling that it had triggered inside him. It had echoes of his curiosity at the Treasury, when his boss was siphoning off a little amount every quarter. The amount was a drop in the ocean compared to figures he usually dealt with but that was irrelevant. It was the principle and beyond that, it was the curiosity of having to know.

Curiosity killed the cat on that occasion and as Gunster looked across at Monica, the gem in his life, he saw a new beginning. He made a conscious decision to quell the urge. Although the newspaper photograph of a dying African child nagged his liberal sensibilities, he decided to let someone else worry about it for a change.

"No darling, I don't suppose it's important at all," he said solemnly. "Nothing's important anymore except you and me."

Again, if Gunster had decided otherwise, The Hacker might have had an ally. But, gradually Bucks Times Bucks faded from his mind. Instead they made plans and shared dreams and ambitions. Monica was keen to get her mother's approval, a prospect that the age-conscious Gunster found daunting.

"Oh leave off, Gunster," laughed Monica. "Me Mam'll be dead chuffed. She liked Mr Goodman. I'm more worried about people in the office. And Office Rule #4."

"Yes, Susan seemed rather distressed today," said Gunster. "A security memo from Head Office and last night's back-up shows more activity on your terminal."

"Does it?" Monica was horrified. It must be Suki's second letter. If only she had not been so obsessed with Gunster and had her brain on the boil, it could have been done during the day and not caused any hassle. "Tiger's going to kill me."

"But no-one was doing overtime last night, so they can't blame you," said Gunster, amused at Susan's unofficial title. "I don't know why Susan's getting so het-up. The memo's just a general warning, it's not anything personal. They're so lax about security at Head Office. Mr Moores' assistant is an arrogant little sod!"

"His assistant?" asked Monica surprised. "Don't you see Mr Moores himself?"

"Apparently, he had an emergency meeting at Bucks yesterday. And you say the computer has a file saying he's from that very company." Gunster recalled again the contents of the newspaper article, the 'bad vaccines' scandal.

"It's strange why a chemical giant like Bucks would want to invest so heavily in Britain," he mused. "No-one else wants to. And why the education system? Still, bound to be some logical explanation," he said, shirking off that irritating itch. He changed the subject to safer ground.

"That's when this computer security thing blew up," sighed Gunster, wondering if he might have pushed Abraham a little too hard into action, producing Susan's anxiety.

But then he remembered the havoc and paranoia when computer-hackers tried to crack open the Treasury's system. "You have to be so careful these days, change your password every week. Do you know what mine is?" Gunster asked playfully.

He leaned over and whispered in Monica's ear. Across the road, Petra's jaw nearly emptied out as she frantically scribbled 'kissing' in her notepad.

"Oh Gunster! That's so lovely!" exclaims Monica. "When did you change it to that?"

"Oooh, at least last month," he said.

"A whole month!" Monica was overwhelmed. "You mean you've been..."

"In love with you," finished Gunster shyly. "Yes, for that long."

Later, they strolled back together to the college, unable to resist holding hands, and Gunster even stole a quick kiss. They tore themselves apart but vowed to meet in the early evening after work. Monica bounced back to the office joyously unaware that Paper Tiger was on the verge of a varicose volcano.

Susan Wallis looked positively ill, teetering on her toes. She was either going to kill someone or commit suicide.

"In here, now," she said hoarsely to a nonchalant Monica.

Mesmerised, Paper Tiger looked blankly at her. This moron had broken virtually every office rule, in efforts to make a mockery out of her authority. How did they manage to let her in to do a degree? The government was absolutely right, standards were dropping like hailstones. But an affair with the Regional Accountant? That was the absolute limit! The thought that Gunster Robbins felt anything for this nasty piece of riff-raff was beyond her imagination. In fact, Susan actually didn't believe it. Impossible. Ludicrous. Her hatred intensified and vented outward.

Monica's glazed expression was the epitomy of self-control. Actually, she had an uncomfortable stirring in her stomach. She really should have gone to the Ladies, but Paper Tiger lacked even a hint of being semi-reasonable.

A conspiracy swelled between Susan's ears. The twilight use of her terminal was obviously a subversive attempt to get her into trouble with Head Office. And if this memo was anything to go by, the plan was working. The continual lateness, just to wind her up, of course. All that rubbish about being arrested for being a terrorist, just to scare her. Flirting with Gunster, Monica had made a play for him and...

Susan's heart nearly stopped beating... Could Monica have inadvertently discovered that she had a severe addition and subtraction problem? And the game plan is to take this information...? Where? Head Office of course, to the author of that horrible memo, and ultimately to Mr Moores.

As her mind made these absurd connections, Susan could imagine what would happen at Head Office. Officialdom would gather around a big oak table, like the one on 'Question Time', and talk about her in that university language that she could not speak or understand. Paranoia was a killer and right now, Susan Wallis was intoxicated. It was for this reason that she made a fateful decision. Taking control made her feel better immediately.

"Empty your desk, sign your timesheet, take your rubbish out and go. We don't need troublemakers like you here," she said briskly.

"You what?" grunted Monica, aware that her concentration had been elsewhere whilst Tiger has been uncharacteristically quiet.

"You heard me. Out, I know what you're up to," started Paper Tiger, alarmed that this demon obviously had no fear.

"Out, like, sacked, man? Why, like? What have I ever done to you, man? Eh?" Monica boiled over. "All I did was ask a few piddly questions about Bucks Times Bucks. You've got something to hide, you have!"

Monica had just about reached the end of her tether. Without realising it, Gunster's love had given her a sense of self-worth. She decided that the first thing she was going to do with it was lose her job in style.

"You are one nasty piece of work, do you know that, eh?" she screamed. "Don't appreciate anyone, always moaning and groaning. I've worked here for nearly six months and not one civil thing's come out of your tongue."

Monica felt French chicken curdling inside her guts. "I feel dead sorry for your cats, man. And one more thing, Personnel gave the job to a brainless moron when they found you, didn't they?" snarled Monica.

She felt satisfied in keeping her promise to say that to this heathen woman. For once, it was Paper Tiger who sat there with an ashen face.

"And one more thing..." began Monica, just as heat rushed through her with scorching power.

Paper Tiger screamed. Papers flew around the room. The involuntary explosion threw Monica on her back. The office door blew outward. Behind it, The Eyes scattered. The staff dismissal of the century was earth-shattering.

"Get out! Get out!" shrieked Paper Tiger in absolute fear.

At Gunster's flat, the sound of her shriek carried an echo in Monica's memory.

"It was horrible, Gunster," she sobbed. "Really

horrible."

"I'll go and see Susan and sort it out," said Gunster soothingly, his arm around his beloved.

"I'm not going back there, ever," spat Monica. "They've hated me from Day One. I'm never going back."

"Where are you going to go?" Gunster asked anxiously.

"I'm going home to see...to see...me Mam," cried Monica. "Straight away. Today, if I can."

"Well, I'm going with you," said Gunster firmly.

"But what about your job?" asked Monica, drying her eyes.

"I can take a month's leave at any time," he said, giving her another tissue. "After that, we'll see. If you want to stay near your mother, I'll see if I can get a transfer or something."

"Oh Gunster! I love you! You're wonderful!" yelped Monica, bursting into a fresh bucketful of tears as she threw her arms around him.

At the office, The Eyes were bloodshot. Petra gave Paper Tiger a blow-by-blow account of the steamy lunchtime date between Monica and Gunster. More importantly, things had calmed down a little in Susan Wallis's mind after she considered her options in the Sick Bay. A student named Preeti Seekh was cleared out when news broke of an unexplained explosion on the RETROBASE floor. Susan decided that Monica was a dreadful security risk who had just been exposed.

The memo had said that in the event of a breach of security, Head Office had to be notified immediately. Susan gritted her teeth. Notified, eh? She'd notify them all right. She made up her mind to nail every little thing she could on that demon. Susan did not appreciate the fact but regulations also stated that any dismissal of staff had to be agreed by Head Office. Sky had made sure that the clause was there because if there was going to be any bad publicity for

RETROBASE, he wanted to know about it before it happened. All this made Paper Tiger's boss want to send a detailed report. Ironically, it was by the speediest technology available. On-line computer transmission.

Petra held Susan's hand as she reeled out "the facts". The report obviously was not the reference Monica might have hoped for once upon a time. Words that kept resurfacing were "late", "terrorist", "Bucks Times Bucks", "unauthorised use of Supervisor's terminal" and "security breach".

"What's Bucks Times Bucks got to do with anything?" asked Paper Tiger's boss, confused.

"God knows, she had a bee in her bonnet about it," grunted Susan sorely.

"Ye-es-ss, sshhee asked Mr Robbins about it-t-t-t," affirmed Petra.

"Is there something wrong with your voice, Petra?" he asked, confused.

"Leave her alone!" snapped Paper Tiger, forgetting his seniority. "She's the only one in that office with any brains."

Petra smiled and patted her hand.

The boss left the office, returning only to ask a simple question. "Susan, how do you spell 'confidential'?"

¥ ¥ ¥

Sky Moores' blue eyes narrowed at the report from Crouch End, glistening at the appearance of the words "Bucks" and "terrorist". He reached out to the intercom and barked sharply for Abraham. "Get me a staff computer file. Name Monica Ruddles. Base: Crouch End."

Minutes later, Sky was looking at a computer record of Monica, her smiling photograph doing nothing to improve his mood.

"She's a goddamn nobody," he muttered. "A terrorist? Come on, gimme a break."

Flicking on the intercom again, Abraham returned to his beck and call. "Get me the list of log-ins, Abraham. And don't dawdle, kid. If I wanted a dawdler, I sure as hell could get one cheaper. Now. I want it NOW."

Sky ran his finger down the list of passwords that people around the country logged-in with as employees of RETROBASE.

"Monica Ruddles," he whispered, moving his finger along the print-out. "Psychokiller?" He threw his head back and laughed with madness in his eyes.

"Line through to Crouch End, Abraham. Like yesterday. And when I connect, no disturbances for the next five minutes. Got that?" Before Abraham could even reply, Sky tapped the telephone receiver. A sweating Abraham gained a connection.

"Get me RETROBASE. This is Sky Moores," he smirked briefly at the thought of having made the telephonist's day.

"OK, I've read the report. Where's this Ruddles woman? Do you guys ever read the regs, huh?" grunted Sky at Susan's boss. "What's the matter with you, huh? Exceptional circumstances, my ass. And what's the connection with Robbins?"

Susan's boss grovelled hard.

"Well, it looks like damage limitation is the only option. Keep it out of the papers," said Sky flatly. "RETROBASE needs no bad publicity. Got that? And what the hell has Bucks got to do with it? Exactly, nothing. Goodbye."

The intercom buzzed again. "Abraham, address and home phone number for Gunster Robbins. Yes, the Regional Accountant. Like yesterday."

"It's ex-directory, sir," said Abraham meekly.

"Abraham, when I hired you, you were an asset. Now, you're just an ass," sighed Sky. "Haven't you ever sweet-talked Directory Inquiries? Forget it, just gimme the address."

Sky noted it down and switched to his private line.

"Oje my friend, urgent job for you. Name: Monica Ruddles," said Sky in a low voice. "I'll fax you the details. Two possible addresses. Now, like yesterday. Report back." He paused.

"Yeah yeah, ten grand," agreed Sky. "A bonus if I get a call today. Ask no questions tell no lies, Oje. Let's just say, she's been asking too many questions. Get my drift? Good boy, Oje. Call me."

¥ ¥ ¥

Gunster had a very private address. His car sat gleaming and unused in the drive-in. Monica gawped at the flat's decor, at the antiques scattered around, feeling underdressed and conscious of her tatty little suitcase as she waited for Gunster to emerge from the shower. She turned over a photograph on the mantelpiece, a picture of a weary Gunster pushing a woman in a wheelchair. As Monica lounged around in luxury, a silhouetted figure silently entered her bedsit through the garden window. The gloved hand rummaged through her stuff, but to no avail. The room was clean. Miss Ruddles obviously knew that he, Oje, the supreme assassin was on her trail. Oje dialled a number on his mobile phone. You had to be quick in this business. Especially when ten grand or more was on the line. He called his accomplice to trace the other address in Hampstead.

"Gunster, let's book the train tickets over the phone," called Monica.

"Card's in my briefcase," he replied. "First class, darling."

Monica opened Gunster's executive briefcase and began searching for his Access card, finding a newspaper article about Bucks Times Bucks instead. Her eyes screwed up in confusion as she scanned the details. Bucks Times Bucks? Bad vaccines? Africa? Asia? Gunster must be concerned about the Bucks connection. The sound of the grandfather clock striking four diverted her attention. It was getting late. She left the photocopy on the mantlepiece.

Monica leafed through the phone books. Her eyesight seemed to have faded in the months of VDU work. She underlined the number for credit card bookings from Euston and reached for the phone. "I'd like two tickets to Newcastle please on the 5 o'clock train. First class. Access. The number is..."

Content that she had covered the preparations for their exit from London, Monica considered how dramatically things had changed. A couple of days ago, she was about as far from being here as she was from passing her driving test. London had been a mixed bag, with some good friends made...

Suki and Amber. This was likely to be her last day in the city and she would probably never cross their paths again.

Impulsively, Monica dialled Suki's number. The sound of Janak's voice on the ansaphone rattled on. "Damn! She's at college." She sighed, waiting for the speech to finish.

"Suki, it's Mo," she garbled quickly. "Listen, I'm not going to be your Student Officer any more. I got the sack. I'm going to Newcastle with Gunster. Amber was right. Paper Tiger didn't stand a chance. She really made me lose my rag, I wrecked the office today. Listen, Gunster's got this article on Bucks Times Bucks from 1976." Monica paused and burst into childish giggles.

"Oh, you don't know, do ya? Gunster and me are like, a couple. He's lovely. Best bloke in the world. Me Mam's going to love him. Guess what his password is?"

As Monica violated another security measure, she heard Gunster coming out of the shower.

"Oooh, I better go but we've got so much in common it's untrue. He hates driving, like I do. So we're going by train. First class, I've never travelled first class before..." Beep!

The tape finished before Monica could. She vowed to write and let Suki know how things turned out. Monica and Gunster shared a loving embrace and departed. The door banged shut and the newspaper article floated off the mantlepiece onto the floor.

Moments later, Oje and his accomplice sifted carefully through Gunster's things. The accomplice was dressed in black, except for one strange detail: a birthday badge with "30 today. Kiss Me or You're Dead" written on it in all the colours of the rainbow. The phone book lay open, inviting investigation.

"Either this guy ain't got no clothes or he's gone to the Bahamas," said the accomplice to Oje.

"Look at this," remarked Oje, holding the newspaper article.

"And this," said his accomplice, pointing to the phone number. "What trains leave from Euston?"

Oje examined the details Sky had faxed him about Monica. "Newcastle is not my idea of the Bahamas. She's taking him home to Mummy. Gimme the blower. Now," snapped Oje, realising that time, and therefore money, was slipping away from him. "Get the car ready. No, we'll go in Robbins' car. What can you buy with ten grand these days?"

Oje called Euston British Rail, as his accomplice drove at high speed.

"The name is Ruddles. I'd like to cancel my ticket to Newcastle," said Oje effeminately, in an effort to mimic a female voice.

"We have no booking under your name, Miss Ruddles," informed the woman from the booking office politely.

"Of course you do. Can't you read?" barked Oje harshly. "Check again. Look under Robbins, Gunster

Robbins."

"Are you a transvestite or something?" snapped the woman. "Yes, OK," she sighed. "We've got two tickets booked under the name Robbins."

"Cancel. Cancel. Cancel," said Oje. "This is a Bomb Disposal Squad matter. Two people posing as Gunster Robbins and Monica Ruddles are coming to collect these tickets. One of them has terrorist connections. Hold them for questioning and I'll come down to take them off your hands."

Monica and Gunster mesmerised in the land of goo-goo stumbled their way to the front of the ticket queue.

"I'm sorry sir, you cancelled your tickets only minutes ago," said the woman politely, from the other side of the glass barrier.

"Excuse me?" said Gunster, confused.

"Listen, right, I phoned at 4 o'clock to book them," said Monica, startled. "We ain't phoned you again."

"There must be some mistake," said Gunster. "Can we sort this out quickly? Our train is leaving in less than five minutes."

"Is that them?" said another woman who had spoken to the Bomb Disposal Squad. She ushered Gunster and Monica into a little side-room. "If you'd like to come through."

The accomplice opened his glove compartment to get his Bomb Disposal Squad name badge.

"Happy Birthday, sir," smiled the woman behind the glass window. He stared stonily and flashed his identification card. Her smile disappeared.

"We're here to escort the suspects back to the station," he said grimly.

Later, Monica and Gunster sat in the backseat of a red Chevrolet, as it sped up the motorway. Oje and his accomplice sat in the front and said nothing.

"I feel like I'm getting an escort in my own car," joked Gunster. "I've got this model in the same colour."

Oje turned to look at them with a sinister smile. "And the same number plate," he said, as the car came to a stop in a country lane.

7

DOWN AND OUT!

When Monica dialled Suki's number from Gunster's flat, the phone rang out into virtual silence. The only vaguely audible sound was a strange humming from the front room, where Shanti sat in a deep state of relaxation. She was enjoying a day of complete peace. No shouting from Janak, no screaming tantrums from Suki, just a sense of inner peace in an empty house. Although she did hear the telephone ring, Shanti suspected that it was an order for carrots or some such materialist interruption. She was having none of it and fixed her thoughts firmly on her favourite mental image, Janak with a gag on, and blocked out the noise. If it was that important, they would leave a message on the answering machine. Reality would have carved little furrows in her forehead. It was important: Monica was saying goodbye to London and unbeknown to her, goodbye to the world.

Shanti was not idle in the least. She was ordinarily a very busy person, always bringing home cuttings and delivering orders and going to meetings about how to save that whale. But today was her day for mantras and lotus positions and day-dreaming about a house in the country. Nothing like a telephone call was going to rouse her into activity. Something happened on Tuesdays and the neighbours always speculated about what it could be.

"I don't even reckon she's up," said Number 42 triumphantly.

"Come on, it's half two," scoffed Number 45.

"Nope. She's in bed. I've done the curtains, baked a cake for Marcus, starched Rob's shirts for the week..." boasted Number 42.

"And she's not even up?" Number 44 was routinely

sceptical.

"It's like this every week," said Number 42. "Maybe she's into Satanic rituals?"

"Probably," agreed Number 46. It seemed logical.

Shanti was a spiritualist, another social group that had fallen victim to misunderstanding. People assumed that spiritualists were brainwashed freaks who roamed around Leicester Square, with hair cropped and little pig-tails in orange robes. A spiritualist faced life's problems by crossing legs, closing eyes and doing nothing.

A belief in the spiritual side of life was the source of her strength in coping with Janak's annoying little ways over the years. Her two children had evolved into quite demanding personalities and well, putting it politely, her husband might as well have been the third. Since Janak's idea of communicating involved throwing his head back and seeing who could shout the loudest, she needed something to keep her ying and yang together.

Stirring from her meditative mood, Shanti spotted a letter on the mat. Another instalment from the college, judging by the postmark. Shanti smiled at the apologetic nature of the contents. Suki wasn't a truant, of course she wasn't. It was all a simple administrative error. Janak was flipping his lid over nothing. He really didn't know his children at all. All that unnecessary yelling. He needed a good shaking to pull his yang back into place.

Shanti opened her larder of herbs and settled down for a nice relaxing afternoon of leg-crossing and working hard at doin' pretty much nuffin' at all.

¥ ¥ ¥

Simeon always generated a sense of ying when he was with Suki. Since this wasn't practical and from Suki's point of view, irritating, Simeon yanged on the excitement of his job. That day, he was on a roll and in true gossip-mongering style, he had struck bingo on our old friend Rupert Mumford, the popular Minister for Education.

With his headphones clasped to his ears, he stood a home-run away from the Houses of Parliament. His hands entwined in the wires of a phone terminal box, he could have been the average telephone engineer doing his job. Inside the box, he held a ham radio, monitoring Rupert's office line. Several phones were making exit calls at the same time, generating quite a bit of fuzz before he could tune purely into Rupert's office.

"Come on Sims," called his workmate, from the van. "No woman's worth this."

"Sssh...I got some action." Rupert's secretary was ordering boxes of aftershave from Harrods.

So that was where the public purse was going! Scandalous. Five boxes of Yves St Laurent. Jeez, you'd think the guy had a heavy duty BO problem! Rupert's wife came on the line. My, she sounds like someone's whipped her jezebels. Obviously don't much appreciate the secretary. Hell, Penny wanted to sue him for divorce! That could wreck the guy. Simeon's mind worked like a tabloid newspaper.

"Sims, come on, man," said his friend impatiently.

"OK OK," sighed Simeon.

Later, Simeon struck a deal with a young telephonist from work. She sneaked in, a worried look on her face. "You got it, Mary?" he asked in a hushed voice. Busby Telecom's staff could get sacked for less than this.

She handed him a copy of one of Rupert's last bills. "One's a mobile. Don't tell anyone it came from me."

"Aw, gee, not a soul, Mary," promised Simeon, slipping the itemised bill into his pocket. "Any time you want me to sit on that baby, just call now."

"You won't be seeing me here no more, Sims," she laughed. "I'm buzzing straight out of here. It's my last day, I don't want no trouble from that," she replied, pointing at his pocket.

"No worries, Mary. Where you headin'?"

"Government company. In the city. Pays better," she boasted happily.

"Yeah?" said Simeon. "Where'd you find that in this recession 'n' all?"

"Some government agency, brings kids back to school," said Mary. "They're so swamped with people calling in, saying so-and-so is on the street, they need people on the phone."

"Yeah?" said Simeon again, raising an eyebrow, his brain working overtime. "You think maybe they'd give me a job, Mary? My Pa's an old man, worrying 'bout bills and dog-food."

"You're never in here are you, Sims? People are running right out of Bus-T. All the vacancies are filled now," sighed Mary. "I'll call you if anything turns up. You can still babysit Mary-Anne, though. That's one vacancy that's never going to be filled."

They sniggered - Mary-Anne was a bit of a brat. Simeon thumped the table. Damn! He could have been straight in there. We just ain't got our finger on the pulse, he said to himself.

¥ ¥ ¥

Suki walked sullenly across the college campus, en route to double Biology.

"Suki! Hey Suki!" called Amber, tearing across the path towards her.

"Do I look deaf?" she asked. "I thought you couldn't be dragged in here kicking and screaming. Who is he?"

"If only. I'm enrolling," moped Amber. "Part-time course."

"Yeah, and I'm a vegan," laughed Suki. "Jeez! What course? A-level Man-hunting? BTEC Population

Control?"

"Ha friggin' ha. Just cos your love life's in full throttle. Simeon looks like he needs a cold shower every three minutes. Dad's driving me up the wall," moaned Amber. She mimicked her father perfectly. "Fry them this way, serve the tomato first, cheese later. Christ, he thinks his burgers are cuisine, not snacks. He's giving me a hard time. I might as well do something."

"Leave him alone. They are cuisine," Suki argued. "And Simeon's working really hard on Bucks. There's nothing else to it."

Suki was lying. Simeon had risen drastically in her estimation. He had been taking the whole Bucks episode seriously and really seemed to be showing an interest in programming. She was even considering telling him about CONTACT. The mere thought of her true love reminded her of her mundane existence. Time was limited and she needed to spend more time to fathom out the inner workings of UNIX. And why couldn't she? Because she was trapped in this mind-numbing college which was predictably grating on her nerves. She was not alone. Teachers were tearing their hair out making up exams overnight to keep pace with RETROBASE's timetable. Apparently, standards had to be assessed at the beginning of a new term. The only standards Suki sought to raise were in her gut, where the gravel still stirred from breakfast. Shanti would undoubtedly have recommended a dose of cleansing herbs but Suki knew exactly the medicine her biological clock needed.

"Listen, all I've got to look forward to now is a rat dissection with maybe a sheep's heart thrown in. Mum would kill me if I didn't protest." She steered Amber back towards the college gates. "College hasn't ever been our scene, has it?" she said. "What say we give a little respect to the animals? Maybe get a little bite to eat and talk about Bucks? Monica hasn't come back to me yet and we could be doing some serious research instead of wasting time."

Amber needed little persuasion. She had only reached the "thought stage" about doing a course. The only plus would be the opportunities to casually bump into Ivan.

Minutes later, Suki and Amber were in The Cave, brainstorming ideas. "Short course," muttered Mr Cavallares, disapprovingly as they entered.

The Burger Bugle Gun had an incredible effect on Suki. She lost her irritation and self-pity and found logic and lateral thinking.

"Monica doesn't know anything," burbled Suki. "Except that this Sky Moores is the bloke at the top of the tree, right?"

"So what do you want me to do?" snapped Amber. "Walk in there, say 'Hi Sky baby, I'm the call-girl you didn't order'?"

"Bit of lipstick and you'd probably pull it off," said Suki sarcastically. "Don't be a moron. You'd probably scare him off, anyway. He's probably really square and has the taste of an accountant or something."

Suki could not yet appreciate that there were interesting, decent and kind accountants around. Like Gunster for instance, who had fallen for an unusually down-to-earth woman like her friend Monica.

"I was thinking more along the lines of a tramp," she said seriously.

"Same difference," said Amber.

"No, a real tramp," explained Suki.

"What, like a tramp from cardboard city?" baulked Amber. "Hi Sky, give us a few coppers, the odd password and I'll leave you alone?"

"Forget MI5, Amber. Frying onions is your scene. I'm on an intelligence-gathering mission and you're in some other movie," sighed Suki, losing hope of any moral support.

Amber exploded. "What you saying, I ain't got no

brains? You cut up rats, write a few programs and you think you've got brains. You? You know nothing. Me, I can be anything. A tramp, a tart, a rose-bush. I'm wonderful. You? You're sick."

A close-up of Amber's face revealed an old, dishevelled woman. Suki made approving noises while smearing the last touches of oil grease on her face, with a pair of grimy fingerless gloves.

"Yeah, do I look good?" asked Amber. "Or do I look great?"

"Really sexy," grunted Suki. "If only Ivan could see you now, he'd be outta control."

"You don't think anyone's going to recognise us, do you?" Amber asked, horrified. "You're OK. You got Simeon."

They cackled at predictable male hormonal cycles, slipping out the back door, armed with the address, an A-Z, a torch and a pair of CB radios. OK and a couple of mucus-dripping Salami Slammers.

Mr Cavallares heard the click of the back gate. "Amber," he shouted. "Gone. The onions? They're going to fry themselves, huh?"

Two very un-drunk, leg-crossing and intellectual tramps discussed the ins-and-outs of computers all the way to Canary Dwarf in the London Docklands. They found that it was a popular haunt for rough sleepers. Suki was slightly embarrassed by Amber's insistence at nodding at every cardboard-holding urchin that passed by.

"We're not family, Amber," reminded Suki.

"Distant cousins," replied Amber, smiling at another.

Suki was grossly offended as a passing executive threw her a coin.

"At least someone's doing their bit, eh?" he smiled, digging into his pocket.

Suki did not need his sympathy. Temporarily forgetting her dramatic garb, she pelted him with his money and screamed up the escalator. "Don't patronise me, scum-drum!"

Moved to stronger measures, she barked sharply into her two-way radio. "Right berk comin' upstairs. Green shirt, beige trousers. Tried to palm me off with a measly quid. Got at least a hundred on him...Don't let him out of your sight."

Executives were pretty well-practised long-distance runners. Partly in an effort to escape the platform "bums" but mostly because the Docklands Railway was so bloody unreliable. That one twitched all the way home.

In the meantime, two other cardboard-holding tramps dived for the pound coin, nearly causing Amber to get into an unseemly row. "Quit messing," snapped Suki, dragging Amber off the platform.

Amber was still sore. "Could have had a coffee with that."

They gawped at the ugliest building in London, a large glass tower-block, visible all around town. The Head Office for RETROBASE was on one of those floors. Sky Moores was up there somewhere, thought Suki. Indeed he was, in the process of screaming intimidations at someone else besides Abraham who looked on, as Sky's nostrils flared and his eyes looked steely. Obviously some kind of crisis and he would probably have to pick up the pieces.

Amber noted that the back windows of the ground floor were filled with fuzzy glass and covered in metal bars. The alley-way was littered with large grey dumpsters, full of rubbish and, hopefully, a few gems.

"How do I know what to look for?" moaned Amber.

"How do I know which one's the right bin, Amber? I'm a programmer, not a psychic!" snapped Suki. "You'll know it when you see it. Anything that looks important, any old manuals, computer print-outs, that kind of thing. Look, we'll split up, OK? Keep in touch on the ham."

"What if they've shredded everything?" whimpered

Amber.

"Then this is all a waste of time!" yelled Suki. "I'm going to shred you if you don't shut up." She started walking off to the other end of the row of bins.

Amber blew. "Can't even ask, can I? Oh no that's just Amber being thick, Amber's supposed to know it all. Next time you want a burger, you pay!" she shouted, irritated. "And no free deliveries!"

"Burgers? who needs your smelly burgers? I'M A VEGETARIAN!" retorted Suki, not to be outdone on the decibel front.

"Ah, go sit on a carrot!" grunted Amber, knowing she was no competition for Suki's practised lungs.

Suki refrained from reminding her that she had no need for artificial stimulants. Amber hoisted herself up on a bin and peered over. The huge metal rim sliced painfully through her multiple layers of good living and jarred against her ribs. She wriggled her large frame around it and held out her arm to grip the other side.

Stan, the security guard, was just making himself a cup of tea and heard the noise. He was aware of the fuss made about security when Mr Abraham was working half the weekend on that memo. Stan was a sensible man and got paid well to take precautions. Just as Amber craned forward to shake some of the surface debris away, Stan clicked open the back door.

"Hey you!" he shouted.

"Aaargh!" Amber toppled with shock, head-first into the bin. Suki pricked up her ears, hearing the unfamiliar voice and hid discreetly behind a bin. Being a midget had it's advantages.

"Come out of there now," said Stan sternly, waving his truncheon.

Amber dangled her legs fiercely and started whimpering. Suki held her head in her hands. Christ, it's not like he had a gun or anything! What was she doing? Suki spotted something under the next bin. It was a flat red and black box. She had seen that brand-name somewhere before. In Dad's greenhouse, of course! The reel-to-reel machine. Years ago, Janak had bought a secondhand one to record his voice at high pitch quality for his plants. Shanti often accused him of speaking to his petunias with more respect than she got. Of course, neither of his children were allowed into the sacred temple on the grounds that his plants wouldn't appreciate them breathing their oxygen.

Suki could not reach the box anyway without exposing herself to this security guard, who was still busy mouthing off to Amber. For some reason, Amber was acting like a total wimp.

"Get out of there," Stan insisted. "Now!"

Amber tried to communicate but doing a headstand with a scrunched up yellow post-it up her left nostril obviously made that a little more difficult. "Sungmaootayear!" translated to "Suki get me out of here!"

Stan, unfortunately, was not a Maori speaker. Suki wondered if she was being a bit harsh. Maybe Amber was hurt.

"Come on now, out," said Stan relentlessly. "Out."

This was easier said than done. Amber was a female Godzilla and gymnastics weren't exactly her speciality. Stan cursed and climbed up on the bin. "Give me your arm," he sighed.

"Nuh!" snapped Amber.

This stupid man had got her into this position in the first place. Now he wanted her to balance single-handed, which was bound to give her a brain haemorrhage.

"Come on, now," said Stan firmly, swiftly realising that his tea was getting cold.

He yanked one of her hands.

"Nuhlegoomeeubater!" or "No! Let go of me you bastard!" boomed Amber.

Suki had enough of being in a dilemma about

whether to show herself or not. Amber sounded like she was being gagged into silence. Suki, luckily, could speak Maori. The sight of an elderly security guard fighting the furious waggling of Amber's meaty legs from the top of an industrial bin was unexpected. If Amber had been under water she'd be treading it, no problem.

"Stop moving!" snapped Suki. The legs stop waggling and Amber's fluent Maori tongue started whimpering. Stan was visibly relieved and even managed to break into a smile at the voice of reason.

Stan and Suki carefully lowered the bin on to its side and Amber struggled out, her eyes streaming and her hands clutching her heaving chest.

"What took you so long?" she blustered and began to brush the rubbish out of her hair and off her clothes as if she had on her Sunday best. Stan felt a pang of compassion. These two couldn't be much older than his own granddaughter. It was a darn shame to see youngsters wandering the streets, in dirty clothes and fending for themselves. For once in their lives, Suki and Amber inspired genuine sympathy in a fellow mortal.

"Lordy lord, don't you two look a right pair!" he laughed, as he turned back to the building. "You won't find any scraps in there. Fancy a cuppa?"

"Well..." Amber hesitated. She was expecting a police caution and maybe even an arrest.

"Don't be shy, I won't bite," smiled Stan. He had been sitting on his own for three hours. It would be nice to chat with someone who was not a patronising executive.

"You just can't leave them alone, can you?" whispered Suki, as they walked behind him.

"Old, young, green, grey, a man's a man," giggled Amber, at this unexpected twist of fate. "And a free cup of coffee's a free cup of coffee. If you don't want it, don't throw it back in his face, OK? Give it to me."

Stan led the way into his security den. On a desk panel, six screens showed the view from camera scanners on every floor. Suki was impressed. She was actually sitting in the target building, about to have tea and toast, and surveying the layout with a walking-talking goldmine of information to give her a visual guided tour. Stan knew every room inside out. She must be on-line to Amber's little brain, who was positively dripping with charm.

"Cor, this is a big building, isn't it?" marvelled Amber, gazing at all the terminals. "Must really have to sweat keeping an eye on all the floors."

"Yep, and I practically handle the whole op myself," said Stan proudly, buttering hot toast.

"Well, you're a pretty smooth operator, catching us," said Suki. "No leftovers in them bins. All office rubbish, isn't? Thanks for this, Stan. I bet no-one sneaks past you, do they?"

"Nope, in twenty years, there's been no break-ins with me on the door. And there'll be none here neither, not with me on the early shift. I just couldn't handle nights any more. Tony does them now. He's younger than me," smiled Stan. He might get a chance to tell his war-stories with any luck.

"No," exclaimed Amber weakly. "You must be all of...forty-five?"

Amber frequently defied the laws of gravity and right now she didn't care if Newton turned in his grave. To anyone with cataracts, Stan easily looked more like approaching sixty. But he appreciated flattering young company.

"Very nice of you to say so. Those night shifts used to add years on me. Mr Moores' assistant really gets on my nerves, staying here till all hours of the night," said Stan. "Course I can't exactly tell him to hop it, can I? Edna just couldn't take it any more. 'It's the nights or me, Stan,' she said. I mean, what choice did I have?"

Suki's ears pricked up like a pair of radio antennae.

"Mr Moores?" she prompted. "Who's he?"

"He's the Big Boss and he don't let anyone forget it. Typical American, always swearing, making you feel small. He's all right if you stay on the right side of him," said Stan. "But you can tell he's got money. And I mean big money. Billions."

"I don't know what I'd do if I had all that money," sighed Suki, knowing full well that she'd go and buy another computer modem and at least fifty Whoppers without a second thought. "I'd probably buy a flashy car and I'd live somewhere dead posh..."

"Yep, he's got a red L-reg BMW with his own personal registration number: SKY. Sick, really, when the rest of us just have enough to get by," said Stan. "I wouldn't swear by it, but I'd say he'd got a private jet or five. And he lives in Holland Park, practically next door to Richard Branson."

He looked pitifully at Amber and Suki. It must really hurt to know that there's this big American bum upstairs with enough money to buy up whole countries. Amber and Suki looked anything but upset. This was wild! This was intelligence gathering! MI5, eat your heart out!

"Another cuppa tea?" asked Stan.

Suki and Amber were overwhelmed by his hospitality.

"Best leave the coffee for Tony," confided Stan. "He'll need it strong and black. I worry about the nightshift, you know. I haven't said anything to Mr Moores. Times are so hard these days. But Tony, he's got two jobs. He's finishing up at Pizza City about now. Don't know how he stays awake."

"Must be really difficult not to fall asleep," admitted Amber.

"But you can't, not in this place," said Stan. "It's dangerous. They say that there was one of them computer break-ins the other week. And of course, Mr Abraham got so big for his breeches and sent a letter to

141

every office in the country!"

Suki froze. Did he mean the hack they had done or was there another hacker out there on the trail too?

"Who's Mr Abraham?" asked Amber.

"Mr Moores' assistant. Mr Pain-in-the-arse if you'll pardon the expression," grimaced Stan. "When that bloke came from the government...oh it was madness. All these blokes in grey suits with sun-glasses on. I mean, if that's their idea of security, how do they see where they're going?"

"Bloke from the government?" Amber looked confused.

"Yeah, he was on TV. Mr Moores gave us time off to watch him. Moores is a funny old fella, kept saying, we're going to watch Rupert the Bear," he chuckled.

"Oh right," nodded Amber, as if it would be strange for a multinational billionaire to get his staff to do anything else except watch cartoons.

A motorcycle drove up and a big strapping lad pulled his helmet off.

"Ah here's Tony," said Stan. "Well, girls, it's been a pleasure."

They nodded vigorously.

¥ ¥ ¥

"What's that?" quizzed Amber.

"A reel-to-reel tape," said Suki. "Might have something on it or maybe Dad can go over it with wind music or whatever he makes his plants listen to. Here, you look after it."

"Stan's great, isn't he?" smiled Amber, stuffing it in her breast pocket.

"There's nothing like intelligence gathering over a cup of tea," admitted Suki.

"So we now know that Sky Moores has an L-reg BMW, he's a power-crazy Yank, with a jet plane and loadsamoney. Your average rich scum-bag, right?"

said Amber breezily.

Almost right. A rich scum-bag with the cunning of a fox. And a temper like a bear...

By now Sky was three miles as the crow flies, sitting in traffic in his BMW and waiting for the lights to change as he screeched into his mobile phone.

"Who's your father, Oje? Saddam Hussein? I hired an assassin, not a goddamn ass. Two for the price of one? I don't want need that kind of discount, you moron! If I wanted two I'd have said two! Goddamn immigrants! You've just killed my best Regional Accountant, you asshole!"

Oje bumbled on at the other end.

"You know who gave me a reference for Gunster Robbins, Oje?" snarled Sky. "The Treasury of her Majesty's fucking Government!"

Oje was silent.

"Yeah, think about it, Oje."

Oje remembered why it seemed logical to kill Gunster as well as Monica in the first place.

"Article on Bucks? 1976? Hmmm...burn it. Now. You're sure it looks like a car crash? Yeah, it figures. OK OK. Just on a general note, Oje, you ever heard of diplomacy? Only arm-twisting, huh. Ha ha ha. Let's call it quits at seven and a half."

Oje was surprised. One minute he'd been called to rescue people from imminent catastrophe and just because he took some initiative, his labour lost all its value.

"Why?" snapped Sky. I'm no grave-digger, I'm a businessman. Pluck your brains out of your ass. I've still got one dead body too many."

¥ ¥ ¥

Suki and Amber stood under a street light at a road junction, looking like a pair of exhausted drug-pushers. Suki's house was minutes away on the left

143

and The Cave was round the corner on Crouch Hill. They were knackered after a hard day's trashing and were about to part company. Amber had only the energy to twitch her bra around, and she was too tired to care who was looking.

"Can't you notice anything different about me?" she asked, still fishing around.

Suki looked puzzled but lacked the zest to undertake an in-depth study of Amber's born-again spots in the dark.

"I could have a Scud missile on my nose and you'd say try Clearasil!" grunted Amber.

Suki tried to be objective. At best, Amber resembled a rough sleeper who had been a resident under Westminster Bridge for at least six months.

"Yeah, that gear does suit you," Suki agreed feebly. "Especially the facial. Mum's always on about mud baths."

Amber gave up and pulled out a bundle of paper that had been trapped under her girdle for about an hour. Her bust shrank in seconds. "God that's better! I didn't want to pull it out on the train. You never know who's who, right? Any good?"

"Where'd you get that?" asked Suki in amazement. The first page was exciting in itself. "Database Management and UNIX 4150 Systems Operations".

"What did you think I was doing in that bin for so long?" Amber smiled triumphantly, handing over the torch.

"Amber, this is wild!" exclaimed Suki, flicking through the pages of commands and system diagrams. "This is like a doorkey to the network, man!"

"Yeah, I figured," said Amber, noticing a net curtain being pulled back. "Old Bumble Puck at 42 obviously agrees."

Suki was pleased that it was Tuesday, as she tried to make a discreet entrance. It is pretty dodgy to come home looking like a tramp at around eight-thirty, without telling anyone. Dad would have an absolute fit. Mum? Well, it was yoga day and nothing would wind Shanti up.

"Oh Suki, you really should have a bath!" said Shanti. "I've made your favourite."

Suki gritted her teeth. Somehow, "favourite" translated into "vegeburger" in her mother's trendy new book on how to "Make Your Teenager Go Green". Vegeburgers were the greatest insult to Suki's intestines, so accustomed to better things.

It degenerated into one of those family entertainment evenings. Suki was hoping to spend just enough time in their presence to ward off any suspicions before sloping back upstairs for some time with CONTACT. Janak was concentrating on the news, which he watched in total silence. Shanti pretended to pay attention to the tanker in the North Sea that had just leaked oil. Her smile revealed that she was not listening at all. As Janak tutted in anger at the story, Shanti was revelling in the homely atmosphere that was resembling a tension free zone. She couldn't be further from the truth. Suki was absentmindedly stabbing the carrots in her vegeburger, twitching about the computer manual sitting upstairs under her bed.

"Suki," Shanti whispered. "Monica phoned. I was in the middle of meditating but she left a message on the ansaphone."

Suki nodded.

"Sshh," grunted Janak.

Suki chewed as quickly as possible.

Trevor MacDonald said goodnight and her father stretched back.

"See we've got another letter from the college about you," he mentioned, motioning towards Suki. "So the first one was a mistake."

"Repeat after me, Janak," advised Shanti. "Sorry. Sorry. Sorry. Say it quickly and it won't hurt. And why must you do it during London Tonight? Local news is the best news."

"Apology accepted," said Suki graciously. "Mum, can I leave this burger? I'm not really all that hungry and I've got loads of coursework..."

"Sshhh..." said Shanti, her eyes fixed on the TV screen. "It's your favourite."

Suki decided that it would be safe to sidle out of the room in a couple of minutes. London Tonight never failed to come up with those really warped news items that her mother adored. Like how Choo-Choo the panda at London Zoo, had failed to get pregnant yet again after Pooh-Pooh, a randy Chinese import, did the business. Those stories gave Shanti a chance to have a rant about zoos being so unnatural and how animals should be freed into their natural habitats and all that Green World stuff.

"How did they expect instant attraction?" Shanti would say incredulously at her Green World meetings. Obviously Choo-Choo didn't have any of Amber's genes. Predictably, London Zoo was the next item.

"Closing down London Zoo?" muttered Shanti. "That's terrible. They can't do that. It's an institution."

Suki rolled her eyes. The moment to escape. She edged out of her seat, her mind tackling the operational problem of how to open the kitchen door discreetly, and stuff the remains of her vegeburger in the organic compost generator without being heard. Her mother had swiftly moved on to commenting on yet another environmental hazard: cars. She talked over a newscaster's report of a fatal collision on the M1.

"See! Another crash. How many more do they want?" she asked, turning to Suki for agreement. "More cars, they want more roads. Give them more roads, they build more cars."

Sighing, Suki sat down again. Caught again. "Mum I really can't eat these burgers," whined Suki.

"What's happened to your appetite, beti?" asked

Shanti.

The newsreader continued. "The two incinerated bodies have been identified as Monica Ruddles and Gunster Robbins."

"What? Sshhh..." said Suki, in shock. She fumbled for the video control.

"You've got to have enough vitamins," said Shanti primly, oblivious to Suki's desperation about finding a blank tape.

"Quiet!" screamed Suki, as mugshots of Monica smiling, and Gunster looking like an accountant flashed up.

Too late, she'd missed it. Ironically, Choo-Choo and Pooh-Pooh would have got more screen time than poor Monica and Gunster did.

Suki stared at the screen but missed the nice little round-off story that London Tonight had managed about Princess Di visiting a mental hospital.

"She should be a patient," said Shanti grimly, picking up Suki's plate. "If you don't like vegeburgers, what's your favourite?"

Her teenager had definitely gone green. Suki could not even stomach the thought of her mother's alternatives.

Her thoughts rattled around something more important than computers, more important than Whoppers, more important than CONTACT. MO IS DEAD, MO IS DEAD, MO IS DEAD.

She pulled herself together. Unlike Simeon, Suki never believed what she read in the papers, saw on TV or heard on the radio. This was partly because Shanti had called them liars so often. Suki consoled herself that there must have been some mistake. Playing the message Monica left on the ansaphone, Suki grew more and more confident that there was no way that Monica had been killed in a motorway accident. It had to be another media cock-up. She pressed the 'play' button on the ansaphone again.

"Suki, it's Mo. Listen, I'm not going to be your Student Officer any more. I got the sack. I'm going to Newcastle with Gunster. Amber was right. Paper Tiger didn't stand a chance. She really made me lose my rag, I wrecked the office today. Listen, Gunster's got this article on Bucks Times Bucks from 1976. Oh, you don't know, do ya? Gunster and me are like, a couple. He's lovely. Best bloke in the world. Me mam's going to love him. Guess what his password is..."

Suki stopped the tape at the mention of the password. Her brain started to vibrate. Password, password, password. Her hand flew instinctively to the computer switch.

"Can you believe it?" Monica's giggles screeched out of the speakers. Suki couldn't, not in her wildest dreams. In one night, she had the manual, the password and her Student Officer had been sacked and was off her back.

"We've got so much in common it's untrue," continued Monica. "He hates driving, like I do. He's had epilepsy and doctors said don't drive. So we're going by train. First class, I've never travelled first class before...Beep!" The tape finished before Monica did.

There, thought Suki satisfied. Monica's alive and kicking and going off with Gunster to Newcastle. She wouldn't be caught dead on some motorway. Would she? There was only one way of finding out. She spoke to a very excited Simeon.

"Come on, Simeon, get real. Murder mysteries in Crouch End? No way, we're just a boring bunch of computer-hackers," Suki smiled.

Simeon was disappointed, but eager as usual to do Suki's bidding.

"Can you get me the number for the Ruddles family in Newcastle? I just want to say thank you to Monica. She's given me Gunster's password by mistake. Yep, the password. Now get the number and leave me alone."

She opened up her computer manual, in blissful ignorance that would shatter the minute she spoke to Ma Ruddles herself.

"My little Monica's gone," she said to Suki.

"You mean it's true?" said Suki horrified. "But she travelled by train. She couldn't drive."

"I know, I know..." moaned Audrey, before shrewdly calculating that no-one knew that Monica hadn't passed her test. "Who are you?"

"Er...I'm one of her students, she made sure I went back to college and er...we became friends," said Suki. Audrey was far too upset to trouble with any more trivial questions about how Monica met her maker - at the hands of a BR 125 or a fuel-injected Chevrolet. Suki's heart went cold as she put the phone down. She knew she'd have to answer those questions herself. There were too many holes in the accident theory. There was something very wrong here. Monica was harmless. But Bucks Times Bucks didn't know that, and the end result was the same. Mo was truly and completely dead.

8

THE INTRUDERS

At RETROBASE HQ the next morning, Pip was surprised to walk into work and find all the computers already up-and-running. The cursor on the screen was whizzing around like a cat chasing a mouse. There seemed to be an extensive file-search in progress.

"Yeah, Mr Jones's secretary phoned this morning. He wants to do a personnel audit, whatever that means," confirmed Jane, her secretary. "The old fool doesn't even know his own password."

"Strange, he's not usually in on Tuesdays," said Pip, glancing out of the window, slightly confused. "His car's not here." She assumed that before anyone started pressing any buttons, she would be consulted about it. Mind you, Mr Jones from Personnel was a cantankerous old fart.

"So, I gave her the password," muttered Jane.

"Who?" asked Pip.

"Mr Jones's secretary."

"You did what?" yelped Pip. "How many times have I told you about that? Don't give out passwords. Hang on a minute, he hasn't got a secretary."

"She said she was new..." protested Jane.

Pip was already reaching for the phone. "See, no personnel audit. No Mr Jones. No secretary. Abraham, I think the hackers are revisiting. This time it is a major security alert, the files they're gatecrashing are highly privileged."

¥ ¥ ¥

Suki had taken a chance by phoning Jane and it paid off. It just proved to her that she didn't need Amber or Simeon. She could work on her own. Shanti and Janak had skipped off to the allotment and, but for the whir of the computer, the house was instilled with an eerie silence. She didn't need any hangers-on. She was a professional. This wasn't about getting a free pizza or tickets to a concert any more. This was for Monica. This was serious. She had hooked on to the system easily enough with Gunster's password. But she needed a password to all privileged accounts to work out Bucks Times Bucks' activities and real intentions. A list of all personnel was a good starting point as it would give her an idea of who was calling the shots and who had system manager status. Suki suspected that it would be Sky Moores who had overall control, but even he wouldn't call himself Sys.man. Stan had painted a picture of Sky as having brains. Sys.man was the password that came installed with the system but Pip made sure it was changed immediately. It would be too obvious for any intruders and would reveal straight away to anyone who was watching that Suki wanted access to strictly confidential information. She would have to gatecrash the files of some of the big names working for RETROBASE.

¥ ¥ ¥

Abraham's hand trembled as he phoned Sky to let him know about this latest crisis with security. Meanwhile, Pip closed off all but one terminal. The system was being assaulted and no work could proceed. The office phones buzzed continually with calls from local and regional offices. Their entry into the network was blocked. Abraham did not know what to say. "Computer security alert" might spark off a panic attack and outrage at the vulnerability of the highly confidential exam results in the system. In Sky's absence, Abraham opted for the "technical problem" explanation and advised them to wait for further advice. His beleaguered confidence was given a boost

151

by his efficient telephone manner, it seemed to transform irate headteachers into confused puppies. After all, even if they taught six-year-olds how to use Wordstar it did not mean they themselves knew anything about computers.

Pip and Abraham watched bemused and bleary-eyed, trying abysmally to make notes on the rapid pattern of files being opened. "What the hell's he looking for?" asked Abraham, irritated that his timetable was being disrupted.

"What makes you think it's a 'he'?" snapped Pip, just as Sky breezed in through the door.

"Abraham, I want you in my office now, with a full explanation," he said briskly. Pip followed him into the glass room without invitation and gave a quick report next to a silent but glowering Abraham.

"So, this intruder...what's the pattern? Is it a smart-arse kid or are we handling someone with a brain?" he snapped. Sky was having a pretty bad week, what with a couple of murders, the loss of his Regional Accountant amongst them and Operation Acid Trip reaching a critical stage of execution. In fact, he was expected to sort out slight teething problems. Pah! He really did not need some hacker snooping around right now.

"It's too early to say..." stuttered Abraham.

"Yeah yeah, Abraham. You wouldn't recognise a brain even if you had one. Well, you'd better find out cos it's your responsibility to catch this jerk. Pronto."

Abraham felt deflated at the very thought of yet more responsibility. Pip was surprised at Sky's tone. As they left the room, she whispered, "Asshole." She smiled at Abraham. He was quite sweet in a pathetic sort of way.

Sky leaned back wearily. He increasingly felt the urge to fire Araham now that Pip could handle responsibility. The only saving grace for Abraham was Sky's other preoccupations. He had more pressing problems than these piffling staff issues.

Suki sat staring at the map of glowing lights on the screen, her bedraggled hair falling over her face. Her heartbeat quickened. This was the climax that Gunster's password had promised. It had opened doors and crevices in the system that saved her weeks of excavating through the manual. Her eyes stared but her brain couldn't register an iota of sense. Her body had fixed in a curving posture for a straight eighteen-hour stretch, the retinas glued to the screen.

What did this map mean? Why was it called Operation Acid Trip? What the hell was Bucks Times Bucks up to? Were those arrows identifying missile sites? Suki then discovered a file of colour-coded keys which identified some of the missing links on the map. Large areas of land were owned by BTB across the world. She presumed that the moving dots on the nautical lines were ships. The land seemed to be ear-marked for some kind of "shipment", a word that came up constantly in budgets and personnel listings. One of the strangest reports amidst a wealth of big words referred to the cost of staff funeral arrangements. It just didn't tally. But the report seemed serious enough and said that this expenditure was "reaching unsustainable proportions". What were they transporting? Coffins?! Suki laughed at her own joke and quickly sobered up, remembering that Monica was probably lying in one and not laughing. She could have sworn that one of the flashing dots moved a millimetre, heading for the coast of the West Indies. She wondered what would happen if she changed co-ordinates.

¥ ¥ ¥

Abraham sat in the cafeteria with Pip over a working bite-to-eat about The Hacker. "I think there's more than one of them for a start," said Pip. "They've been at it for hours."

"Great. Not only do I have to hound down one, there are twenty of them."

"Not I, we," said Pip. "Haven't you ever heard of teamwork? Anyway, we'll have to have a detailed look but I think I can see a general pattern emerging."

"You can?" Abraham was doubtful. All he could see was a haystack with no needles in sight.

"Look, if you were a kid, you'd be more interested in the school files, changing a few exam results here and there. But these are professionals," Pip concluded excitedly. "They're looking for financial files, reports, minutes, particular personnel. It's like they're a rival company or something."

"Great. It's not a couple of schoolkids. It's a business cartel." Abraham was depressed.

"What are all those references to Bucks Times Bucks? What's that all about? Bucks is a chemical multinational or something, isn't it?"

"Bucks...oh that. That's where Sky has all his meetings," explained Abraham, letting go the burden of confidentiality. "That's why he's never in the office. He's at BTB."

"So how did he get to run RETROBASE?" asked Pip. "I mean chemicals and education are a bit different, aren't they?"

"God knows, but there must be lots of money in it for him," said Abraham. "If there's one thing I've learnt about him and BTB it's that they go where the money goes."

"You don't like him very much, do you?" remarked Pip.

"I'd say he's the most patronising, insulting, greedy, selfish, thoughtless, cruel bastard I've ever had to work for," said Abraham easily. "But otherwise, he's

154

fine."

They laughed and walked back towards the office. Secretaries with their coats on were shuffling past. "Mr Moores is having a breakdown," muttered Jackie. Through the double doors, they found Sky sitting in front of the computer screen in a cold sweat, his tie loosened and face red.

"Something up, Mr Moores?" asked Abraham. "Shall I call a doctor?"

"Look," squawked Sky weakly. The screen filled with a map of the world, with co-ordinates and highlighted spots. Operation Acid Trip was on the screen, although it didn't mean much to anyone else except him. Things were going desperately awry. Earlier that day, one of his gypsy vessels reported difficulty with custom officials about docking in the Bahamas. It had not been a serious issue, but the captain did not know that.

Sky had vouched to co-ordinate a different route, arranging another more agreeable destination. Now the thought occurred to him that The Hacker's timing with his mini-crisis in the Bahamas was no accident.

"The plan, the plan. On the other hand, don't look."

His sensibilities had caught up with him and he turned to face Abraham, his cold blue eyes slanted with sheer madness. His voice masked fear with a familiar rage.

"Listen to me, sonny, you are going to get these bastards, if it's the last thing you do. And I mean the very last thing. Hear me? When I get back from the john, we're going to make a plan to get these guys. All our lives are at stake. Got that. In my office, both of you."

When Sky returned, they saw a very presentable, spruced up man with his tie in place and his hair greased back. They would have been shocked to know that Mr Moores had just been shaking in his shoes and resorted to dragging his nostril over the ceramic toilet flush, consuming his every last granule of cocaine.

"I'm ready for anything this Hacker throws at me," he grunted, his eyes glowing red. "Now, Abraham, got any ideas?"

"The intruder or intruders are very smart," said Abraham. "They've by-passed every security check we have. If we do a back-up for the day's computer activity time, we might find their point of entry, what files they've accessed and what they're looking for. This should help us identify who they are."

"Excellent, superb, I knew there must be a good reason for employing you, Abraham," beamed Sky. "I'll leave it in your capable hands."

"I'll take that as a compliment, sir," Abraham said stiffly.

Pip ripped the computer page and peered closely in disbelief. "Gunster Robbins. It's his password, his user ID..."

"But he's dead, isn't he..." faltered Abraham. For amoment, Abraham had a vision of an ashen-faced Gunster twitching in a computerised coffin.

"Assholes!" screamed Sky. "It's someone using his password. I'm surrounded by complete dorks! You guys are the techno-experts, not me. The guy's just died in a car crash. It can't be him. Someone's using his password."

He paused to consider the implications. Someone was obviously hot on the trail. It couldn't be Oje, could it, a little perturbed at the cut in fees? Na, the only technology he knew how to use was a Kalashnikov.

"And I want to know how they got it. And who are they anyway? Something tells me that you're not going to be able to suss anything out without me telling you how to spell 'potato'. I want the exact details of what they're going for. And I'll work out why! Give it to me like yesterday!"

¥ ¥ ¥

"We can change the password when they get off the system. But I doubt whether that will stop them. Whoever the intruder is, they sure know about the system. They're penetrating weaknesses in the program I didn't even know about," said Pip in admiration.

"What do you mean? A program is a program, isn't it?" asked Abraham.

Pip had a chance to impress him with her expertise. "Don't be a dodo. This program is designed to meet our needs. We need to store lots of addresses, exam results, attendance details for each student in the country. They get fed directly into the RETROBASE system through the local and regional network. So we have to be flexible to keep those channels open. It also means..." she said, "that the door is open to abuse if a terminal gets into the wrong hands."

"So you're saying it could be someone at a local office that's doing this?" said Abraham.

"Exactly," said Pip triumphantly.

"But why?"

"If I knew that dick-brain, I'd be home and putting my feet up. It's obviously somebody who's very interested in Bucks Times Bucks and who knows there's some information about the company on our files."

"Can't we put some kind of trace on the line and track them down?"

"I suppose so, but we've have to get the police and Busby Telecom involved."

"No police," said Sky adamantly on his tannoy phone. "It's a goddamn embarrassment to confess to being a victim of espionage. No cops till we know who's doing this, what they're getting out of it and why. And that's final."

"Well, Busby Telecom have been instructed to put the line trace in," maintained Pip.

There was no telling what this madman would threaten next. She certainly had no intention of crawling through potholes in the middle of the street looking for the right telephone lines. And, besides, there were more fundamental questions to answer.

"Mr Moores, the pattern so far shows that the hacker's going for stuff on Bucks Times Bucks. What's the connection with BTB and RETROBASE?" she asked squarely.

Abraham felt like praying. Sky paused. Well, you had to give it to this woman, she had bottle.

"A purely business arrangement. An exchange of materials, one might say," he replied briskly.

¥ ¥ ¥

Simeon woke up with a throbbing headache. He'd spent most of the night awake and agitated. Suki hadn't answered her private line and refused to respond to his coded flashlight signals. She had the password and was obviously making use of it. He phoned his workplace and took the morning off work. He would rather keep a close eye on Suki any day of the week. It was guaranteed to improve his health.

"I didn't realise you were still with us anyway," said his supervisor gloomily.

He was losing half his best staff to other companies and the rest of them were feigning sickness. Meanwhile the workload showed no signs of stemming. He'd just logged an emergency call from a government company for a computer line trace.

Simeon caught sight of Amber as he was stepping out. They both looked pretty exhausted from the previous day's excesses. They spoke simultaneously.

"She's going for it."

"With the password..." said Simeon.

"Yeah? And the manual..." added Amber.

They stopped.

"Without us..."

They quickened their pace across the alley-way. "No way!" they screamed and frenzied their way to Number 39.

Number 42 was having a breather. "Don't kids have anything better to do?" It sparked off the 'youth in society' doorstep conference.

"Let us in for God's sake," Amber panted into the ansaphone. "OK fine, Suki. I'm going to do my ranting 'Jehovah coming to save you child from the hell of earth, AIDS and the electronic age' routine." Amber braced herself for a bellowing performance. "You have been warned. Thou shalt denounce blood transfusions in the name of the Almighty and declare war on every meaty morsel that enters thine orifice..."

The buzzer saved Suki from an earful worse than death.

"Always works," scoffed Amber. They scarpered upstairs, unaffected by the aghast neighbourhood watch.

"Christ, you've been up for a long stint," she remarked casually at Suki's glowering eyes. "So the manual gave some joy. Another Cavallares victory in aid of the human race..."

"Make it snappy. I'm busy," said Suki flatly.

"Yeah, too busy to remember your buddies. I was up all night flashing at you..." moaned Simeon.

"Didn't have much impact, eh?" giggled Amber, playfully poking at Simeon's ribs. They began a quick exchange of abuse, which Suki broke up with sharp clarity.

"Monica's dead," she said quietly. "I spoke to her mother last night. They'd been fed the accident story. Bucks killed her because she was asking too many questions."

After a respectful silence, Simeon pressured for the details. "And Gunster's password..."

"You two better keep out of this. It's dangerous,"

said Suki, turning her back on them and heading for the computer desk.

"Get stuffed!" snapped Amber. "I'm OK to go trashing around town diving into dust-bins risking hepatitis but it's t-ooo-ooo dangerous to sit in front of a screen."

She parked herself on the swivel chair, signalling that her departure was simply out of the question. Her legs lounged over the arm and she chewed a toothpick. She was about to motion a prayer to Screen Mecca when the colourful world map caught her attention.

"Yeah, gimme a break," said Simeon, trying to be assertive. "I've taken a day off to dig into this life and death gig and I'm going to get my hands dirty, OK?"

He pressed the play button on the ansaphone. Monica's voice reverberated across the room.

"Take a hike, this is my baby!" growled Suki in the face of dissent. Her throat was throttling for a scream. She stopped the tape.

Simeon pressed play. Suki pressed stop. They alternated furiously until Suki reached the point of total exasperation. "We're finished unless you leave me alone, you nerd!" she hissed.

Amber oblivious to the fraying tempers and straining relationships around her, stayed glued to the screen. "What the hell are these shipments, Sucks?"

"Get your nose out of it, Amber!" shrieked Suki.

Monica had waffled considerably despite constant stops and starts and was just about to confide in the password, when Suki lost all control and pressed the erase button.

"That's vital evidence, you little shrimp!" yelled Simeon.

"This is a no fingerprints operation. No fingerprints and no amateurs," yelled Suki. "So get the hell out of my life!"

His eye was caught by a momentary distraction of

his bleeper, signalling that he should call his office. Suki took her chance to communicate decisively and belted her metal leg implants into Simeon's vital organs, finally arousing some attention from a distant Amber.

The pair of them stumbled out of the room, Amber falling easily into a nursemaid role. Suki returned to immobility in front of the screen, unable to comprehend Amber's abuse about lost manhoods and friendships through the intercom. Her glazed expression gave no emotion and she ventured deeper and deeper, beyond the realm of reason. Suki had stepped into the unknown before. This was the first time she'd cut her ties so completely. The rift had been declared irreparable with that final kick.

¥ ¥ ¥

Simeon was in considerable pain and aroused much suspicion in the street, doubling over and hobbling home.

"Satanic rituals. See, I was right..." came the murmur.

"Give me the phone, Amber," he stammered. "Yeah? Simeon here. Aw come on, man, you thought I was sick? I'm practically disabled now! I've got groinaritis."

"I don't care if you've had a stroke." His supervisor had wisened up to contemporary staff management skills. "Simeon, if you don't do this job, you're out. And that's final. It's an emergency."

"OK OK, you got me by the balls. As long as I get full sick pay plus a day's on top," relented Simeon.

"Hey Sims..." protested his supervisor. "All right, it's a deal. Here's the details..."

"They can't make you work!" Amber was horrified. "You should be in casualty."

"Yeah, I know. I should have asked for severance

pay." He glanced at the address, twinging with every agonising movement into his van. "Damn, this job's all the way into the City too. It could be a long haul."

¥ ¥ ¥

Simeon negotiated a hamburger with the go-slow on the North Circular and abused various slow drivers going down one-way streets before finally arriving at his destination. He was going to nail Suki's butt to the wall. She was just getting too cocky for her own good. Ah, here it was. Return to Basic Education HQ. It sounded vaguely familiar but a sleepless night prevented him from being able to place it. Just as he was getting directions from the receptionist, an old flame tapped him on the shoulder.

"Mary! How's it going? So this is where it's all happening!" Simeon clicked. Suki was mainlining into this place. And, as irony would have it, they wanted him to pull the plug out. He had to get to a phone. "Hell, no, I'm still with Busby but they've just called me in to do a line trace here. Give me the low-down, Mary."

"Yeah, some problem with the computers. It's some young punk who doesn't want to go to school, wrecking the system," said Mary. "I haven't been able to do a dot of work all day. Top floor, Room 208. Mr Moores' office. He's the main man himself. Let me show you the way. Something wrong with your leg?"

"Ah, I was just playing baseball and stretched too far, that all. Scored one too many. These things happen. I haven't slept for nights since it happened," he lied.

They talked about the trials and tribulations of being a working mother and how Mary never got any sleep any night of the week, as they headed for an encounter with Sky.

162

¥ ¥ ¥

"I feel like we're dealing with a robot. These guys just don't have a break," moaned Abraham, looking dishevelled and cross-eyed from looking at a VDU screen. Suki certainly was hammering away relentlessly, not caring who was watching her.

"Simeon De Vere, Assistant Telephone Engineer from Busby Telecom. How may I help you?" He beamed at Abraham. "Are you Mr Moores?" This approach always assured him of getting the exact details of the job over a nice cup of relaxing coffee.

"Why would anyone want to hack you to death?" continued Simeon. "Oh, hang on, I've heard about you guys. You drag kids back into school, right?" he smirked. "Looks like this kid's got the better of you, though. Ha ha."

Pip and Abraham didn't laugh. They didn't have the energy. "We don't think it's a kid. It's more like a sophisticated business cartel, trying to get our database," they murmured lifelessly.

They were off the scent completely. Simeon continued to listen sympathetically to Pip and Abraham, whilst memorising the office floor plan. You never knew when it would come in handy and plus, it would make Suki green with envy. Simeon left the building armed with the phoneline number and got to work in the depths of the telephone system. Predictably, Suki wasn't taking any calls. He had no choice. He couldn't keep warning her. This was his job and this is where he was happiest, in the mesh of lines and wires. And of course, he had his little black book of important phone numbers...

¥ ¥ ¥

"The trace will take about an hour to catch and the number will come up on your screen, OK?" said Simeon cheerfully. "Any more problems and just call."

"We've got it!" Pip excitedly called Abraham. A number had appeared on the screen just as the engineer had predicted.

Sky smiled. At last, this nightmare was over.

Rupert Mumford, our rejuvenated man of the people, was caught in a passionate embrace with Schister, his German secretary, when the phone rang. "Leave it, they'll ring back later," he pleaded with Schister.

"No Rupee, it may be important." Schister pursed her lips and spoke with practised ease, "Minister for Education's office, I'm afraid Mr Mumford's in a meeting..."

Sky exploded. So it was that slimy schmuck from Paperlace that had wrecked his life, his database and was trying to expose the plan. The diabolical sweating machine-on-legs was responsible. And if he thought he was going to get away with it... "Get that asshole on this phone, with his flies done up," he snarled patronisingly. "Darling."

"Rupert, it's an American heavy breather!" squeaked Schister.

"Ah Sky, what can I do for you?" asked Rupert, pleased to hear from the man who had enabled his rise to fame and aftershave.

"Fancy a dive off the Canyon? Listen, what the hell are you doing with my database? I've traced the line to you and if you think you're going to slide your way out of this one, you're going to be blasted out in the open. Get my drift?"

"What are you talking about?" Super Rupert was puzzled. "What line? Database? Blasting what?" This sounded like warfare.

"You've hooked into my computer system and I'm going to nail your butt for it," snapped Sky. "Simple, you try to hoodwink me with MI5, gatecrashing my system and I'm going to pull the plug on you, you goddamn aristocratic paperchasing piece of dog-shit."

"There's really no cause for such abuse, Sky. Someone has been tampering with your computer system, is that it?" Rupert was finally catching on. "Yes that's very worrying, you do have confidential departmental information on those files. What on earth makes you think I've got anything to do with it? I'm the Minister for Education, for God's sake! I'm hardly going to sabotage my own operation, am I? Give me some credit, Sky!"

Sky resorted to silence. Danger signals were scanning Sky's brain. If Rupert hadn't even come close, he was pretty inept after all, then who had? The Hackers were exposing the trail of deceit, unravelling the objectives of Operation Acid Trip, one by one. First the murders, then using Gunster's password. Now the trace leads to Rupert Mumford's office. It was clear that they were teasing him, distracting him, leading him on to the point of self-destruction.

Sky murmured words of consent and put down the line. Rupert was fast becoming paranoid. He rang back.

"Who's doing this, Sky? Do they know about Bucks investing in the Education Plan? My reputation is on the line here! You're the Director, do something!"

"I've got it under control. Now get off my case, you wind-bag!"

The trace hadn't worked. The hackers were smarter than that. There was no way he could compete with them on the technological front. There had to be something simpler, something logical he could do to draw them closer. Close enough for identification, close enough for an interrogation, for a trade-off. Or, despite the taste it left in his mouth, it might be another job for Oje...

The master of psychological warfare rose to stare out of the wall window and consider his plight. The same question burbled around his head, circling and resurfacing. Who? Who was doing this to him? Could it be someone inside BTB? One of the other people on the Board? They'd all love to see him fall, he knew that. But not before Operation Acid Trip was up and running and profit-churning. Even if it was, they had evidence from elsewhere in BTB and wouldn't bother to disrupt the RETROBASE database. Was it Skull, Bell or any of the other chemical manufacturers? Like BTB, they had similar long-term staff and commodity problems but as far as he knew, Operation Acid Trip was the best kept industrial secret. Top insiders knew that a cure for AIDS had been suppressed, everyone knew that a water-fuelled car engine had been invented and destroyed. But no-one knew about the revolutionary concepts in Operation Acid Trip. No-one else had a plan that would see them into the next century, richer than any multinational corporation. No, it couldn't be a competitor.

Sky glanced down at Pip's last report on his desk. Whoever the hackers were, they were looking for evidence. Evidence of a connection between BTB and RETROBASE.

He took a moment to call the captain of the ship, Cayon Seas. It was best to check what was going on in these treacherous times.

The captain was confused. His plans had been torpedoed with new co-ordinates. "Fuck the computers," ordered Sky. "Take your direction from paper unless you hear otherwise from me. OK?"

His suspicions were confirmed. The hackers were interested in what BTB was really doing. But they obviously didn't know what the hell they were doing. It wasn't industrial insiders. He'd use that to give them exactly what they wanted. Confidential information.

Set the bait, dangle the hook, drag the line in and catch the fish. Sky Moores sat in his glass fishbowl office, fingering the sails of a glass ship on his desk and made a decision. RETROBASE would lead the way with a breakthrough in combating computer crime. The plan was to catch The Hacker by laying a trap.

9

SWALLOWING THE BAIT

Simeon discovered that a new weapon had arrived in road traffic control. In times gone by, drivers used to disguise their activity under their dashboard. It was history when drivers tried to sneak a pick surreptitiously by being first off at the lights. Now it was roll the window down, dig openly into one's nostril and with words that promised mindless violence, flick snot of stupefying proportions towards the offending driver in the hope that they got the hell out of the way. It was a fighting strategy to get through the traffic with your nose clean.

The Bus-T van at the head of the traffic lights seemed to be immobile. Cars beeped and drivers flicked their snot in anger and glared, but to no avail. Simeon was getting an anxiety attack. Suki was not taking any calls. The hurt unrivalled any previous pain he had experienced, including the groin kick. At least she was acknowledging his existence then. Worry lines crossed his face as he finally shifted into gear and screenwiped the green slime. Suki just could not afford to be on-line for such long periods of time. They might think it was a cartel for now, but there was no doubt in his mind. They were hunting down The Hacker with a determined vengeance. She was teetering on the edge of big trouble and her senses were closed to all the warning signs. He could still feel the dull twinge aching down below as he parked outside 39 Lime Road.

Janak and Shanti were raging through a family dispute. Threats of divorce, ineptitude and diminished responsibility were flung around the frontroom tennis court. They paused for a let at the sound of the doorbell.

"Gee, you mean she's not at home?" asked Simeon, puzzled.

"And she hasn't been to college either," grimaced Janak. "I knew I was right but her mother can't accept that her daughter is a layabout good-for-nothing..."

The ball was thrown back into play and Shanti was going for an ace. "She's your daughter too..." she shrieked. Simeon left hurriedly in case he was drawn into the fracas as an umpire between a pair of total fruit cakes. It was pointless explaining that their daughter was in life-threatening danger.

¥ ¥ ¥

Despite her delirium, or perhaps because of it, Suki discerned that she had to get closer somehow and penetrate the very heart of the beast: RETROBASE HQ. She had done remarkably well to establish from a remote terminal that a multibillion dollar scam was in progress, but she knew little of the motivation behind it all. The twilight hours had arrived and shadows of dumpsters crowded around. The only tweek of light was from the back door where Stan had welcomed them so warmly. Lack of sleep had not detracted her will to crack this case.

It had got personal now. Monica's face and the sound of Audrey's distressed voice came into her mind. "Who are you?" she'd asked Suki. "Who are you?" Suki didn't know how to explain how her accidental association with Monica had led to her death.

¥ ¥ ¥

"What's the big mystery?" said Amber with simple logic. "Silly mare's gone to RETROBASE. She's probably sitting in front of Stan's computer screens right now."

"You just don't get it," Simeon said, urgency lumped in his throat. "She might get caught."

"Relax, she'll be back," replied Amber. "Dad's takings are going down the shoot. She hasn't had a burger for twenty four hours."

Suki did not need any reminders. Tony had returned from his pizza job, with a box strapped to his motorbike. Soon, he was snoring with his head dipped into an olive and salami pizza. Suki's rumbling stomach would have registered on the Richter scale but in Tony's case, it fell on mushroom-plugged ears. After sneaking out a rasher of salami, it was easy to slip past and weave her way to the deserted computer terminal room. Six hours after cruising in and out of the system, collecting passwords and entry codes she heard Tony stir. Suki sneaked into the corridor and after opening several unmarked doors, she finally collapsed in a cloakroom full of overalls.

Meanwhile, Amber assessed their options. "What we know about computer programming would be difficult to balance on a pin-head," she acknowledged gracefully, picking up her diary. "There's only one thing for it! Simeon, you're not going to like this, but the family business is at stake. I have to take drastic action. If burgers are ever to be consumed again, it's a small sacrifice."

"Gee, what can we do? I'm ready to try anything," moped Simeon, contemplating life without his loved one.

"Give me the phone... Can I speak to Ivan?"

"Hell no, not the bagman! Not the jailbreaker!" yelped Simeon. "Gimme a break."

"Where would you like it this time, sweetie?" smiled Amber, barely containing her animal excitement.

¥ ¥ ¥

The following morning, Sky was in a breezy mood.

170

After a good think about how he was going to trap and torture The Hacker, he had slept soundly. The other staff were still miffed by their boss's schizophrenic behaviour, and nervous in case they got another display. He called in his half-asleep and dishevelled experts, Abraham and Pip, for a planning meeting.

"The hackers are into BTB and that's exactly what I'm going to give them," Sky said briskly.

Abraham was aghast. "But, Mr Moores..."

"Shut up, you dingbat, I'm in charge now," he smiled. He was back to normal.

"I want you to print out this list of files and then delete them. I want them to be listed as strictly confidential and given straight to me." He handed out copies of a report. "Now, this is seriously classified information that needs to be input into the computer. Any suggestions for a filename? Nothing too obvious, but nothing too obscure either."

"I take it this information is junk," said Pip, putting two and two together.

"So there is a braincell out there!" sneered Sky, with something approaching good humour. "Correct. This carrot should be so tantalising for these nosey jerks that they're going to stay on-line for a direct trace. Get Bus-T in on it."

Flabbergasted by Sky's good spirits, Abraham and Pip left to drum up a file that seemed genuine with an accompanying password, filename and memory space. "Operation Secret" and other such imaginative operatives were being muttered when Simeon arrived to set up a fresh trace. A rendezvous with an eager Ivan the previous day had put him in a bad mood.

"Just a goddamn crook! Get me a floorplan, get me this, get me that," Simeon muttered to himself. "Get me a job will be next. Jackass!"

He dutifully noted the dimensions of the floor and then pursued his own agenda. He scoured the building, hoping to smuggle Suki out, but failed to check out that obvious hideaway, the closet full of dirty overalls.

The hackers seemed to have lost interest for now, which was convenient in one sense, as it gave Pip and Abraham time to assemble the "dummy" file. Pip was supervising the input of Sky's "dangling carrot". Statistics on BTB streamed from page to page, with reports inter-breeding. If she hadn't been so exhausted, she might have been interested. Every other line mentioned the secret Operation. "Pure myth-making," smiled Sky cynically.

The challenge of capture had exhilarated Abraham and Pip. They had been reduced to a pair of giggling buffoons. "This time, we're hot!" they informed Simeon gleefully. He smiled back weakly.

After some twilight activity, the computer lines had only the quiet buzz of day-to-day office work. Miserably Simeon left the building with the trace genuinely in place. There was nothing else he could do to defend Suki, except install a signal that would tell him when the trace had been a success. He left it up to her good sense to realise that if she didn't quit now, they'd be on to her.

¥ ¥ ¥

Suki awoke, initially disorientated. She was hungry and shivering with cold, but resolved to warm up under a set of over-sized overalls. She sneaked past Stan's door, stealing a sandwich, and made her way through the corridors to the terminal room, entering the system program with practised ease. She knew she was getting nearer to finding some answers.

The facts flashed through her mind. A chemical multinational company investing some heavy duty bucks in a government education programme. A Student Officer asks some questions about this unprecedented finance policy and gets killed. She has a relationship with the company's accountant and he gets knocked off too. Land has been bought in all the poor places around the world and shipments are heading in that direction. A nuclear warhead was spotted on the computer map of the world. A chemical company with shipping interests and lots of money...Drugs, warfare, murder. Hardly a bunch of do-gooders...And the government had sat back and let it happen.

She had the right to be here, she told herself firmly. They dared to get a file on her and she was getting her revenge. Her eye caught a new file. It had been loaded and was plastered with confidential information on BTB... She had to check this out.

"They're on," whispered Abraham, his eyes transfixed by the screen.

"Are they taking the bait?" asked Pip.

"Yes, yes, yes!" rejoiced Abraham.

"We're going to get these sons..." muttered Sky. "What are you doing about it, boy? Get a troop of security guards and get on the trail!"

"We need the number. Come on, baby, give me the number..." said Pip, speaking to the IBM like a nurtured plant.

Amidst a troop of rough-looking bouncer types, Abraham, Sky and Pip were still waiting an hour later. "It takes time," explained Pip.

"Too goddamn long," spat Sky. He had the urge to strangle someone right now.

As clerical staff left the office and security guards indulged in widespread snoring, a telephone number popped up on the screen.

"That can't be right," said Pip, looking down a list of internal telephone numbers.

"Why not?" snapped Sky. "We're nailing their butts and it's not right!"

"But it means they're in this building," protested

173

Abraham.

"Even better. Right here under our noses," Sky gritted his teeth. "Wake up you dozy mares! Get those suckers now!"

¥ ¥ ¥

The security operation got under way. The boys in black, armed to the hilt, had surrounded the terminal room. They were frustrated by the fact that the security camera in the terminal room refused to activate.

"Some mean professionals we got here, man," muttered one. "Might be an Argie," agreed another.

The security guards were unemployed soldiers, virtually redundant after the Falklands War. They frequently reminisced about the Argie-bashing days and regarded everything that came their way as a picnic in comparison. This was a challenging placement as they had strict instructions to hold back from outright murder and just apprehend. After being trained to kill, it was a strain to survive without the pleasure "of doing the job properly".

"Just ain't no such thing as job satisfaction any more," was the usual lamentation.

They lined the stairs leading to the terminal room, ready to do their stuff. Stan was bound and gagged on the premise that he had let the hacker in. Visors were down and radios were whispered into. The silence outside the room was broken by the sound of an approaching motorcycle. The guards clicked their guns like a reflex. Tony had arrived for his night shift.

"Hey, what's going on?" he asked sleepily. He was drowned out by the screams and shouts of frustrated security guards forced to wait around. Their training came to force as they dived on him in a military ambush. Tony had just stuffed a free sausage and pepperoni pizza and proceeded to throw it up in the enclosed space under the torsos of hardened war-mongers. From behind the door, it all sounded very messy. Suki had got this far and she wasn't about to give in now. She took her chance at the diversion Tony had created and went for a bust.

Holding a computer disk as her only weapon, she screamed out a stream of obscenities and rushed out of the door to the alleyway. Bashing defenceless Argentineans had been a pleasant pastime. The guards were not geared for an unarmed and wildly threatening, red-eyed, disk-holding midget who was freaking out.

"I've got some of the biggest industrial secrets on this disk and if you so much as breathe, the computer's going to self-destruct and blow up the building!" screamed Suki. "Get my drift, assholes?"

They stared at the scrawny, anaemic-looking kid with Gandhi glasses mounting the motorbike. After a moment of stunned silence, the guards sought to give chase. One of them was hindered by the sickly stench of pepperoni vomit and proceeded to add to the mess. The others slipped and slided in an effort to recover position. "It's a bust," they yelled up to Sky's office on their radios.

"Get her," screamed Sky, reaching for a pouch of white powder. The levels of incompetence surrounding this whole episode were driving him crazy.

¥ ¥ ¥

Suki had never driven a motorbike before and it showed. The fact that she nearly crashed into a Bus-T van on her exit out of the alleyway didn't exactly inspire her confidence. Simeon and Amber were elated to see her but they only understood her reluctance to hang around for a casual chat about coming here often when they saw a procession of security vehicles giving chase at top speed into Docklands High Street. If they'd been in "Terminator 2", traffic wouldn't have been much of a problem. She might have been tempted to ride rough-shod over the streams of cars ahead or at least skirt at 60 mph in the middle lane, leaving behind a stream of drivers wishing they could trade in their cars for a bike. But her lack of movie-star qualities forced her instead to wobble from litter-bin to litter-bin since her feet didn't even touch the ground.

"I want the bitch alive!" screamed Sky into radio controls every so often. "I want that disk!"

"We ain't even in shooting distance," bemoaned one guard with regret.

Suki was conscious of being pursued by all and sundry. She half-expected to see her mother and father on their bikes any minute now. She criticised herself for not being able to get Shanti and Janak's banalities out of her mind even though she was firmly in the grip of a gravestone situation. They'd still be able to have a row, lament her lack of interest in things academic before catching the drift that a bunch of madmen in fast cars were trying to kill her. After slowly edging forward an inch at a time Suki realised that the traffic was not going to be her saving grace. Her horror intensified when she caught sight of an armed guard in her side mirror, on foot and edging slowly forward. She veered on to the pavement, revved up the engine and nearly mutilated a few pedestrians en route.

"Damn!" screamed the guard.

"Damn!" Sky reciprocated.

"Yahoo!" screamed Amber.

"Great!" screamed a policeman, lolling back to life in his Metro. He might get home for tea yet.

The siren blazed and drivers dug deep for a snot attack. Someone was jumping the queue and it wasn't them. This was a conspiracy against the ordinary motorist. Suki was flying past the shops and heading for the crowded roundabout. She had throttled past queuing cars, dodging on and off the pavement, cursing herself for now having set another party on the trail.

"On the Docklands. Motorbike. Driver looks under age. Probably a member of the Joy Division. No helmet, speeding at over 80 miles per hour and driving very dangerously," spat the policeman into his radio, unable to hide his glee. "I want a chopper seeing this."

The security cars were following Suki's trend. They'd made the unpopular decision to mount the pavement and were facing a twin sideline attack by angry pedestrians and drivers. "Get back on the road, you jerk!" screamed one elderly woman, pelting tomatoes from a nearby greengrocer's.

"Piss off, grandma!" yelled a guard, rolling down a window. "I'm a war hero." He got a humiliating cabbage thrown in his face.

"Yeah, and I was at Dunkirk!" balled a learner driver, in the middle of her test. She'd given up trying to pass and already had her fingers up her nostrils, ready to cloud the guard's vision with a sticky green mess. Someone else got there first and visibility was down to zero.

"Get that girl!" screamed Sky. "Or you're not getting paid."

Nothing was going to deter these rough and tough guys. Not being bathed in pizza vomit nor having their windscreens smeared with green slime. The prospect of living with the fact that some midget Argentinean armed with nothing but a floppy disk had beaten them on their own turf was the very last straw.

Meanwhile, the police Metro was closing on Suki, who sought to take the nearest exit and head for cover in the safety of traffic. Unfortunately, she'd squared into the exit that led back into Docklands High Street.

It was downhill all the way to a mini-roundabout. Her hands were burning on the steering grips. The tyres felt bald and her eyes were streaming with the smell of hot tarmac. Perhaps it was the sound of a helicopter buttressing above her, but Suki found herself going too fast and unable to turn left or right. She was on a collision course with the concrete verge of the roundabout. Behind her was the police car and in front of her was a string of security cars that had caught on to her. She was boxed in and flaking out. Suki came to a skiddy halt. Police officers homed in, and led her away with a book full of offences. And the approaching Bus-T van could do nothing about it. She was well and truly caught.

¥ ¥ ¥

"Get me a file on her," said Sky grimly. "And the number for the cops. I want to make a donation to police funds."

Theft of a motorbike. Riding without a licence. Breaking and entering. Trespassing on private company property. Use of technological equipment belonging to a private company without permission. The charges floated over Suki's head as dawn broke over the Docklands city skyline. Suki did not know whether it was day or night, Monday or Sunday, in the strangely empty world of the police interrogation room, which was bare except for a table and chairs, and a fluorescent light with an irritating fly in it. The only remotely human company Suki had was the less than tolerant WPc Crisp and Sergeant Marsden. And surprisingly enough, they wanted to start at the beginning of Suki's strange and twisted tale.

"Right at the beginning?" asked Suki.

"Yep," said the burly Sergeant Marsden, flicking open his notebook.

"Well, I can only remember as far back as 1977 when I..." she began.

"Less of the cheek, kid," snapped WPc Crisp with such force that the glasses nearly toppled off the end of her nose. Her life before the police as a matron in a girls' boarding school had not granted her with much of a sense of humour.

"Cheek? I'm surprised I've got any left. I feel like I haven't seen a burger since the beginning of time. I'm totally emaciated," sighed Suki. "And isn't it just my luck to be landed with a pair called Crisp and Mars. A right little packed lunch-box. Rubbing it in or what!"

"Listen you cretin," spluttered Sergeant Marsden. "This is a soundproof room. If you screamed your guts out no-one this side of the river would hear you."

"It's no use prattling around," said WPc Crisp. "Let's get back to Monica Ruddles. You said you hated her?"

"You should see a doctor about your hearing," advised Suki. "I said I hated being chased back into college. It was Monica's bad luck that she ended up having to do that horrible job. She hated it and we became mates. It was when she got bumped off by Bucks Times Bucks that all this started."

"So according to you, your friendship killed her?" asked Sergeant Marsden hopefully.

Suki groaned.

"Your school and college records show that you're a truant," affirmed WPc Crisp. "Now you've graduated to joy-riding, information theft and back-chatting to the police. Can I add wasting police time to your charges?"

"Monica left a message on my ansaphone," explained Suki.

"She said that she'd got sacked and was going back with Gunster to Newcastle. She hadn't passed her test and Gunster didn't like driving so there's no way she died on the motorway. She told me she was catching the train from Euston, right? Then I heard that she's crashed on the M5. Pretty weird, I thought to myself. Like maybe you would, if a mate of yours suddenly got the urge to tear up the motorway when she was scared of changing into first gear. But then again, you probably haven't got any mates!" Suki was now getting exasperated.

"You are heading for a bloody good hiding, girl!" spat WPc Crisp.

"There's a simple way of sorting this all out," said Sergeant Marsden, who was pretty exhausted himself. "Where's the ansaphone tape?"

"Bit of a problem there, I erased it," said Suki sheepishly.

The Sergeant laughed. "Nice one! Well, we can always check whether she's passed her driving test on her work records, can't we?"

"Yeah, and maybe I can get some sleep," murmured Suki.

"Only when you tell us what you're interest is in Bucks Times Bucks..." demanded WPc Crisp.

"Yeah, and what a huge chemical giant like that would gain out of killing off a pleb like Monica Ruddles?" continued Sergeant Marsden.

"And what the hell were you doing inside the RETROBASE building and exactly why you were approaching a roundabout at 60 mph on a stolen motorbike?" added WPc Crisp.

"When grown men are puking up around me and walking around with shot-guns, it tends to rattle me and I get this urge to leave. You've obviously not been listening to a single word. It's that old hearing problem again," snarled Suki. "Right, I'm not saying another word till I get three Kingsize Macs, hold on the mayo, loads of ketchup and throw in some fries! You got that all down?"

Sergeant Marsden clenched his fists. WPc Crisp gritted her teeth. "Get her the stuff, Ray," she said.

"Crisp is a bit of a sad name, isn't it?" commented

Suki, in an effort to break the silence. "Were you a packet of Walkers in your last life or do you find it tough on the beach without sunblock ten?"

WPc could stand it no longer and left the room. The desk sergeant looked surprised, having just seen Sergeant Marsden come out with a similar expression. "I swear, Sarge, if she doesn't have a criminal record, I'd bet my truncheon that she's been through this all before."

¥ ¥ ¥

Although the meat did not compare to Mr Cavallares' standards, Suki devoured every last morsel and snoozed off. Sergeant Marsden and WPc Crisp took the chance to bend their Chief's ear.

"We're at the end of our tether," explained WPc Crisp. "The little shrimp's coming out with some garbled story about a chemical multinational killing off Monica Ruddles and Gunster Robbins, both employees of RETROBASE."

"They were in a motorway crash so it seems like a pretty tall story from the midget," continued Sergeant Marsden. "We've done what we can with her, sir."

"First offender?" asked the Chief, practising the famous arching of his hands in tandem with the chair swivel.

"Yeah, though you'd never guess it," muttered Sergeant Marsden.

"Needs a bloody good whipping, in my opinion," agreed WPc Crisp.

"Your opinions on corporal punishment won't be necessary, Crisp," said the Chief. "The parents?"

"They know she's under questioning, sir," informed Sergeant Marsden.

"She hasn't exactly been pleading for mummy," grimaced WPc Crisp. "They're probably glad to get rid of her."

"Well, in that case it seems like the girl's going to be facing some pretty hefty charges besides the joy-riding and trespassing," commented the Chief. "I've just had a call from a Mr Sky Moores, the Director at RETROBASE. The girl's a known truant who's been mucking around with their computers. They want to know if she's wrecked their systems. I think letting the men from RETROBASE interview her would be a good idea, don't you? It looks good on our CV to be helping government agencies."

Sky Moores promise of a substantial contribution to the police coffers made this inter-agency co-operation seem all the more beneficial.

"She's as mad as a coot." WPc Crisp and Sergeant Marsden were pleased to get the little terror off their hands for a while. "I'll tell her she's going," volunteered Sergeant Marsden.

"Good luck. I'm off to bed," said WPc Crisp.

Sergeant Marsden picked up the fax from RETROBASE HQ regarding Monica's driving status and examined it with glee. The Ruddles woman could drive! The little immigrant didn't have a hope in hell.

"You haven't got a leg to stand on, if you'll pardon the reference to your disability. Monica Ruddles could drive," grinned Sergeant Marsden. "And Mr Moores has got a few questions to ask you about their computers...you're sinking pretty fast, aren't you?"

"You what?" yelled Suki as the sergeant disappeared out of the door. "Come back! He's the murderer! Don't send me to him, you jerks."

Sitting in the empty locked room, she suddenly felt very sick.

¥ ¥ ¥

The following morning, Suki felt like a convicted prisoner with no hope of jail-break. She was shoved in the back of a police security van and carted off in handcuffs to RETROBASE Head Office to meet the notorious Sky Moores.

"Nervous?" laughed Sergeant Marsden.

"Get knotted," sulked Suki.

Her legs had started shaking. The enormity of the situation had hit her. She had broken in. She had stolen information. She was on the trail of a multinational with millions of pounds and government support at its disposal. She didn't even have the freedom to nip out for a burger. This was trouble on a scale she had never imagined for herself. The sight of daylight burned her eyes as she entered an airy interrogation room, equipped with only a table and chair and an ominous looking reel-to-reel tape, much like the one her father kept in the greenhouse.

Sky Moores looked like the Godfather from the back, parked in a swivelling chair, facing the window. He just couldn't believe the reflection in the window. Was this goggled brat the cause of all the trouble? She was the business cartel, the vindictive competitor, the insider on his trail, the threat to Operation Acid Trip. He was going to mutilate her.

"Ms Samra. Date of birth 15 February 1976. Address: 39 Lime Road, Crouch End, North London. We have a very interesting file on you. You are just the kinda scum the government wants to be rid of. I call it 'scum', the government calls you a truant."

Suki sat in silence. So this was the powerful man behind it all, she thought. He was the one calling the shots. He was the one constantly mentioned in minutes, with his name on the bottom of reports, littering fear like confetti. She noticed the awe he inspired in everyone around him. She put down her own quivering to the air-conditioning.

"The cops ripped your tongue out? Damn, I told them to let me do that!" he smiled menacingly. "Who are you working for?"

Sky was losing patience. He had given up valuable

hours away from Operation Acid Trip to get some answers. And none were forthcoming. "Listen, quit the Gandhi routine. If you don't talk you're not going to see mama and papa again."

"I want a lawyer," blurted Suki.

"You're going to need one too," smirked Sky. "I'm going to nail your butt so hard on the stand, you're going to find it difficult - or should I say more difficult - to walk! No lawyers, no life and no mama and papa till you spill why you've been poking your nose around my computer system!"

The pleasurable thought of life without Janak and Shanti after days of a never-ending nightmare seemed like the promise of Nirvana. Something snapped inside Suki. "You're a murderer, you stupid Yank! You stick me on the stand and I'm going to tell them! Just you try it!"

Sky's eyes glinted. Suki's attempt to brave it out left him in no doubt that she knew something all right. And no way was a goggle-eyed mutant from North London going to screw up the work of a lifetime. He was going to appoint the best lawyers and blow this irritant away.

¥ ¥ ¥

The first BTB ship had arrived in Columbia and was in the process of being unloaded. Customs officials were not too happy with the contents of the barrels. It was clearly illegal but the discreet opening of briefcases containing thousands of US dollars removed any consternation. Thousands of miles away, the Director of Security for the shipping operation was a man in great demand. The phonecalls to RETROBASE Head Office had not stopped, since rumours had it that Sky Moores had apprehended a computer-hacker. Companies dogged with the problem of computer sabotage in the worldwide club of the rich were

184

phoning to congratulate and hunting for tips. It was a problem that cost the business world billions of dollars and pounds every year, but the desire to preserve their reputations had prevented them from admitting it. Now RETROBASE's success led to a watershed!

Rupert Mumford had got wind of the capture and was impatiently anticipating a phone call from Sky. Abraham looked a nervous wreck. He could hear the sound of bells ringing in his head and found himself picking up phones to find nobody on the other end. Having been reduced to an overworked telephonist, Abraham now found that his boss wanted him to set up a press conference.

RETROBASE intended to portray Suki as a prime example of Enemy Number One to the education system and the social fabric of the country. Catching computer hackers was a difficult business, very few companies admitted that they had suffered the scourge. RETROBASE could lead the way. It was also a perfect distraction from ships docking illegally in bays around the world. Moores was patted on the back at dinner parties for his business acumen and chuckled to himself at his skill in abusing the situation to the best commercial advantage. This made him feel like a pretty cool person and a smooth operator since it was better than the option of being caught for abetting the murder of two of his employees (the unions would have a field day), let alone having the notoriety of orchestrating a scheme to buy the future of the planet. Getting caught red-handed on that one would have made life pretty difficult. Now, no-one would ever know because the spoke in the wheel was fixed. Apparently...

10

OUTSIDE OPERATORS

Simeon was getting a bout of machismo fever. He had arrived to meet Amber and Ivan at The Cave in black leather trousers and a jacket with tassels. He looked more like the average nob in a 1970's Littlewoods catalogue than a man with a death wish.

"Cool," muttered Ivan sarcastically.

"I bought the gear with my pay cheque," emphasised Simeon. "Do you know what one of those things looks like, jerk-off?"

"You look like the sexiest king in town, Simeon. If only Suki was here to see it. And Ivan, nine-to-five just wouldn't suit your lifestyle," said Amber with brisk diplomacy. "Now..." she paused, "What the hell are we going to do?"

"I know what I'm going to do, man. I'm going to kill that Yank! Nail his ass to a Minnesota tree and whip it till it's red!" glowered Simeon.

"Hey Amber, come here," called Mr Cavallares from the back.

"Dad, I'm busy," groaned Amber. "You know, busy trying to save a friend from being put through a meat grinder." She imitated her father. "'Do this, cut them, find this, you've burnt this, buy me this, what do you mean you want money? You don't do no work!' This is exploitation, man."

"It's about Suki. Something on the TV," called Mr Cavallares.

The three bundled hurriedly into the back room. They found Richard and Judy interviewing someone about computer addiction, following the well-publicised case of a computer-hacker. The portrait of the hacker was much like a drug-addict or a criminal. The so-called expert sounded like he wished he could have pulled off a few digital bank robberies but armed solely with the knowledge of Word Perfect, he could only make a living by spreading treacherous fears. Bit like Andrew Morton wishing he could be someone on the civil list, but since the chances of that were non-existent, he had resorted to publishing books about the Royals.

"Prat!" remarked Ivan.

"Ssshhh..." whispered Simeon. "Quit the commentary."

They waited anxiously for the news bulletin. "They can't do nothing in the courts. Computer evidence doesn't count," sneered Ivan. "They're just trying to scare us."

"Well, it's working," said Mr Cavallares. "Look at you all, wasting your time in here."

"Dad..." warned Amber.

"'Dad...'" mimicked Mr Cavallares. "Look, this is a recession and I miss Suki. She eats like a horse and I want her back in here. Go out and do something to get her back."

"Dad, gee, that's a really clever idea," said Amber slapping her head forcibly. "Why didn't we think of that ourselves?"

"You! I give you advice, you don't want to listen. I say start a campaign..."

Amber looked at Ivan. Ivan looked at Simeon. A campaign to free Suki. It was a brilliant idea.

"I give you all the ways and you laugh," continued Mr Cavallares. "Huh! Out of my way, I've got people to feed!"

"Dad, you're a genius!" said Amber, grabbing his cheeks.

The news gave a thirty-second report of a computer hacker, a renowned truant, being held by police in connection with the break-in at RETROBASE and the high-speed chase in Docklands. Rupert Mumford's head materialised to add to the rhetoric.

"The Government's plan for Education is obviously weeding out these menacing elements," he said cheerily.

"Get knotted!" sneered Ivan.

"We're coming after you, man!" grinned Simeon, charged with a sense of purpose. "We're bringing the government down, you gook!"

"So guys, let's get to work!" said Amber charging off. "Today is the beginning of the campaign. Suki is innocent!"

"Suki is innocent!" they cheered in unison, fists humped together in unity. Simeon was repulsed by having to make physical contact with Ivan but the good of the cause propelled him.

Permy, the Prime Minister's right hand, brain and soul had also seen the news. "What the hell's going on, you nincompoop?" he growled.

"It's all sorted," said Rupert effortlessly. "The perpetrator's been caught and the matter is going through legal proceedings."

"Really?" said Permy, sitting on an adult swing in the middle of the PM's office. "And how legal are you in all of this?"

"Well," spluttered Rupert. "What can you mean, Permanent Secretary? I certainly had nothing..."

"Who gives a toss about your wheeler-dealing with the Paperchase contract?" snapped Permy. "You, dear Rupert are dispensable. What have you done to make sure that nothing is revealed about the Bucks investment? Because it is the Government's neck that is at stake in these legal proceedings, Minister."

"Why should that emerge, sir?" asked Rupert meekly.

"It shouldn't," agreed Permy, patronisingly. "But it might, if you don't make sure, don't you think, Rupert? Apologies for making assumptions there, Minister. Of course you have little capacity for thought. How presumptuous of me!"

"What do you suggest, Permy?" pleaded Rupert. "I couldn't bear to be hauled up in any public scandal. I really haven't done anything wrong..."

"All right all right, stop that sniffling. It's a most irritating habit, if I may say so," said Permy curtly. "I would suggest that the Home Secretary bring charges forward as soon as possible and make this a test case. Don't you agree, Minister?"

"Most certainly, Permanent Secretary," said Rupert through his tears. "And perhaps, we could have a nice, sympathetic judge too."

"Agreed. Right, now piss off," said Permy in a parting gesture.

¥ ¥ ¥

"So what are we going to do?" asked Amber, after the declaration of togetherness and undying love was over.

"I thought we were mounting a campaign?" said Ivan confused.

"Yeah," said Simeon, surprised to find himself in agreement with the Lower Life Form.

"Well what the hell does that mean?" snapped Amber impatiently. "Where's the nitty gritty, the abc, the 123? Can you see the Muswell Hillbillies coming out for a march? What's that going to do anyway?"

"We've got to let everyone know..." said Ivan slowly. "That Suki is innocent, right?"

"Well yeah, like eureka," said Simeon. "Einstein was a brainless dork-shattering amoeba compared to you, right jerk-off?"

"Amber...I can't work with this fool," Ivan said. "I came in on the condition we were doing a hack-job and this cool sucker with an elephant hide crawling on his back is getting on my..."

"Knock it off, guys," said Amber sweetly. "Or somebody's going to get injured. Suki had the right

189

idea, know what I mean?" She stared indiscreetly at Simon's leather trouser pockets.

The threat of endangered manhoods brought about an immediate silence.

"Hey you still here! I'm busy, you know," called Mr Cavallares. "One minute it's 'I love you, Papa' and the next..." he said to a customer, giving him a serviette embellished with The Cave logo.

"Hey Papa, I've got an idea!" yelled Amber. "Give me those tissues!"

The local printers ran off 2000 serviettes for The Cave marked with a slogan: "SUKI IS INNOCENT. WANTED: THE GOVERNMENT." One went with every customer, who got a special "Free Suki" burger for signing the INNOCENT campaign. A petition had begun to rescue the local girl from the jaws of government bureaucracy. Mr Cavallares was pleased, his business takings were going up and at least Amber and Ivan had stuck around to help shift the grub.

He was less pleased when an elderly resident from Highgate came in at lunchtime to complain at the proprietor's support for youth who were guilty of crime. "I'm Mrs Doolally, the local Neighbourhood Watch Chairman," she said, pulling forward her glasses to inspect Mr Cavallares.

"Well lady, congratulations," said Mr Cavallares briskly, in the face of widespread interest from his clientele. "Chairmen these days wear rollers, huh?"

There was a hoot of muffled laughter.

"I'll ignore that superfluous comment, sir," she said haughtily, thrusting forward a campaign serviette. "I am merely drawing to your attention the fact that you are perverting the course of justice!"

"What do you know, Mrs Chairman?" laughed Mr Cavallares. "The girl is a valued customer and I want her back. And she's innocent."

"Your defence is baffling," said the pensioner, aghast. "I saw the high-speed chase on the television with my own eyes. She's guilty as the day is long."

"Well, Mrs Chairman, I would like to draw something to your attention!" snapped Mr Cavallares. This woman was now overstepping the boundaries of civilised conduct. She was also holding up the queue and a couple of customers were leaving.

"People do small bad things for good big things. Don't you remember the war, girl? Thirty thousand Greeks killed German soldiers to fight Hitler. Now, this is my shop and I will support any campaign I want. Are you going to buy something or is this conversation history?"

"Silly cow," he muttered when she had gone.

That night, Amber pulled down her charred hands on the shutters of The Cave. "This is only the beginning," she said. She and Simeon were heading for Ivan's King's Cross flat, where amidst the general squattish atmosphere, sat a large, probably stolen computer. Ivan skirted into the local school and college computers to insert a small program that was designed to have an impact.

The following morning all the computers in the Maths block were found to be switched on and reading the message: "SUKI IS INNOCENT! MISCARRIAGE OF JUSTICE IN PROGRESS! SUPPORT THE COMPUTER GENIUS'S CAMPAIGN NOW!"

The Headteacher and the College Principal were informed, who in turn, reported the incident to the police. The Hornsey Journal reported yet another break-in by a "notorious gang of computer thugs". It was hardly the publicity that Suki needed.

The Campaign Crew were depressed. They'd had two knockbacks out of two. Admittedly, no-one else except the Highgate Neighbourhood Watch Association had complained about the serviettes. Then again, those who had signed up for the campaign were just doing it to get a free burger.

Community spirit seemed to have died in some previous age.

Simeon, in particular, was feeling the loss. Suki was probably getting tortured by some vicious police guys who had been trained in Los Angeles and here he was, sitting on the outside unable to generate a wind-bag of support to get her out. The reality of her driving the coppers round a very sharp bend and stuffing her face with her fifth successive burger was unimaginable. The bruises in his lower region had now disappeared and he had forgotten that their last words were acrimonious. His vision of strolling out of court with her on his arm to a groovy candlelit dinner by his favourite telegraph pole seemed to be fast turning into visits to Wormwood Scrubs with smuggled copies of computer programs.

And having to work with Ivan just added to his insecurity. Perhaps all his feelings for Suki were in vain if she could go for a schmuck like him. If her idea of excitement was dating a crook with no dress-sense (ie no leather trousers), no prospects and no detectable brainlife, then maybe he was barking up the wrong pole. But the feeling of sheer longing for the sight of that irritating little midget showed no signs of quelling.

"We're getting nowhere," he muttered.

"We've been concentrating on the local scene too much," said Amber. "People round here don't care. Wait until something happens to one of them." She naturally slipped into a conversation with the absent pensioner. "'Oh Mrs Doolally, so you've had your pension cut, you've got a motorway being built through your front room, you've been robbed by some hooligans. So sad, so sad. Well, I must rush, I've got onions to cut and tomatoes to slice. Do let me know your new address when they shove you in a b & b.' Stupid woman, didn't even want to listen."

Ivan was the only one who seemed unaffected by

depression. After all, his work was just about to begin...And it was a challenge. "We've got to know what this Bucks lot are up to. It's what Suki's found out that's got her into this trouble. We need to dig it out too..."

"So that we can find ourselves in knee-deep shit..." grumbled Simeon.

"Hey man! You want to save your girl or what?" Ivan said, allaying Simeon's fears of competition.

"She ain't nobody's girl, Suki's her own person, right!" snapped Amber. "This 'goo-goo ga-ga dribbling around for love' scene is getting on my goddamn tits!"

"That's cos you ain't got nobody!" blurted Simeon.

"Yeah, too right," said Amber. "And I ain't missing a thing! So let's get on with it, shall we?"

"You mean you're not seeing anyone right now?" asked Ivan, surprised.

"No!" yelled Amber. Were these guys revelling in her misery or what?

"Hmm...so, yeah as I was saying..." continued Ivan. "Suki must have stored stuff on her system, right? Any good hacker keeps stuff for future reference. So we've got to find it."

"Yeah, I've been meaning to go to Suki's place for a while anyway," said Amber. "There's this reel-to-reel tape she wanted to give to her dad."

"Yeah, and I'll need that manual eventually. It seems to me that Suki's got a lot of stuff that we could be doing with," said Ivan after some pondering.

"It's only for borrowing," remarked Simeon protectively. He looked at Amber. "Her dad don't like you, does he?"

"Yeah well, I'm trying to rescue his daughter from jail," smiled Amber. "That should swing round the pendulum. I'll tell him I'm a vegetarian or something. The worst weapon he could come up with would be a pair of lawn clippers. So no worries."

¥ ¥ ¥

Shanti was pleased to find The Crew on her doorstep the following morning. She desperately needed to vent her feeling of horror on someone besides Janak. Yoga did not even begin to help her cope with the fact that her own daughter wasn't only a truant, but a joy-rider and now, according to the latest police briefings, an information thief. Janak was totally unable to adopt anything but a negative outlook on the whole situation. Their last clash had been about finding a lawyer.

"Is there any point?" he had said. "She's as guilty as hell."

In the face of this submission to forces at play, Shanti was impressed by Amber's keenness to help Suki.

"We think that there's something very fishy going on," confided Amber, in a responsible tone. "Did Suki ever mention Bucks Times Bucks to you?"

"Well, I remember her asking me something about them, yes. They got into a lot of insurance trouble in the 1970s..."

As Simeon took notes during this history lesson, Amber and Ivan ventured upstairs to Suki's room. She had left a complete tip, with burger wrappers openly littering the floor and computer print-outs hanging from the lampshade.

Ivan switched on the computer and flicked through the manual.

"I'll go and check out the reel-to-reel tape in the garden," said Amber.

"Mrs Samra," called Amber. "Is it OK if I go into the greenhouse to see Mr Samra?"

"Yes, but be careful of the plants," replied Shanti, before turning back to Simeon.

Amber carefully followed the narrow footpath to the greenhouse which housed so many plants that the windows were steamed up. It was impossible to see anything or anyone. She opened the door. The sound of sea waves emanated from the reel-to-reel machine in the corner. She negotiated the jungle-like overgrowth and eventually reached the machine, turning it off. The silence was eerie. The plants seemed almost to turn towards her asking, "What the fuck did you do that for?"

"Sorry guys, better check this out before giving it to the boss," apologised Amber, aware that Suki would never have ventured this far into her father's sacred temple. "It could be full of steamy sex scenes or something."

Her fingers shook as she fiddled with the tape reel in her pocket and she had considerable difficulty mounting it on the wheels. "Come on, come on," she whispered impatiently. The tape finally clicked into place and rewound to the beginning. A twig snapped outside and Amber nearly dived behind a yucca.

She pressed the play button. It sounded distinctly like that prattish MP, Rupert Mumford, talking about RETROBASE! "Well, I have read all the papers if that's what you mean."

"Cough cough cough." A door closed.

"If I've read it all correctly, Mr Moores..."

"Oh please, Minister, call me Sky." It was Sky Moores on tape!

Janak walked into the greenhouse, horrified to see another human being.

"What the hell are you doing here?" he boomed, risking angina for his beloved plants.

"Ssshhh...I'm coming to a good bit," snapped Amber.

"Uh, very well," Rupert's voice continued. "As I understand it, the plan is that you...or rather Bucks Times Bucks...will invest ten billion pounds in an agency that runs the British education system."

"The agency is called Returning to Basic Education,"

said Sky. "RETROBASE."

"Yes, yes, yes..." rejoiced Amber.

"Just you hang on a minute!" yelled Janak. "You are trespassing on private property, you probably had meat for breakfast, lunch and dinner and you are endangering my plants!"

"Oh no, Mr Samra! Suki found this for you and I was just checking to make sure it was OK," explained Amber.

The voice of reason seemed to have no notable impact on Janak. His eyes bulged wildly.

"I'm also trying to save your daughter from prison," reasoned Amber. "This is vital evidence and I was trying to find you..."

"That stupid woman would let thieves in the house if they asked her!" spluttered Janak. "Get out! Get out!"

"I'm just going, Mr Samra. I really wasn't doing anything wrong!"

"It's all because of you and your lousy family! My daughter's been arrested because of the likes of you! She deserves every kind of punishment she gets!" he snapped. "Get out!"

"I'm going, all right! I just want the tape back!" she said, pulling the spools out.

"And don't come back," he said, chasing her across the garden and into the kitchen.

Ivan had opened the window to check out the commotion in the garden. Seeing an unknown face in his daughter's bedroom did not ease Janak's temper. He collided with Ivan and Simeon in the hallway, as they were hurriedly trying to make a discreet exit. He had an additional freak-out.

"Who the hell are you? And what were you doing in my daughter's bedroom? Do you know this boy?" He motioned to Shanti.

"Chill out, man, I'm trying to find some clues," said Ivan.

"You jerk!" hissed Simeon. "Respect!"

Janak would have been inclined to agree. This was a mass invasion of his home and Shanti had let them all in! His life was going to pieces. His plants might never recover. Shanti refused to take the blame for something that was not even a misdemeanour. Inevitably, a row ensued.

The three of them piled breathlessly into the street.

"Jesus, man, that guy needs help!" said Simeon, panting.

"A lobotomy for starters," agreed Ivan.

"We've got it!" Amber cried. "We've got Sky Moores and the Minister of Education on tape." They headed for The Cave for a conference and a burger celebration.

"We need to get into Suki's computer," said Ivan.

"But we've got the tape," said Amber. "What more evidence do we need?"

"We need something more solid," insisted Simeon. "The tape only tells us something that we've known for ages. What's it going to do for Suki?"

"It'll show that Suki got into the whole thing because Monica was checking out why Bucks was investing billions in the Education system," said Amber impatiently.

"Yeah, but why? Why would Bucks want to kill off a nobody like Monica?" persisted Simeon.

"And a somebody like Gunster," added Amber. "He was the Regional Accountant."

"Exactly!" triumphed Simeon. "It had to be because they were asking questions they weren't supposed to. And Suki must have found out some of the answers and they nailed her!"

"Back to square one," interjected Ivan. "We need to get into Suki's computer. There's no two ways about it. We need the password that Monica gave to Suki."

"It'll have to be a hack," said Simeon miserably. "There's no way Mr Samra's going to let us near that house."

Returning to the house of squatters, Ivan was puzzling over the list of files in Suki's computer directories.

"Hang on a minute, what's in that file?" asked Amber, pointing to the listing on the screen. A lot of memory space was allocated to a file called CMB2000, so Ivan agreed to pursue it. "Some kind of program that she was working on. It'll take me days to work it out. Let's stick to what she's been working on recently."

Records showed that she had off-loaded a huge amount of information in the days before her capture. Teasing open different files, the screen finally panned out in the shape of a world map, with flashing signals and moving dots.

"Bingo!" Ivan cried. "God, I'm brilliant..."

"And modest," said Amber, smiling. "Yeah, that's the map we saw on her screen once. What the hell does it mean, is the question. Is there any clue in any of the other files?"

"Give me a chance," muttered Ivan, concentrating on his selection. "There's one called 'keys'..."

They retraced almost the same steps as Suki had in deducing the constant reference to land masses, target areas, delivery dates and shipments.

"What are they transporting, I wonder," said Ivan. "Let's get into the live sequences and see what happens when you change the co-ordinates."

¥ ¥ ¥

For Sky, the hacker incident was a thing of the past. It would now be a matter for the courts to decide. Rupert was pleased that the offender had finally been caught and the sooner the little brat got convicted the safer the climate would be for them all.

Sky was more anxious about the latest mini-crisis brewing in the South Pacific. A ship, called the

Zanoobia, was departing from its Venezuelan port of destination with its barrels still on board. Something in the pyramid of bribery had obviously gone wrong. The officials in Venezuela were known to accept any cargo as long as the price was right. And of course, BTB had the money to buy the land and pay off or, if necessary, dispose of anyone who was proving difficult...

Operation Acid Trip was Sky Moores' brainchild. In the early 1980s, Bucks was experiencing a number of problems. The people who worked in the Bucks laboratories were mysteriously dying off. There had been the eminent scientist, Professor Snade, who was dead within six months of his arrival at the company and people on the ground were snuffing it in big numbers. The public story blamed the stress of the job, but like many other issues in the accident-prone life of Bucks, those at the top knew the real reason. At the same time, Bucks was making too much money to throw it all away because of a few operational difficulties, like lack of staff. There were lots of people in the world to replace them, weren't there? The company had to establish a way to find the best brains and keep them on file, headhunt and prune them over a number of years, if necessary. Hence the finding of a solution: Operation Acid Trip. There were people in the upper ranks of Bucks Times Bucks who said the plan could not work - it was too risky.

So Sky, in defence of his project insisted that any plan needed the right leadership and the right investment. In a private seminar for the Board of Directors, he argued his case. "We need to invest in people. They're the ones that make our bread and butter. How many of you have worked in a laboratory in the last ten years? Not one! Not a single one. We're dealing with a dangerous commodity and we're only going to carry on if we've got the manpower. We don't need bozos, Lord knows, we've got enough of them."

He paused. No laughter. They had obviously taken it personally, as he had intended. "We need the cream of the crop. We need to penetrate the education system and prune them right from birth so...that they're ours."

His hands grasped the air. He knew by the frightened look in the eyes of the grey men around him that he had won their hearts. Operation Acid Trip got the go-ahead. Sky was given the money and the power to see it through. And now, as Director of Operations he was supposed to ensure the safe delivery of the cargo from factories, companies and military bases all around America and Europe to destinations around the world. Barrels numbered in their hundreds of thousands and had to be co-ordinated with pristine efficiency. Right now, Sky didn't look like a piss-up in a brewery was in his command. Shipping crises were happening to him as a matter of course. Well, at least one thing was sure, it couldn't be The Hacker, could it?

¥ ¥ ¥

"I can't seem to get any further," said Ivan, after the buzz of watching a ship change its movements had subsided. "We need the password."

Simeon returned from work and interrupted the search with some good news. "I went back to RETROBASE today! Got rid of the trace."

"Whoopee!" said Amber sarcastically. "Did you find the midget and drag her back here? Save us a lot of hassle."

"Nope, but I did look through their trash bin," said Simeon excitedly. "And I found this!" He held up a yellow note from a post-it pad, with two telephone numbers written on it.

"Wow, that's just smashing, great, amazing," said Amber flatly. "Even pregnant elephants are faster than you. Get to the point, Sims."

"The number at the top is Rupert Mumford's. The number underneath is a bloke called Oje Zamira. He's a contract killer. How much do you wanna bet that this Zamira guy bumped off our amigos?"

"How do you know that?" asked Ivan, sceptically.

"I called him," said Simeon coolly. "He's Greek, he's been a mercenary and offers a full range of services..."

"Yeah, I thought I'd heard of him," murmured Amber.

"You did what?" Ivan was incredulous at the depths this macho freak was willing to go. At one time, he himself might have confessed to fancying Suki but calling up contract killers was a bit much.

"So what did he say?" asked Amber, relatively unimpressed. She had spoken to Mick Jagger personally and nothing was going to top that.

"I said I was the minder for a rich Greek woman whose husband owned a casino chain and she wanted him bumped off. I said she was rich but she could only afford ten thousand quid. He was more than happy! He said his last employer was really stingy! Then he said, 'Bloody Americans!' and then apologised. I told him I wouldn't take it personally."

Amber laughed. "Cool! That sounds like Sky Moores to me!"

Simeon continued breathlessly. "I said he sounded OK but the woman wants to know this is going to be a sure thing so she wants to know if you're good."

"He tried to tell me he'd killed JFK but I told him he was talking bull and I said what about recent work. Did he do car crashes? Then he got really cagey and said he wasn't interested in them any more! It's a cert. He did Monica and Gunster over!" finished Simeon. "I wish I'd taped it. But we've got the number anyway."

"Jesus!" exclaimed Ivan.

Amber smiled. "Well done, mate. I wish we'd had as much good news for you. This hunt-the-password gig is doing my head in."

It was nearly time for the news. "We've got to do this with some logic, man."

"Do I detect a massive ego under the hide?" remarked Ivan.

This jerk might be good with telephones and contract killers but computers were most definitely his scene.

"Well, yeah, telephones are very logical devices and I'm a logical dude, you know," agreed Simeon modestly. "If we print out every file, it'll be somewhere. We can eliminate the junk and try out the likely candidates for Password of The Year. The trace I've set up doesn't take for the first 180 minutes, so as long as we don't go over that time, we should be OK."

The nine o'clock news bulletin spurred them into action. A reporter, yep the usual dick with the bad taste in ties, stood in front of a court house. He prattled on about how the Government's concern for rising levels of youth crime had prompted a hurried court appearance for The Hacker, a seventeen-year-old charged with numerous offences including joy-riding, trespass and information theft. The next court appearance was scheduled for March 1st, when the perpetrator would be sentenced. It was to be a trial like no other with computerised monitors for the jury to consider the evidence. Experts would demonstrate how The Hacker had got access to RETROBASE's database.

"Hmmm...sounds interesting," said Ivan. "Let's have another look at Suki's file list."

"March 1st is only a week away," said Simeon. "We better get a move on."

After four hours, Amber stopped. "This is exhausting. She's got about ten thousand files in there and counting. It could be anything and nothing."

Ivan was hungry for some on-line action. "Why don't we go for the main chance, guys?"

"Those morons have still got computer security in

the office," cautioned Simeon. "They're watching the system for as long as possible."

"Twenty-four hours round the clock?" asked Ivan.

"No, they finish at about midnight," admitted Simeon.

"Well, we can wait, guys!" he said, thrilled at the prospect.

¥ ¥ ¥

"I'll start and you say the first thing that comes into your mind," explained Ivan. "Monica."

"Fat," said Amber.

"Newcastle," said Simeon.

"Brown ale," replied Amber.

"Come on, Amber, switch to green, will you?" begged Ivan. "You've got to get inside Suki's mind and think like she does."

"Listen Ivan, I can do a lot but a psychic, I am not," said Amber. "Anyway, it's Monica's head we've got to get inside. She's the one who knew the password, not Suki. I met her once. She had a thing about red clothes, she's fat, she's from Newcastle, she wanted to go out with Gunster... Yeah, it's probably not even her we should be bothered about. It's Gunster. It was his password! And the only thing I know about him is that he's dead. Right?"

"Slow down, red clothes, Newcastle, what else?" asked Ivan.

"Try her date of birth," said Simeon. "Suki had that somewhere in a file. But I'm sure that whatever file Suki put the password in would have meant something to her. Something about RETROBASE, maybe. Maybe something about us."

"Something like what?" Ivan was interested.

"Leave the room," insisted Simeon. "It's private."

"Hey, man, nothing's private in the Crew," said Amber, curiously.

"It's worth a try, isn't it?" pleaded Simeon.

"OK, OK, just type it in and press the <Enter> key, OK?" conceded Ivan.

"I know how to use a keyboard, right?" glowered Simeon.

He heard the door close behind him. Part of him did not want to go through this exercise. He preferred not to tell the others because it was indeed a private and personal matter between Suki and him. "Please Lord, let it be," he whispered as his fingers covered the keyboard.

Amber would have cackled, he knew, but he had to find out. <Simeon> flashed up on the screen. Seconds later, so did <Incorrect Password Try Again>. Simeon felt his chest tightening. He had to know, he had to check. It might break his heart but at least he would know. He typed in another word. <Ivan>. His finger lingered on the <Enter> key. It was now or never. <Incorrect Password Try Again> returned to haunt them but at least he knew. He breathed a sigh of relief. He had been itching to find that out for hours and his mind was put to rest in minutes. He wished she was there to squeeze tightly.

One filename was keeping him from her. In the universe of words there was one that might stop her going to jail, that might make him the hero and he must have heard it a thousand times in conversations. She would have picked something so obvious, like 'door' or 'burger'...

Hey what about the second love in her life, after him? A Slammer!

"Haven't you finished yet?" called Amber.

"Give me a minute," muttered Simeon.

The slammer idea hit the same brick wall.

"Come on in," called Simeon.

That attempt had failed but the trial date had given them incentive. The countdown had begun. The Campaign Crew began a rota system with Suki's filelist. Years of working on a computer had generated a vast array of information. Most of it was useless. The Crew would often reach points of irritation because each of them realised they needed just one word.

"It could be anything," sighed Amber in one of these moments. "It could be cabbage, has she got a file called cabbage? She might have wanted a burger and couldn't get one, so she looked down at her plate and saw..."

"You need some rest," said Simeon. "We all do."

Even though they would have declared the strongest words of allegiance to Suki, at that historical moment in their friendship, she was a complete pain in the butt. Four days and nights passed glued with curiosity to a computer screen that seemed dedicated to rejecting their efforts.

"Tonight's going to be the night," Amber declared.

"Don't say that, man!" tutted Simeon. "We're doomed!"

It had become a matter of superstition. The ritual would begin by Ivan looking on the list for a filename. Amber would type it in and Simeon would sit around moaning, or as he called it after the event, "giving you all motivation".

"If only she'd listened to me," moped Simeon, recalling their last conversation. "I warned her, I told her to let us in on it. But oh no, Little Miss Muffet, wanted no amateurs...no fingerprints and no amateurs. D'ya remember that? Right before she kicked me in the goolies! She's left fingerprints all the way to the dock, man." Simeon shook his head.

"Hey! Hey, that's a file on the list, I've seen it!" yelled Simeon excitedly. "Try it man, try it."

"Chill out, guy, we've been through this scene before," muttered Ivan.

"Hurry up man!" yelled Simeon. "No fingerprints! NO FINGERPRINTS!"

"Yeah, I saw the filename. So what?" said Amber,

sleepily.

"She told me, she told me she'd leave no fingerprints," said Simeon mechanically.

An uncharacteristically long moment passed before the computer registered the filename. <SMART BASTARDS!> flashed up on the screen.

"YES!" screamed Simeon.

The nut had been cracked. Gunster's password for some reason was "Psychokiller" just like Monica's.

Its emergence on the screen quietened the hysterical celebrations with relative speed. "Bloody ironic, if you ask me," said Amber. It left a chill on the spine just to think about the implications. "Now let's get on and use it, guys."

11

TRIAL ON A TIGHTROPE

The Campaign Crew stared with bated breath at the computer screen. Gunster, as the Regional Accountant, would have had something approaching super-privileged access. Had he been a hacker he might have used it to its maximum capability and avoided an early cremation. The fruits of finally knowing Bucks' real intentions hung like grapes in a desert. But, to their dismay, the Crew found that anticipation was a cruel thing. The password was invalid.
:<Psychokiller>:>Invalid password

"What!" screamed Simeon.

"I just don't believe it," groaned Amber.

"Maybe it's a reception problem with the computer," said Ivan, crestfallen. "We're hopping from my system to Suki's to RETROBASE's and then onto Bucks."

"So we're stretching it too far?" said Simeon hopefully.

"What do you expect?" snapped Amber. "They're not going to open the gangway and chauffeur us in. The password's been changed and we've been wasting our time."

"OK, we're doomed. Suki's doomed. Bucks has won. Happy now?" retaliated Ivan. Amber was not alone in short-circuiting.

"Hey, come on," soothed Simeon. "We're so close. There must be something else we can do."

¥ ¥ ¥

Sergeant Marsden did not rate Suki's chances. "Nothing she can do now," he smiled. He was looking at Suki, holding the number five, alongside several others through a one-way screen. Stan was on the other side, pondering which little midget with glasses to choose.

"I'm really not sure, you know," he admitted. "It was dark and her face was covered with muck and rags."

"Listen, Stan. You look like an intelligent man," patronised Sergeant Marsden. "What's four plus one?"

Stan ignored him. "I reckon it's a toss-up between five and seven..."

Sergeant Marsden was gratified. "Number five, can you turn sideways?" he called into the microphone. "What do you reckon? A pretty damn cert, isn't it?"

Stan had his mind elsewhere. "Yep," said Stan. "Number seven, it is."

"Great! What? What happened to number five?" asked Sergeant Marsden baffled.

"Number seven," insisted Stan. "She looks like a nasty piece of work. Aren't you going to ask her to do a twirl?"

Sergeant Marsden groaned. "Forget it, Stan, it's over." This was supposed to be a formality.

¥ ¥ ¥

The Campaign Crew were seeking some means for justice to come their way for a change. Time was heading for the wire and Suki was going to get it in the neck if something did not break.

"We've been sticking too close to the local frontier, man," asserted Simeon.

"That's original," sighed Amber.

"We've got to go bigger," continued Simeon. "National, international, interplanetary."

"Yeah," boasted Ivan, seizing on the concept. "We know the telecommunications scene better than anyone who works in the system. We're the best..."

"Yeah, I know, we're wonderful, amazing, stupendous. Let's get practical guys," pleaded Amber. "Why don't we take the story to the national papers?

It's the only thing I can think of."

"It's got spice," admitted Simeon. "A bit of death here, a bit of investigation there...I can get the fax numbers."

"Let's go!" said Ivan, snapping his fingers.

An hour later, Amber was staring at the computer screen. "I always did hate essays," she said uncomfortably.

"We've got to write it so that it has impact, style, punch...I've got the first line on the tip of my tongue," Simeon said. "Dear Media Moguls...The Crouch End One is becoming a heavy-duty victim of the whole injustice scene."

"Stick to the telephone, Simeon," advised Ivan, uninspired by this unShakespearan outburst. "That's your only tool of communication."

"Hey! You think you can do better, you unemployable bagman!" said Simeon.

"Yeah, I reckon keep it short and sweet. Miscarriage of justice. World exclusive. We have reason to believe... Here's the evidence. Blah, blah, blah."

"Blah, blah, blah. Great headline, I can see the Financial Telegraph going for that one in big print," said Amber sardonically. "Why don't I dictate and you do the shorthand?"

It was the best solution. Three hours later, each of the national dailies found their faxes generating a five page article that made gripping reading. Journalists crowded the Editor's office to have a look-see at this incredible story. The silky pages convincingly listed the financial connections between the government's Education Plan and Bucks Times Bucks.

A financial journalist at The Parent instinctively picked up a phone to check out the details with someone in the investments market. Her editor clamped down on her quicker than a traffic warden in Oxford Street.

"Josie, this is a hot story right," Jacob acknowledged.

"But if we get sued by Bucks, we're screwed. I'll bring it up at the Editor's Forum today."

The pages almost radiated heat with the references to the apparent murders of Monica Ruddles and Gunster Robbins by the chemical multi-national.

"I'm not going to let this one slip," vowed Josie, over a lunchtime drink with a colleague. "There's too much detail in the story, there's even a phone number for the contract killer. Jacob is just playing chicken."

"It's so frustrating," agreed her friend. "I walked into his office once and he was sitting there, about to put on a muzzle."

"Oh that old thing! That's nothing! Have you heard those rumours about the PM wearing baby clothes? He gets complimentary tickets to every kids' film, and then someone forgot to book Jurassic Park. State of emergency..."

"Come off it," laughed Lisa at the ludicrous thought.

Whenever Jacob got the twitches with a story, the 'should I, shouldn't I' syndrome, he would put on his muzzle and immediately feel better. It gave him a sense of symbolic relief somehow, knowing that even if he wanted to say something at that moment, it was physically impossible. The muzzle absolved him of all responsibility. This Bucks story brought out those insecure feelings that yearned for the odour of leather round one's mouth. The Chairman of the Board at The Parent owned a large stake in the chemical industry. "You can never pin these things down," muttered Jacob. "Who knows, it might be connected?"

It was not, since the Chairman was a Skull investor, but the eyes behind the raw donkey-hide mask were watering with fear. In fact, the Chairman may well have been interested in the enormous funds that Bucks had dedicated to the government. It was a curious financial decision since everyone who was anyone knew the government was on a sticky wicket.

The Editor's Forum gathered together to

ceremoniously bury the story.

"Stick it in the 'futures' file, Peter," lamented the man from the Daily Window.

"A cracker of a story, but just not enough tits and bums," read the minutes of the meeting.

It was a quiet night in the police station, with most officers either on leave or in the canteen. Burglars and drunk drivers were either taking the night off or getting away with it.

The only audible sound was Suki munching into a second- rate burger with surprising enthusiasm. She was treated with more leniency by some officers, much to the annoyance of Sergeant Marsden and WPc Crisp, possibly because she was one of their more interesting detainees. Her eccentric appearance and of course, the leg, gave other more naive officers the impression that she was harmless. Just a kid who had somehow got into a mess.

The way she had given Marsden and Crisp the runaround was the source of much rib-tickling and leg-pulling in the canteen. The officers even devised a rota for regular trips to McDungs to indulge her insatiable appetite. So, all in all, it was of little surprise that Suki often spent her evenings with the desk officer rather than in a cell.

Seargent Davis felt a strange fascination for Suki and as there was often no competition for doing the evening shift and he jumped at the chance to spend time with her. He unwittingly found himself staring at her whenever the computer registered a criminal incident. A stolen car, a break-in, an arrest of some kind, would loudly generate print, cracking the silence of the lobby. Suki twitched every time, and so did Sergeant Davis.

"How did you do it, then?" he asked eventually, with a false air of nonchalance. He had been saving the question for a while, waiting, lingering, hoping to build a sense of familiarity with the convict. God knows, she must be used to his face by now. Suki certainly was but was nevertheless uncomfortable in his presence. It always seemed to be him on desk duty in the evenings, though she presumed it was by accident, not design. His eyes fixed on her, making her eat slowly, which only served to remind her that her mouth was chewing a poor cousin to The Cave's produce. Luncheon meat as opposed to ham. Do what? she thought to herself. Pretend that I'm a vegetarian? Pass exams without thinking? Have parents that belong to another age? But she knew what he was talking about: computers, hacking, delving, ducking and diving and not getting caught for so long. He was giving her a chance...

And having been away from a keyboard for what seemed like a lifetime, Suki was not going to miss the opportunity to show off her wares.

"I'll show you if you like," she said, jumping off the counter and dusting her hands.

"What?" he seemed shocked, turning instinctively to check who was listening. The station was deserted.

"That's what you want, isn't it? You want to know how, right?" Suki's blood was starting to boil. Was this fool just pulling her mouse? "Look, quit jerking me around. You want to know how I hack and I'm ready to show you, right?"

"OK OK but be quick. I don't want to get caught," he whispered hoarsely, his head almost spinning.

"Do you know any passwords?" she grunted, without much hope, lifting up the counter.

Nervously, Davis pulled open the top drawer of the desk next to the computer. Various officers names, next to cartooned faces and doodles were passwords, written plainly and openly for anyone to see. Suki marvelled at the lax security. She glanced at Davis. He watched her like a hawk.

"Can you get into the National Police Computer?"

he whispered.

"I should get paid for this." Suki was tempted to giggle. Davis was obviously riveted by the whole experience. Like most hackers in the underworld, venturing inside the gateway of criminal activity where no seventeen year old had a pass, Suki was in paradise. And sitting by her side was a police officer, sanctioning her every move...

She got to work. He wanted to be impressed and she would oblige. Having done the standard amount of research, Suki knew that the NPC would have to be a high calibre system, capable of handling vast quantities of data on individuals. It would have to be an ICL model, probably in the 2900 series. Sure enough, it was a 2980. The same thought kept inventing itself in her brain. Here she was, virtually convicted of every sin, satisfying her craving for the very thing that had led to her downfall. Suki quickly calmed her performance nerves and logged onto an available computer network directory to find out where exactly the system sat in relation to others like it. That discovered, it was simply a matter of finding out which operating system was on 'go' and who was calling the shots. Chief Superintendent Clarke. Davis bolted when he saw the name, it obviously referred to God in the police world. Suki shrugged her shoulders. Every human was the same. Computers made them accessible. She reached for the phone. Davis plumped his clammy hand on hers.

"What are you doing?" He nearly wept.

Suki growled. He let go, dumb-struck. She dialled the number for Scotland Yard, posing as the Chief's secretary, to find out who was in charge of a secret compartment of files on the screen, entitled "Foreign Operations". Taking on a different persona, Suki was courteous, even talkative with the switchboard operator. "Of course, it's Chief Superintendent Monk. You know, I'm working too hard, I can't even remember his assistant's name."

"You mean Hilary Hudson," said the operator helpfully. She now had the key to open that last door. Using a police telephone directory, Suki by-passed the switchboard by calling direct to Scotland Yard's computer section. Davis was mesmerised. "Hilary Hudson here, Chief Super Monk's just called me at home. Can't seem to get access to his account. He wants to know why!"

The poor VDU operator at the other end threw a wobbly and started to stammer through the manual. It wasn't getting Suki anywhere fast. Davis was starting to twitch badly.

Suki sighed, as if she'd been here before. "Darling, the man's wept in my arms. I'm his secretary not the KGB." Her voice dipped with sarcasm. "I presume you'd like to get up to work in the morning."

It worked. Security was broken and the password given gladly over the phone. In a mere thirty minutes, Suki was engrossed in reading details of international criminals listed by Europol. At the sound of officers returning from grossly extended tea-breaks, Suki logged off and the computer resumed its normal print-outs. Davis was nearly in tears.

"Oh for God's sake, pull yourself together," snapped Suki. "I did all the work." She wiped her brow. "See - no sweat."

¥ ¥ ¥

The Campaign Crew hung around King's Cross till midnight, waiting impatiently for the following day's papers. They snatched a copy of each of the tabloids with tearful ferocity and rifled through each of the pages.

"It's not there!" yelped Simeon.

The front pages glowed with a picture of the Queen spanking one of her grandchildren. The headline read,

"Is this the way to treat our little 'uns?"

"These fools can't smell a corker when it's handed to them on a plate!" cried Ivan angrily.

"Must be in the 'serious' press," said Amber, incensed.

"If the papers don't take it," groaned Ivan. "Neither will Oracle or Teletext or the TV stations."

"You can't make that kind of assumption," glared Simeon. "How the hell do you know?"

"Bus-T's a monopoly right? No-one interferes on their turf," said Ivan. "It's the same with the media. Everybody knows everybody and when one doesn't do something that everyone wants to, then nobody does what they ought to. Get my drift?"

"Yeah, that's a pretty cool résumé of the whole gig," said Simeon impressed.

"And exactly what are we going to do about this really 'cool' pile of shit?" asked Amber.

"I was just coming to that..." said Ivan. "We've been too nice about everything. I don't get nothing done when I'm with you lot. Everything is ten steps forward, eleven steps back."

"Don't you start getting all..." began Amber.

"Hang on, I want to listen to this tap dance," intervened Simeon. "Then we'll thump him."

"Thanks mate. We're giving these people choices and look what they're doing with it," explained Ivan. "I know the truth and I'm telling it. They don't want to listen. So we've got to cut out the choice and make them open up."

"I smell a dirty deed," cringed Simeon.

"Well, I'm game. Murder ain't exactly small fry in my book," said Amber with a glint in her eye.

Simeon put his head in his hands. "We better get cracking then," he said resignedly.

Unbeknown to the Campaign crew, the newspapers had caught wind of a story of a ship dropping its cargo off the coast of Colombia. Apparently, it had great difficulty docking in at its destination in Lima, and had ventured up the coast but was turned away from each port of call. The ship was a mere rusty shell, half the crew were dead and the other half sick. On his last ebb, the captain had ordered that the barrels be dropped overboard in the Pacific Ocean. Fish drawn from those waters were neon. The main point of interest, however, was that the ship was owned by a company in Illinois, registered in Liberia, insured in Britain and drawing its cargo from Italy and other European countries. The name that glowed in the dark on Josie's computer was Bucks Times Bucks. Bucks Times Bucks.

Wood Green Crown Court was not renowned for its verdicts, nor its caseload. A divorcing couple forgot their acrimony in the midst of a packed corridor for the next case: The Crown v Samra. Today, the court was filled with more than its fair share of distraught people, some of whom had staked their reputations on the verdict of The Hacker and some who had more of a personal interest in Suki. Either way, neither party was going to leave.

A bamboozle of journalists, pressed like sardines against the Victorian panels of the press gallery, unwittingly frustrated the path of police and security guards chasing a convict who had only just been sentenced. He managed to disappear without trace in the crowd amassing outside the lobby. This showpiece trial in suburbia had enough nervous energy to electrify Piccadilly Circus for a week. Josie was excited, despite the fact that her face was glued sideways to a picture of an eighteenth-century lord.

"This is what journalism's about," she whispered to her friend, who was slightly distracted by a sound cable round her neck.

Jacob was bound to disagree. Today would go down as a nightmare in his diary. Tomorrow would probably be the first day of his experience of unemployment.

Somehow, he did not dare to think how the paper he had edited yesterday had not been printed. In its place, was the very story he had shunned at the Editor's Forum. He was shaking in his boots, partly because he had not spoken to a single Government department about it to check whether the facts and the full-stops were in the right place, and partly he was staring a 'should I or shouldn't I' syndrome in the face. Should I behave as if the article was intended or should I be outraged at its discovery on my front page? The talons of an editor's nightmare had gripped his life. If only he had his muzzle for these public appearances, it was where you needed them most, or so he'd read. The only consolation was that the other editors looked like they wanted their muzzles and body belts too.

Amber and Simeon had argued frivolously all the way to the court house. They emerged out of the Bus-T van still at logger-heads.

"You could have done better," moaned Amber. "What will Suki think? Where the hell's Ivan?"

"She's gonna be too embarrassed to look at you. You are really outrageous, girl," replied Simeon. "This ain't no rave, it's a court, you know like the gallows, the guillotine." He motioned a slit throat. "No-one is going to be in red. No-one."

"Exactly. And who's going to be in overalls? I would have honestly preferred the black leather stuff, Simeon," ranted Amber. "My, oh my, it's busy today, isn't it?"

They decided to hang back in the hope that Ivan would turn up soon, particularly after Janak gave them a vicious glare. Shanti was dressed for a funeral parlour, almost in preparation for the verdict. She seemed immersed in a copy of The Parent but after a while, lifted her veil.

The judge, Lord Clapperton, was similarly more concerned with his attire than the case. There was some kind of furore in the gangway, but that was none of his concern.

He had been briefed by the Permanent Secretary and that was enough. The essence of Permy's message had been to keep it short and sour. The good Lord jumped at the unexpected sight of the Minister for Education, of all people, lurking in the back-chambers.

"Rupert, you scared me. What in God's name you doing here?"

"Have you read the papers today?" hissed a decrepid Rupert. "Have you switched on the TV?"

"No, I can't say I have," smiled Lord Clapperton. "No news is good news, as they say. You look like you've had better days."

"I have," wheezed Rupert. "Look you have to send this one down. You have to send her down. I've just got shot to pieces."

He held up a copy of The Parent, headlining with 'The Truth About BTB' followed by The Daily Window and The Financial Telegraph bearing even starker statements about Suki's innocence.

"Well, that's preposterous," blustered the Lord, skimming over the article. "I'll sue them, we can't have the course of justice pushed aside!" He vanished into the main chamber.

"Thank you, thank you," said Rupert before flaking out. All he heard was the voice of the court usher. "All rise."

"Call forth the defendant," said the judge, amidst the hushed silence. "Let me start by saying that this is going to be a trial by jury, not a media trial."

Suki walked forward to stand in the dock. She looked thin and pasty. An uproar went up amongst journalists, who were craning their necks to see The Hacker. That little mite? Who'd have thought? Look at her, she couldn't harm a fly. She must be innocent! The story was right! Their story was right. The judge mistook the mayhem to be in response to his opening statement.

Josie took the opportunity to edge closer towards Jacob, who looked like he was about to faint. "Jacob, come outside."

"Josie, what am I going to do?" he grieved, still in a complete state of shock. "I've got a wife, kids..."

"You're going to shut up and listen," admonished Josie. "For once."

She poured the details of her discovery about Bucks Times Bucks into his burning ears. A smile slowly grew on his face. He kissed her in a rare moment of elation.

"Ugh!" said Josie, wiping her cheek. "I could do you for harassment!"

"So we're allowed to go to print, we've got the facts. In fact, it's a world exclusive," beamed Jacob. "This is wonderful news. I was about to commit suicide a moment ago, now I'm ready to walk on the moon. I'll do anything, anything you want, Josie."

"Right, I want to be appointed Chief of International Affairs," said Josie.

"Josie..." said Jacob, looking injured. "What about Bill?"

"Bill's a jerk. And I can always take the story elsewhere," warned Josie.

"OK, it's a deal," conceded Jacob.

They returned to find the Crown's lawyer in the middle of making a complaint.

"M'Laud, the newspapers seem to be having a field day," he said. "We haven't had any of this published material to view in advance. If it has any substance, which we very much doubt, then we'd like some time..."

The Editors minus one shook violently in their shoes.

"I vehemently agree," said Lord Clappeton. "I'll grant a recess till this afternoon."

A hubbub overtook the court as people poured out. The Editors ran for a mini-conference. Shanti hit Janak over the head with her newspaper before rushing over to embrace Amber and Simeon.

"Nothing's certain yet," Amber warned Shanti. "There could be a last minute hitch. Where is Ivan?"

Ivan failed to materialise until after the afternoon session had begun. Simeon looked like he was going to hit him when he did turn up.

"Sorry guys, late night, early morning," said Ivan apologetically. "Leather's at the cleaners, is it? About time too, you've been wearing nothing else."

"Silence in the court, please," called the usher.

"Whoops!" cringed Ivan. Courts were not his favourite places.

Janak took another opportunity to turn and glare.

"Now, members of the jury, we're about to indulge in some computer-generated evidence," said the judge. "Is all this really necessary? Won't paper do?" Lord Clapperton sounded exasperated. "I myself am illiterate with these ghastly machines but I'm told they are easy to operate. Proceed for the Crown."

Giggles ran through the court. The Crown prosecutor undertook a step-by-step explanation of what would follow.

"The Crown has felt it appropriate, M'laud..." The jury yawned simultaneously, "Given the vast amount of information..."

"We all know the whys and what fors. Get on with it," muttered the judge impatiently.

"The instructions are as follows," said the lawyer, reading with nose-peak glasses. "Please press the <Enter> key, to find Exhibit A."

The jury members dutifully pressed the <Enter> key on their keyboards. "Now, as you'll see, the document that appears on the screen shows that the defendant hacked into the RETROBASE system a total of..."

"There seems to be a slight technical hitch, counsel," motioned the judge. "Exhibit A has not appeared on my screen."

"Very well, we'll proceed, M'laud," said the lawyer, slightly flustered. "Exhibit B will appear if the members of the court press the number 2."

Suki turned her head towards The Campaign Crew. Simeon was certain that he detected a wink.

"No, it doesn't," snapped the judge. "This is obviously a complete waste of time. Can't we have the paper documents, counsel?"

"There are no paper records," stammered the lawyer for the Crown. "They were all inputt-tt-tt-ed on computer and shredded for security."

"Well, where's the evidence? We can't have a trial without evidence!" bellowed the judge.

The noise levels in the chamber hit decibel level. Clearly, the much-publicised case up for prosecution that had rocked lawyers, educationalists, police officers and Ministers, was in a complete shambles.

The judge snapped. He had only agreed to take this on for Rupert's sake, and as usual that bumbling fool couldn't organise a game of conkers. "Court dismissed!" yelled the judge, in need of a good strong whisky. "This is a complete waste of time!" he rumbled before shuffling off into the chamber.

Rupert emerged from his snivelling stupor to hear only those final words. "Thank you, thank you," he smiled. It was so quick and easy when you had power, he thought.

It would not be seen as professional to be seen with the judge now. It might seem a little orchestrated, especially when the place was crawling with cameras and journalists. Ah! Yes, the cameras. Well, since he'd been vindicated, he could face them with nothing to fear, couldn't he? Rupert the lamb went to the slaughterhouse.

Suki was elated as she walked out of court, arm-in-arm with Simeon on one side and her mother on the other. "I need some food, man," she grinned. "Amber, you didn't bring any with you by any chance?"

"In the van," whispered Amber.

"I've got plenty of food waiting for you," said Shanti.

"Mum, there's something I've been meaning to tell you for ages..." began Suki.

After a midnight feast, Suki lay gorged on her belly and made an entry in her diary:

"A pretty close shave. But look, no hands! No fingerprints!"